400

Date Due

The
HOPE
And The
PROMISE

HUGH GREIG

STAGECOACH PUBLISHING CO. LTD.
P.O. Box 3399, Langley, B.C. V3A 4R7

Typesetting, layout and design by
Mainland Graphics, Langley

Printed in Canada by
D.W. Friesen & Sons Ltd.

First Printing — October 1977

Fic
Gre   84   467

Canadian Cataloguing in Publication Data

Greig, Hugh, 1912-
   The hope and the promise

ISBN 0-88983-017-7

I. Title.
PS8563.R449H6   C813'.5'4   C77-002192-1
PR9199.3

Copyright © 1977 by Hugh Greig

Contents

Dedicated to:
NELL

Introduction

I approached the writing of this, my first novel, with many fears and great trepidation. How do you portray a folk-history, so complex, so fragmented, so at variance with today's life-styles, and yet, somehow, reveal the truth, the beauty, and the abiding faith of a loveable, industrious, dedicated peoples?

In my judgement, the traps that lay in waiting for the unwary writer were two-fold. On the one hand, maudlin emotionalism, glorifying a tradition and a belief that needed no such glorification. Or, on the other, dwelling on, and exaggerating the sensational aspects of the few, while ignoring the efforts of the solid, stable majority. In my earlier years as a playwright, I had been found guilty of the latter. I am deeply ashamed. If this novel should meet the criteria set by my many Doukhobor friends, then I offer it as my apology for those productions of the past.

This is not the "Great Canadian" novel we writers dream of. In truth, I am not even a clever writer. Words do not come easy. I have no earth-shaking philosophies to expound upon. Rather, may I lay claim to being a simple story-teller? Therefore, in light of the above, I decided to relate this history as viewed through the eyes of one family—a family history encompassing the pageant of events that saw them exiled from their homeland, and settled in Canada. Outside forces, over which they had no control, constantly buffetted them, sending them off on futile pilgrimages, and, when the occasion demanded, protest marches and meetings, always in peace and in prayer—protests, which I may add, were the inalienable right of all citizens as incorporated into the very fabric of our democratic society. Their nudism, as reported by the lurid press headlines in our daily papers, was nothing more nor less than an act of protest, with religious overtones, indulged in by a small minority of the more fanatical of the Sect.

It is inconceivable that a naive, harried peoples such as these could enter into a young, hustling and alien society, and not have some setbacks. The excesses of stupidity, and deliberate misunderstandings indulged in by both government and business, eventually triggered an era of terrorism in the Kootenays. In the beginning, at least, these were the acts of frightened, disillusioned, homeless men, and at no time did they number more than a few hundred or so, a mere fraction of the estimated twelve thousand Brothers and Sisters residing in Canada, who patiently, and with stoicism, endured the hardships and the pain inflicted upon them. Further to this, I must state, that at no time did they wilfully take a human life, other than on the sad occasions when a home-made bomb exploded prematurely.

That they became the pawns of elected politicians, and the victims of avaricious, greedy businessmen is recorded fact. To us, the paternal Canadian, who accepted these weary, suffering exiled children into our midst, must go a great portion of the guilt and shame for the deliberate, forceful assimilation of a viable culture, and a religious belief which we did not try to understand, nor appreciate. This loss of a vigorous, meaningful lifestyle is Canada's.

My sincere thanks to Messrs. Woodcock and Avakumovic, co-authors of *The Doukhobors,* which book was one of my prime sources of research, and to Mr. Koozma J. Tarasoff, author of the *Pictorial History of the Doukhobors,* from which, by means of his excellent collection of photographs, I was able to picture these peoples in an earlier time. Finally, to the British Columbia government for their *Blakemore Report on the Doukhobors* [*1912*], thank you.

Foreword

Doukhobors, a name given by the Russian Orthodox clergy to a community of non-comformist peasants. The word signifies, "Spirit Fighters," and was intended by the priesthood to convey that they fought against the Spirit of God. The Doukhobors themselves accepted it as signifying that they fight, not against, but for and with the Spirit, though they later decided to give up this name and call themselves, "Christians of the Universal Brotherhood."

The community was first heard of in the middle of the 18th century. By the beginning of the 19th, their doctrine had become so clearly defined, and the numbers of their members had so greatly increased, that the Russian government and Church, considering the Sect to be peculiarly obnoxious, commenced an energetic campaign against it.

The foundation of the Doukhobors' teachings consists in the belief that the Spirit of God is ever-present in the soul of Man, and directs him by Its word within him. They understand the coming of Christ in the flesh, His works, teachings and sufferings, in a spiritual sense. The object of the sufferings of Christ, in their view, was to give an example of the suffering for truth. They believe Christ continues to suffer in us, even now, when we do not live in accordance with the behests and spirit of His teachings.

The whole teaching of the Douhkobors is penetrated with the Gospel spirit of Love. Worshipping God in the spirit, they affirm that the outward church and all that is performed in it, and concerns it, has no importance for them. Church is anywhere two or three are gathered together; i.e. united in the name of Christ. They pray inwardly at all times; on fixed days they assemble for prayer meetings, at which they greet each other with fraternal low bows, thereby acknowledging every man as a bearer of the Divine Spirit.

Their teachings are founded on tradition, which is called the "Book of Life," as it lives in the memory, and in the heart. It consists of sacred songs or chants, partly composed independently, partly formed out of the contents of the Bible, which, however, has evidently been gathered by them orally, as, until lately, they were almost entirely illiterate, and did not possess any written book.

They founded their mutual relations, and their relations to other people, and, in fact, to all living creatures exclusively on love, and therefore hold all people to be equal and brethren. They also extend this idea of equality to governmental authority, obedience to whom they do not consider binding upon them in those cases when the demands of authority are in conflict with their conscience. In all that does not infringe upon what they regard as the Will of God, they willingly fulfill. They consider killing, violence, and, in general, all relations to living beings not based on love as opposed to their conscience and to the will of God.

Industrious and abstentious in their lives, when living up to the standard of their faith, they present one of the nearest approaches to the realization of the Christian ideal ever attained. In many ways, they have a close resemblance to the Quaker Society.

For these beliefs and practices, the Doukhobors long endured persecution. Under Nicholas I, in 1840 and in 1850, when, on religious grounds they refused to participate in military service, they were banished from the District of Taurus, whither they had been previously deported by Alexander I to Transcaucasia near the Turkish border. Neither the severe climate, nor the neighborhood of wild and war-like hillmen, shook their faith, and, in the course of half a century, in some of the most unhealthy and infertile land in the Caucasia's, they transformed a wilderness into flourishing colonies, and continued to live a Christian and laborious life, making friends with, instead of fighting, the hillsmen and tribesmen of the frontier.

The wealth which they attained, weakened for a time their moral fervor, and, little by little, they began to depart somewhat from their beliefs. As soon, however, as events occurred among them, which disturbed their outward tranquility, the religious spirit revived.

In 1887, in the reign of Alexander III, universal military service was introduced in the land; even those who, as in the case of the Doukhobors, had formerly been banished, were now called upon to serve. At first they outwardly submitted, but later refused to serve, and brought the wrath of the government down upon them.

By the decision of certain government officials, the right to possession of public property of the Doukhobors, valued at about 50,000 (Pound Sterling) passed from the Community to one of their members who had formed some of the more demoralized Doukhobors into a group of his personal adherents. These were henceforth called the Small Party. Soon afterwards, several of the most respected members of the community were banished to Archangel, a Siberian type labor camp. This series of calamities were accepted as a punishment from God, and a spititual reawakening of a most energetic character ensued. The majority, about 12,000, resolved to practise the traditions left them by their Fathers, which they had renounced during their period of opulance. They gave up tobacco, wine and meat, and every form of excess, many of them dividing their property, in order to supply the needs of those left in want. They renounced all participation in acts of violence, and so refused all military service.

In confirmation of this sincerity, in the summer of 1895, those of the Large Party, as they were called (as distinct from the Small Party), burnt all the arms which they, like others, had taken up for protection against wild animals and the fierce hillmen. Then, under the reign of Nicholas II, they became the victims of a series of persecutions. Cossak soldiers plundered, beat, and maltreated men and women in every way. More than four hundred families from the province of Tiflis were banished to Georgian villages. Of the 4000 thus exilled, more than 1000 died in the first two years from exhaustion and disease.

All would have perished had not information reached Tolstoy, and, through him, the Society of Friends in England, when funds were immediately raised towards alleviating their sufferings. At the same time, an appeal written by Tolstoy and some of his friends, requesting the help of public opinion, was circulated in St. Petersburg, and sent to the Tsar and higher Russian officials. The Doukhobors themselves asked for permission to emigrate, and the Society of Friends petitioned the Tsar to the same effect.

In March of 1898, the desired permission was granted, and the first party, 1126-strong, were able to sail for Cyprus, sufficient funds not being available for transfer to any other British territory. Later it was found possible to send two parties of more than 4000 to Canada, where they arrived in January, 1899. They were joined in the spring of the same year by about 7800 others, the government alloting them land in the province of Saskatchewan, near Thunder Hill, and Yorkton. Some settled around Prince Albert, and in other various localities. They were cordially received by the populace of the port cities.

In April, 1901, in the Canadian House of Commons, the Minister of Justice issued a statement, in which he said that "not a single offence had been committed by any Doukhobor, and that they were very law abiding, and that, if good conduct was a recommendation, they were the best of immigrants. The large tracts of land demanded population, and as they were not given to crime, the conclusion was that they would make the best of citizens."

Nevertheless, the Canadian government has had difficulties with this Sect, owing to their age-old beliefs and objections to acknowledge any allegiance other than that of the Law of God, and the teachings of Christ, together with the dictates of their own consciences. However, they willingly fulfill, and abide by, any law or government ruling which does not contradict nor conflict with their teachings.

BOOK
I

It happened on June the Twenty Ninth,
Eighteen Hundred and Ninety Five,
The Caucasian hills of Russia
Seemed to come alive.
Great tongues of flame swept skyward,
Near the midnight hour:
A plea to Brothers round the world,
Defying Tsarist power.
Destroy all weapons; Live in peace;
Let wars on earth, from this day cease.

1

The Burning Of The Guns

In the early morning light, flocks of wild pigeons whirled, now coming to rest on rocky banks, now wheeling overhead in tight rapid circles, now vanishing from sight. Although the sun was not yet visible, the upper crests of the ravine were beginning to pale. Yellowish-green moss covering grey-whitish rock, dew-covered bushes of Christ's thorn, dogberry, and dwarf elm all appeared startlingly distinct and vivid in the golden light. On the far side of the ravine, wrapped in thick mist which floated in uneven layers, sombre fingers of night still clung, presenting a contrast, an indefinite mingling of color: pale purple, dark green, splotched here and there with the white and cream of opening blossoms. Up ahead, rising starkly against the dark blue horizon, could be seen the bright, dead masses of the snowy Caucasian mountains, their shadows and outlines exquisite in every detail. Crickets, grasshoppers, and thousands of other insects awoke in the tall grasses, filling the ear with clear, and ceaseless sound. The air was full of the perfume of water, of grass, and of the mist — the perfume of a lovely summer morning.

This one morning, the routine of everyday living had been broken. Throughout each village, in every farm nestled close around, from each small stone house, from each tiny adobe hut, pillars of light wood smoke could be seen lazily curling upwards. From small windows, soft gleam of lamplight illuminated lush gardens, neat yards, the shadowy forms of neighbors urging sleepy horses into harness. Sensing the hustle and bustle of villager and farmer alike, the subdued voices, as if each were

14

engaged in their own solitary act, gave one a feeling of excitement and urgency, as if all were acting from a common compulsive master plan — a pact over which none had control, yet in which all were caught up.

Huddled together under bulky sheepskins, the family Obedkoff, perched on the high seat of a two-wheeled farm cart, quietly observed the flurry of movement and activity around them, their voices muted in the predawn hush.

"Father?" Peering round the small form of his sister, a young boy, of about ten, gazed up at the dark, bearded features of his father.

"Yes, my son."

"Must we burn all our guns?"

Soft brown eyes momentarily swept the grave face of the young boy, then moved to the mother, sitting stiffly against the far side of the cart.

"I'm afraid so, Paul."

"Even my small pistol? The one you gave me last birthday?"

As if awakened from a deep reverie, the mother jerked erect, one hand gripping the seat rail, her eyes never leaving the way ahead.

"All must go. Our Beloved Leader in Christ has written... 'Thou shalt not kill.'

Her voice, suddenly loud in the stillness, softened.

"Young...so young. Some day Paul, you will understand."

Sensing his perplexity, she gently placed an arm around the thin shoulders.

"We live by God's will. So you have been taught...and so you will live."

Paul made no reply, his eyes on the ever-changing scene. They were travelling now on a rough cart track which wound its way upward along one bank of a swift noisy stream. Tumbling through the centre of a broad steep ravine, the mid-summer flood carried the icy touches of upper snows down to the placid warm Black Sea.

Paul's thoughts were akin to the tumultuous rush of the waters. He puzzled at the obvious contrast in the routine day-to-day behaviour of his dearly-loved parents. They differed so in their outlook on the somehow other worldly nature of the events that were to occur this day.

For this was St. Peter's Day, June the Twenty-Ninth, Eighteen Ninety-Five, and although he had no way of knowing, this would be a day long to be remembered in the annals of his people. His mother had so often chattered of this day. Although it had been a secret, known only to the village Elders, somehow, in the last few days, rumours had been whispered about. Rumour had become a certainty, then accepted fact, and now common knowledge. As this day neared, his mother, in rising anticipation, had recounted with greater frequency and fervour, exciting tales of other days, some far in the past.

Again and again she had related how, with patience and resignation, his forefathers, in their continuing troubles with Church and State, tenaciously held to their belief that Christ lived within all men, and that His commands took precedence over that of any official. Stubbornly, they refused to work with, or assist in any way, a State at war. Because of their strict adherence to pacifist views, coupled to their firm denial of the need for structured religious dogma, pomp, and ceremony, a callous Tsarist regime, aided and abetted by a vengeful Orthodox church, had meted out many forms of brutality and degradation on the persons of this rebellious sect. Many were the stories of exile, kidnapping, rape and execution. All of these were depicted in his people's Book of Life: a simple history of the Doukhobors, passed on orally from one generation to the next. Many of the more graphic tales took the form of Psalms sung at every Sobranya.

The one incident Paul never tired of hearing, occurred some time before his birth, when the more wealthy Brethren, now known and despised as the Bad Ones of Horlovka, had, to avoid trouble, decided to obey the will of the government and supply much-needed food and transport to the army. Succumbing to official pressure, these Bad Ones, with an irony difficult to comprehend, joined forces with the Tsarist regime against their own Brethren, to throw them off the communal lands, and forcing them into a rigorous exile in the barren reaches of the Caucasia's.

Here, in these mountainous regions, totally alien to their ancient established ways, the Brethren had managed to eke out a comfortable living, raising cattle and horses on the many highland pastures. Although, in the first few years, an attempt had been made to introduce cereal crops, the mainstay of their former life, they were soon made aware of the fact that a short growing season, combined with the harsh terrain, negated mass communal cultivation.

Always, she had impressed on his receptive mind the unwavering courage with which his forefathers had met each and every appalling edict. In fact, it would seem that their farms and their faith thrived on misery. He felt, ever anew, a wonder and a pride as, daily, he observed the continual growth of a true spiritual communal life. Not once could he recall his mother speak with rancor or bitterness, though he knew that she, like so many of the Brethren, past and present, had lived a life of constant sacrifice, persecution, and hardship.

In fact, he mused, his mother seemed to find an inner peace, a serenity that radiated outwards, illuminated her features, softened her voice to a fervent whisper. Her one reality — prayer — was that her people, now referred to as the Mad Ones, would forever and against all odds, keep and live within the True Faith.

Although he knew that his mother had been too young to take part in the day of exile, he liked to picture her as one of the women who went into the fields they had known so well, and, pressing the rich earth to their breasts, cried aloud, threw their beseeching hands to Heaven in supplication, sang their mournful Psalms, and prayed for justice. But, the earth which they pressed to their breasts, and the men who should have heard them, all remained deaf to their sorrows.

Curiously, Paul glanced up at his mother. Some peculiarity, something inherent in the early morning light made him see her as if for the first time. The small perfectly-boned features, oval grey eyes accentuated by high cheekbones, were framed by a thick mass of coal black hair — a face more Oriental than Caucasian — a legacy of Tartar forefathers who had come sweeping across these lands many hundreds of years in the past. Thoughtfully, he studied the contours of her well-shaped mouth, which he knew, to his cost, could cut as scathingly as the finest-edged knife. In total, it was a face that gave the lie to her inner nature — a nature as hard, as ruthless, as the toughest of men.

The querulous voice of his sister broke into his deep reverie.

"Poppa. Put your arm round me. I'm all shivery."

Gently encompassing his small daughter, the father drew her close to his side.

"Poor little Nastasia. Up before the birds. Never mind, my pet. Soon you'll be as warm as toast."

With a quiet chuckle, he chirped to the horses, which were steaming from exertion.

As it left the ravine, the road became more tortuous and steep. A breeze, stirring against his face, made him aware that the higher they climbed, the cooler the air became. But then, this had always been a time of day he loved — the few minutes before dawn. How often, he wondered, had he paused in his tasks, sensed the cool flow of moist air whispering down the craggy peaks of the Treeless Wet Mountains and timidly brushing the few scraggly pines that struggled for life on the harsh slopes. Silently stirring the tall dew-laden grasses of the upper meadows, then, as if in vain attempt to soften the grim valleys, it wandered ever more softly over the undulating foothills, to reach and cross the flower-blanketed pasture lands, the dirt brown barnyards surrounding his village—the village of Orlovka, one of the many Doukhobor settlements dotting the mountainous slopes of Southern Russia.

Leading away from Orlovka, on the few tracks and narrow roads winding upwards, the harsh ring of iron wheel being hauled over rock, the metallic jingle of harness, the muted clip-clop of hurrying hooves, all so foreign to the early hour, added to and heightened a sense of urgency, a mood of excitement, as had the early rising and the preparations for the trip.

"Look Father, daylight creeps over the plateau."

Quietly, Nickolai glanced around.

"We have time, Paul."

He noted, however, dark outlines of the higher crags were now softly profiled against an ever-increasing luminosity. As he watched, a faint rosy glow mingled with the luminous halo.

"Late. Always and forever late. You know, Paul, that father of yours will yet be late for his own funeral."

Shrugging, Nickolai made no reply, other than to crack the lines smartly across the backs of the laboring team. Sleeping birds, hidden in the long grass by the side of the road, disturbed by the passing of many vehicles, began to make themselves heard.

The sudden, startling jar of a musket shot, echoing loudly in the morning air, caused all eyes to jerk ahead and upwards, to where an ominous glow surmounted by a thick pall of black smoke, appeared from behind a hill well above them. Excitedly, Nastasia started to speak, but was quickly hushed by her mother.

From the vicinity of the blaze came the sounds of many voices singing in unison; faint, hauntingly sweet, giving voice to an age-old hymn. It was evident that they were late for whatever lay ahead.

"Old fool, Nickolai Obedkoff." Her voice a snarl, the eyes of the mother surveyed her husband. "I urged you to make a start earlier. Now we will be too late. Did I not tell you the burning was for the midnight hour?"

"We will not be the last to arrive, Elizabeth. The way is long and the road steep. Now quiet yourself."

But he found no peace. His wife's voice, nagging, petulant, made him resentful. For the first time, he reached for his whip, slashed it once across the backs of the team. The sudden, violent lunge ahead almost unseated the mother. Furious, she turned on him.

"Faster. Make them move faster. You will yet shame us with

your tardiness."

"'You wish me to kill them perhaps? Patience woman. We will be in time."

Paul, his eyes on the red glow and smoke, broke into his mother's tirade.

"It will be a great fire, Father?"

As if in answer to his query, tongues of flame shot straight up, lighting the area, and tinging all objects to a dull red blush. Several more rifle shots, louder now, echoed throughout the foothills. Instinctively, Nickolai flinched as he answered, "It will reach right up to Heaven."

"Aye, and beyond. Over the mountains, and across the steppes of Mother Russia."

Her face hardened, her voice became ominous.

"Into sinful Moscow. Through the gates of the Tsar's fine house. Yes, it will reach even there. Now, still your idle tongues."

Her voice dropped to a low murmur.

"This one St. Peter's Day will not soon be forgotten."

Other than a quick glance at her face, Nickolai made no reply; his energies on the sweating, heaving team. The road had become steep and rocky. Ahead, a two-wheeled cart, pulled by a slow lumbering ox, blocked the way and slowed progress to a crawl. Impatient now, all eyes peered ahead to where long tongues of flame could be plainly observed. Again, shots rang out, followed by a rumbling explosion, which sent sparks and embers far up into the sky, momentarily obliterating the chorus of voices. Nastasia, comfortable and warm against the side of her father, whispered dreamily, "The singing's so nice. I like singing."

Humming to herself, she picked up the melody, a sad, touching Psalm which echoed loudly round the carts and wagons. The voices were sweet, vibrant, and melodious in the dawn air, seeming to reverberate as if a large pipe organ were being played. The odd shot still rang out.

"Those shots, Father? Should they not unload the bullets?"

Nickolai glanced around uneasily and muttered darkly. "Our Brethern have about as much patience as your dear Mother. In their haste to destroy the weapons of death, they will yet end up killing each other."

Sensing her husband's unease, the mother turned to Paul.

"Climb in back. See no bullets remain in..."

With a quick restraining hand on the boy, Nickolai morosely interrupted, "Have no fear. I took good care of that last night."

Further conversation was stilled as the wagons rounded the last rocky shoulder of a low hill, and drew to a halt. In front and to all sides, a large plateau stretched to high escarpments which marked the steep sides of the mountains. To the right, an enormous conflagration radiated heat waves, warming the air for many yards around. As each wagon entered the plateau, they moved to form a rough line some distance away from the fire, where the teams contentedly nibbled at the sparse foliage, thankful that the steep ascent has been completed.

Nickolai guided his team into line beside the others, jumped to the ground, and reached up to lower an excited Nastasia down. Tugging at his coat, she followed him as he commenced to tether the horses.

"Poppa. Remember, you promised."

As he dropped the heavy tether-block, he good-humoredly patted each horse. Then he picked up his daughter, and drew her face close to his. "What promise did I make, Little One?"

"The fire Poppa. And the singing. You promised...last night."

His eyes, filled with worry, moved to the fire. Figures of men and women could be seen hurriedly approaching the flames. Each would pause just long enough to heave assorted weapons into the inferno. The intense heat kept all at a distance. With care, Nickolai deposited Nastasia into the wagon bed.

"You cannot come with me to the fire, my pet. Would you have your pretty hair burned by the flame?"

Giggling, Nastasia reached up, encircled his head in her arms, rubbed her small face against his beard. "No, Poppa. Nor would I have you burn your beautiful beard."

The affectionate gesture was returned by Nickolai. He smiled, stroked her long silky hair. "Later, my pet. Once the burning is done, you may join the Elders."

At this moment, the mother and son, immersed in the scene around them, moved to join Nickolai at the rear of the wagon.

"Enough Nickolai. Get these devil weapons into the fire where they belong. And you, children, remain here in the wagon."

From the wagon, Elizabeth seized an armload of assorted weapons, then paused: "You know, Nickolai, the children should have remained at home."

"You would have left them alone, by themselves?"

About to turn away, she again paused, impatient, her eyes on her husband.

"No, but if you had listened to me, we would have arrived for the midnight burning."

"The cows had to be milked. The horses fed. You know that, Elizabeth. And anyway, was it not decided that the burning would go on till noon?"

Abruptly, Elizabeth turned and moved towards the fire.

Nickolai dragged out a large, old fashioned musket, and cradled it in his arms. For a long moment, he stood gazing down at it, then, with a sigh, turned to follow his wife.

They approached the intense heat as close as they dared. Losing no time, Elizabeth heaved her load into the flames, one by one. Beside her, Nickolai made no move. Again, his eyes searched the old gun, noted the finely-carved stock, the intricately hand-worked trigger guard.

His wife turned, glanced, half amused at his thoughtful features.

"What ails you, old fool Nickolai? Do you yet believe our dear Leader in Christ makes with foolish words? Feed it to the hungry flame."

A shrug his only reply, Nickolai, with a sudden savage move, whirled the gun above his head and sent it crashing into the fire.

Only the children, standing in the wagon bed, witnessed Nickolai's agony and hesitation, so engrossed were the others in the work of the flames. Rifles, muskets, swords, weapons of all description crashed into the inferno, and were quickly reduced to heaps of charred, indistinguishable globs of molten metal.

The task completed, both parents retreated away from the heat, panting from their efforts. As if to soften her husband's obvious distress, Elizabeth gently encircled his waist with her arm as they walked to join the large group of neighbors gathered to one side of the fire, the source of the singing. The air was heavy with loud commands from late arrivals, as voices guided and halted teams of steaming horses, greeted neighbors. Over all was the rushing roar of the conflagration. The odd shot still rang out, but, from their infrequency, clearly indicated some had taken the precaution of unloading their weapons.

As was their custom, on reaching the singing group, Elizabeth parted from her husband to join with the women, while Nickolai mingled with the men. Both groups stood facing one another across a long table over which had been placed a snowy white cloth. On this, sat a loaf of rye bread, a jug of water, and a small container of salt.

Poignant notes of a Psalm floated away in the morning air. The first probing rays of the rising sun bathed the singers in an aura of red and gold. Then, a male voice, deep, sonorous, achingly sincere in tone and quality rang out, subduing all other sound, until it seemed that even the fierce roar and crackle of the fire fell under its spell, and died to a faint murmur.

"Our Father, who art in Heaven."

With one accord, the multitude sank to their knees, their voices united in chorus: "Hallowed be Thy name...Thy Kingdom come." The age-old prayer of the Christian world was recited to the final Amen. A pregnant hush settled over the worshippers.

Again, the male voice rang out, "Oh Lord God in Heaven. Look down on us, your repentant sinners. See how we, your obedient children, this day, obey Your commands." Loud, fervent shouts of, "Slava Bohu. Slava Bohu," issued from many throats.

The thread of the prayer was picked up and continued, this time by a female voice. Forceful, urgent, the words tumbled out, "Never again, Oh Lord, shall we, your children, kill nor maim man nor beast. By way of this hot flame, do we send you, our Heavenly Father, the wicked knives, the cruel guns, the harsh swords. Take them, Oh Lord, take them."

Again, the multitude cried out in a rhapsody of emotion. Once more, the two thousand voices blended in an ancient Psalm of hope and of promise.

Into this harmony of hymn and prayer, a new, alien sound filtered — the thunder of many horses approaching at full gallop. A hoarse command, followed by a bugle blast, brought silence. A troop of two hundred Cossacks slid to a halt, facing the kneeling worshippers. Quietly, slowly, they rose to their feet, their eyes on Captain Praga, the troop commander, as he rode forward to halt between them and his troop. His voice, harsh in the silence, rang out commandingly.

"You there. You people. What foul deed brings you out here at this time of day?" His words were greeted by a stony silence. "Well? I am Captain Praga, and I demand an answer."

From somewhere within the crowd, a male voice humbly replied, "We come only to worship. And to destroy our weapons."

At this, the captain peered intently into the inferno, studied it for a moment, unbelievingly, and murmured, "You what? Those twisted pieces of metal... Sergeant, were those really guns?"

The troop sergeant, who had ridden close to the fire and stared at the charred bits of metal, returned to the side of the captain, his face red from the heat. "I think so, Sir. Looks like there might be swords in there, too."

"My God, wait till the Governor sees this." Yelling threatingly, he rapidly strode forward, "Send me your leader, at once."

A female voice rang out, calmly, assuredly, "We have no leader. We re all equal in the sight of God. No one of us is better than the other."

Before the captain could reply, his attention was drawn to the sounds of horse and carriage rapidly nearing the scene. With a jingle of harness, and slamming of doors, the governor of the Province of Tiflis jumped quickly to the ground, followed by the grave-faced Count Kripinski. Both men stood for a moment, surveying the scene. Dress dishevelled from what was obviously a fast, rough trip, was hurriedly adjusted. They had rushed out of Horlovka hours before, and driven hard and fast to reach this scene of a rumoured revolt. Spotting the captain, the governor called out authoritatively, "Captain Praga. What the devil goes on here? What were those shots we heard?"

The captain rode towards his superiors, halted, saluted. "Good morning, Governor. And to you, Count Kripinski, a good morning also."

The governor's irritation was visible in his scowl.

"Never mind the morning. What goes on here? What are these fool fanatics up to this time?"

"Celebrating St. Peter's Day, Sir."

The captain could not resist a glance back to the fire, evidently relishing this moment: "By burning their weapons."

"Burning their—Captain, did you say weapons?"

"I did, Sir."

Beside himself with rage, the governor stamped his foot and waved threatingly toward the assembly, now very quiet, watchful.

"But, but, they cannot do this. This is impossible. Sheer lunacy. I thought, in fact, I was assured, that they were preparing to attack the good folk of Horlovka."

"That was certainly the rumour, Sir."

"Then what are they doing? Oh, never mind." Voice rising, he stabbed a finger at the crowd. "Captain, order these people to disperse at once."

"Very good Sir."

Grim-faced, he rode back to his troop, as, thoughtfully, the Count studied the silent, unmoving assembly.

"I could not believe that they were preparing any attack. Not these Douhkobors. You know, Governor, they do have strong pacifist views."

"My dear Count. Those Horlovka people were so sure of it. Ever since they chased these fool fanatics off their land, there have been bad feelings."

"No matter, Governor. These people shrink from violence in any form."

Shouted commands interrupted further conversation.

"You people. Hear me. Go home. Your Governor has ordered you to return to your homes. Now, go. Start moving."

The assembly, silent till then, replied, but only with the commencement of another Psalm. Thoroughly enraged by this token form of rebellion, the governor screamed, "Very well, Captain, ride them down. Ride them down, I say!"

With a restraining hand on the arm of his companion, the Count quietly protested. "Oh, come now, Governor. These people mean no harm."

The governor shrugged him off, spat out his reply. "You, Count, are here as an observer, not as my adviser. You would do well to remember that."

Baffled and defeated, the Count silently watched the troop deploy. Over the notes of the Psalm, the brassy notes of a bugle sounded, clear and urgent, followed by the thunder of many hooves, which increased in tempo until they reached full gallop. Yells and shouts of fast riding troopers filled the air. The singing died away to a low murmur. Slowly the worshippers sank to their knees, mouthing unheard words of prayer.

When it seemed that the troop must surely trample the kneeling group into the ground, the horses, of one accord, slithered to a sudden halt—almost on top of the sea of bodies—some rearing high on their hind legs, others sliding and shying to one side. This abrupt move, so unexpected, threw a few of the troopers to the ground. For a split second, there was dead silence, broken by the nearly incoherent voice of the furious governor.

"Move, dammit. Make those horses move. Ride on. Use your lash. Into them!"

Troopers' curses, intermingled with the sharp crack of the lash against horsehide, accompanied the frantic neighing and whinnying of the terrified beasts. Still, they would not budge into the bowed forms of the people.

"Captain Praga, Captain Praga. I ordered you to ride these people down. What are you standing there for? Ride the fools down."

The captain's desperate shouted reply came back over the bedlam, "I don't know, Sir. The horses just will not move."

"You idiot. Make them move. Try again." To himself, he muttered, "Horses won't move. Never heard such nonsense."

Puzzlement apparent in his eyes, the Count stood silently observing the action.

"Well, well. I can't believe it. Those horses just will not move past the front rank. You know, Governor..."

Vicious words of the governor cut him off. "I'll move them. Just you watch, Count. Captain Praga, stand your ground. Use your lash on those fanatics. Use your lash on them. Now!"

At this new threat, there was a quick shifting and movement amongst the villagers. From the solid, massed, kneeling position they had assumed to meet the charge, they rapidly rose to form a human triangle. Closest to the menacing troop, the apex was filled by older men and women. The younger people moved back to form the base of this triangle against a rock cliff.

The feared sound of the lash changed, became heavy, thudding down on unresisting backs. First one, then two, three, until the air resounded with the thud and crack of many lashes being used cruelly and effectively on human flesh. Muffled cries and low groans were the only indication of the pain and torture, as if the sufferers in their agony sought to prevent any outcry. As one fell, they would be tenderly lifted, and with gentle hands, passed back to the base of the cliff, and another of the Brethren would step forward to fill the place of the fallen one.

Ashen-faced, the Count cried out in despair, "Governor, I urge you, put a stop to this."

Savage-voiced, face contorted by rage, he replied, "It is the only language they understand. Force."

Unable to meet the disgust and loathing in the Count's eyes, he moved away, only to be halted as his companion roughly grabbed him by the arm and forced him to stand face to face. "This has gone far enough. In God's name, order your men to cease. Why must we always brutalize ourselves? I plead with you, stop this carnage." In his fury and desperation, he vigorously shook the struggling, enraged governor.

Startlingly, the high-pitched scream of a terrified child tore through the bedlam. Surprised by this unexpected development, both men turned to the source of the scream. It happened that Nastasia, unnoticed by Paul, had jumped from the wagon and somehow made her way round the milling troopers in search of her parents. Caught in the press of people, Paul tried vainly to reach her. Jolted by her scream, he saw her fall, shaking and sobbing under the restless hooves of a frightened horse. The animal, looming above her crumpled form, shied violently to one side, ears back, eyes dilated by fright and confusion. The young trooper, almost dislodged by this unexpected move, reached quickly down, instinctively clasped the little girl in one arm, raised her out of harm's way. As if regretting his action, he thrust her roughly into the upraised arms of Nickolai, who had raced to assist her.

Reacting to the scream, the Count had also moved to assist the child, but, noting that her danger had been averted by the actions of the trooper and her father, returned to resume his position beside the now very calm governor, as father and daughter were lost to view in the surging crowd.

Safely away from reach of the stinging lash, deep in the midst of the Brethren, Nickolai gently lowered Nastasia to the ground. Unbelieving, he raised his hand to stare at a deep red stain of blood covering his palm. Turning her over on her side, he found the cause of the stain. A large rent had split her woolen shawl, gray pinafore, and undershirt, revealing a diagonal, ugly whip weal running from shoulder to waist. Mercifully, she sank into unconsciousness.

Starting back in a rage such as he had never before known, Nickolai clenched his upraised fist, shaking it in the direction of the perspiring laboring troopers. "You cowards! Animals! Swine!"

As he attempted to push his way forward, a restraining hand clasped him by the shoulder. A soft voice interjected, breaking his tirade. "Calm yourself, Brother Obedkoff. Calm yourself. Live in Christ. Did he not say 'Turn the other cheek to those who would smite thee!'"

Defeated, realizing the futility of revenge, Nickolai gathered Nastasia up in his arms, pushed his way back to the base of the triangle, calling for his son, "Paul...Paul...Over here. Come quickly."

Struggling through the massed bodies, Paul forced his way to the side of his father, took in the stricken form of his sister. Gently, He stroked the quiet little face. "I could not stop her, Father. I tried. Is she hurt bad?"

Then, overcome by the shock of events, he became incoherent, sobbing quietly. Shocked and grief-stricken, he could only stare into the eyes of his father, who savagely thrust Nastasia into his arms. "Get her out of here somehow. Quickly, now," he shouted. But, realizing the boy's hurt and confusion, he moved with a now softened voice to comfort him. "Gently son, gently. Your Mother?"

"I tried to help her Father. The Brethren carried her out of harm's way."

For a moment, he stood watching his son carry Nastasia farther back, to where many of the younger women were busy, tending the wounded. At a shouted command, his eyes fell on the troop. Men and horses were breathing heavily from exertion. Slowly, they turned away from the people. Now, the sudden quiet broke. As if they would taunt the might of the Tsar, the defiant sect again raised their voices in hymn. Without any understanding of language, there could be no misunderstanding of the meaning of this reckless singing. The fervor of song bespoke, clearly, contempt of government, the use of force and of brutality.

Striding forward, grim-faced, the governor eyed the defiant throng. Halting, he commandingly raised his hand. The singing gradually died away. All eyes focused on the stocky form.

"Listen to me, you fools. I give you one more chance to return to your homes." Sullen silence greeted his command. "Very well, then." Turning rapidly on his heels, he moved to stand beside the now dismounted troop. "Captain Praga, have your men fall in line order, and unsling carbines."

Over the dry rustling of carbines sliding from holsters came the shocked voice of the Count, "My God, you must not. You cannot do this."

Glancing briefly at the face of the horror-stricken Count, the governor turned his back on him to face the troop. Very calm and determined, his voice rang out, steady, cold.

"Ready."

Two hundred carbines swung upward, to point menacingly at the determined, silent group. A horse shook its head, the jangle of chain and bit loud and clear in the stillness.

"Aim."

In the pregnant quiet, not a movement, not a sound. The world froze for an instant. For an eternity. There could be no doubt now that the governor fully intended to shoot down these recalcitrant fanatics. Nor could there be any doubt that, before they would give in, they would be willing to die.

Before he could utter the fatal order to fire, the voice of the Count, sickened and horrified, penetrated the silence. "Give the order, Governor, and I shall cleave you in two where you stand."

Withdrawing his sword, he raised it high above the head of his companion. The hiss of pent-up air issuing from two thousand throats, came out like a pressurized steam valve. Someone coughed. A woman cried hysterically. Others called out over and over, "Slava Bohu... Slava Bohu."

Again, the chorus in the morning air, triumphant, jubilant. Thankful, the volume of sound almost obliterated the orders of the captain to his men. The governor, defeated, shaken, and now very quiet, addressed the troop. "Have your men return to quarters, Captain."

He then turned to the Count, "You have not heard the end of this. I will of course make a complete report of your interference. Completely unwarranted."

The Count shrugged slightly, but walked with evident relief to the carriage, accompanied by the governor. About to enter, he laid a restraining hand on the arm of his companion, his eyes on the worshippers.

"One moment, Governor. It would appear you have a delegation to meet with you." His eyes were on a group of young men approaching the carriage, and his tone dripped sarcasm. "Probably come to offer their thanks."

"Well now. You see? I told you that force was the only way. Beat them now and then, and they'll fawn all over you."

Slowly, his smile changed to a scowl. The group halted in front of him, reached into their coat pockets, withdrew pieces of paper, and threw them at his feet.

"Take these papers back to your Tsar. We'll have no further use for them."

Defiant, they marched back to rejoin the group, passing on the way many other young men, all bent on a similar mission.

The governor's eyes jumped from one group to the other. Fuming, blustering, he called out, "Here now, what's this, eh? Why do you throw these papers at my feet?"

He received no reply. Only the flutter of falling paper, and many footsteps approaching, then receding.

Amused, the Count watched the ritual. "Apparently, conscription has just ended. At least, for them. And, after today, who can blame them? Poor devils. Look, my friend. The young dogs approach. So many of them."

Disregarding the amused Count, the governor continued in his blustering.

"Here now. Stop this. Stop, I say. Count, tell them to—oh, never mind." Taking in the amused expression on the Count's face, he shrugged and entered the carriage. "Come, let us go, I am famished."

About to follow, the Count paused and surveyed the littered ground: "Like pure snow. Never have I seen the ground around your feet so white."

Then, jumping into the carriage, he sat watching as they moved off.

The crisis over, many of the people moved to the wagons, some assisted by others. Some, too injured to walk, were carried in the arms of the stronger young men. Others, in pure defiance, renewed the Psalm singing.

In the rising heat of the morning sun, Paul, gently cradling Nastasia in his arms, knelt at the side of his prostrate mother. Gingerly, Nickolai searched the back of her head with his fingers. Small rivulets of blood oozed down both sides of the white neck, seeping into the sheepskin cloak. Satisfied, Nickolai murmured, "She will soon recover. No broken bones." Tenderly raising her in his arms, he started for the wagon. "Come Paul. Let us get away from here."

Nearing the outer fringe of the crowd, they were stopped by one of the several women tending the wounded.

"Your Elizabeth, she is hurt bad?"

"Only a head wound." Nickolai's voice, reflecting his anger and impatience, was loud and overly rough.

As he attempted to push past her, she laid a hand on him,

impeding any further progress. "Peace, Brother Obedkoff. She suffers for Christ. Only for Christ."

Angrily, he pushed his way past her, brushed her arm to one side. "And my little one. Must she also suffer for Christ?"

The old woman's eyes followed his retreating back, "Aye, even the little ones. All must suffer."

Eager to escape the scene of soul-sickening and unwarranted horror, Nickolai loaded his little family into the wagon and headed for home. As is the way with horses, upon sensing the return journey, they broke into a rapid trot, and bounced the occupants roughly about. Elizabeth, gradually awakening, lay stretched out in the back. Paul, white-faced and drawn, clutched the seat rail beside his father, and grimly held onto his sister, who still remained oblivious to her surroundings.

Though busily engaged in restraining the eager team, Nickolai brooded on the morning's events. As they crossed the lower meadows, his eyes followed a fleeting cloud shadow. High above in the blue, a lone white cloud played tag with the sun, casting a racing darkness across the land it touched. As he watched, the edge of the shadow sped across the meadows towards him, touched the cart, then engulfed it, permeating the occupants in an aura of sudden gloom — a twilight zone of clammy greyness in the noonday heat, that sent a tremor over perspiring arms and faces. A premonition. An omen of evil yet to come. Then it passed. Nickolai shuddered in the heat.

Travelling in the opposite direction, the carriage of the Count bounced and swayed as it moved rapidly along the high road toward Horlovka. The two men, lost in thought, sat in their respective corners, eyes unseeing as they stared through the small windows. They were totally oblivious to the brilliant June sunshine flooding the gently flowing hills. As it moved down from the highlands, the carriage rumbled along a broad, smooth highway that stretched the length of a green, lush, fertile valley. This had been the previous home of those Douhkobors now living in Orlovka.

Governor Nakashidze, his small pale face reflecting anger and frustration, turned to the Count.

"You know, my dear Count, I still feel your interference this morning was unwarranted and entirely uncalled for."

The sound of the Governor's voice, loud after the prolonged silence, startled the count. He turned with a jerk from his musings. For a long moment, he surveyed the sullen, irate governor. When he replied, it was with the soft, thoughtful tones of a man well-versed in the ways of justice, though somewhat saddened by its ironic twists.

"Sorry, my friend. Just thinking. You know, I have known you for many years. As a friend, as the husband of my dear niece. Your two children are of my blood. Until today, I had always thought of you with respect. The dedicated, loyal servant of the Tsar. Now..."

Shrugging, his voiced trailed away to silence, the agony in his eyes all too evident.

The face of the governor flushed in anger at his old friend's remarks. He did not, however, give way to the furious retort so evident on his lips and in his heart. It was as if he realized that such could only lead to a bitter quarrel. He paused, took a deep breath, then with a voice straining for control, said, "Yes, my friend. Dedicated. Loyal. A servant. That, I am. And that is all. I carry out my orders to the letter. And my orders today were precise and to the point. At the first sign of defiance, disperse those fanatics, and send them back to their homes."

"Did your orders, Governor, empower you to shoot down defenceless men and women?"

"My orders, Count, gave me full power to deal with the situation as I saw fit."

Suddenly, the effort to contain himself became too great. Voice rising, urgent, compelling, sincere, the governor leaned forward and brought his face close to the startled Count.

"Can you not understand, my friend, that, at this very moment, the fabric of our nation is being torn apart by revolution? Strikes and uprisings in every city. In Kiev, in St. Petersburg, in Moscow. Workers are taking to the streets, day after day. Waving red flags. Howling out their insane demands. More pay. Less working hours. A say in government. Where will it stop? Next thing you know, why, they will be demanding to run the country. It just cannot be allowed to continue."

"Those were not factory workers you faced today. They were simple peasants. And, governor, compose yourself."

Momentarily taken aback, the governor answered quietly, "Simple peasants, Count? What has been the history of the peasant over the past few years? Burning, looting, stealing. Murdering the land owners and their families. This is the simple peasant? I tell you, we have open revolt across the land, and it will be put down. At any cost."

Wearied by an exchange with one so set in his ways and opinions, the Count turned once again to stare out the window, his voice a low murmur. "Lootings? Burnings? Murders? I cannot deny this. Yet, are these not the acts of desperate men, beaten, hopeless men, men who once had hope, who were given a promise? How else would you expect them to act?"

"Riddles, my dear Count? I am afraid you have lost me. Their only hope lies with their father, the Tsar. Their only promise is that by toil, by the sweat of the brow, why, then, someday Russia may stand as a giant among the nations of the world."

This turn in the argument awakened a new spirit in the Count. He turned to the governor, his deep emotions sobering his voice.

"That is not quite what I had in mind. Thirty years ago, Alexander the Second abolished serfdom. Men were free for the first time in their lives. Free to marry as they pleased. Free to own land. That is, if they could afford it. Free to practise any religion they choose. Free to send their children to school. He gave them a hope. He made them a promise. Now his successors have taken away those freedoms. No, Governor. Without hope, without a fulfilled promise, all your bullets will not stop them."

Quickly, voice quiet, the governor replied. "And so, my dear friend, what was his reward? An assassin's bullet through his chest. That, I can assure you, will never happen to Nicholas."

As if groping for words, the Count closed his eyes. That this assassination had been an undeniable, unexplicable, useless act, he knew to be true.

"That, I have never been able to comprehend. On the very day Alexander decreed as law the rights to a Representative Assembly, the very thing that the people had been fighting to accomplish for years, that was the day he was shot down. I will never understand the mentality of the working man. The senseless, wanton destruction of their one benefactor. It baffles me."

"And yet, these are the very people you and other moderates would place in power."

For the first time, the voice of the Count rose. He had felt the sting. "No. I want no such thing. And, Governor, do not place words in my mouth. My sole concern at this moment is the unnecessarily harsh treatment of a small religious sect, whose only offences are their refusal to abide by and recognize the Russian Orthodox Church, and their refusal to kill their fellow man."

Dogmatic, the Governor broke in. "There is only one Tsar. Only one Church."

The sudden clatter of wheels over cobblestones brought the discussion to an end. As the carriage pulled to a halt, the Count, turning to his companion, smiled, "Oh, Governor?"

About to open the door, the Governor turned towards the Count questioningly.

"I feel that I have been overly critical of you this morning. For that, I apologize."

Somewhat mollified, the governor shrugged, opened the door

and stepped down, followed by the Count who, in a gesture of friendship, placed an arm around the shoulder of his companion. Together, they moved up the stone flagged walk towards the large double doors of a rambling village hostelry.

"And to show there are no hard feelings, you will lunch with me?"

"My pleasure, Count." Pausing by the door of the hostelry, one hand on the massive wrought iron opener, he turned to face the Count, again serious, sombre.

"There is one factor you have not taken into account. Possibly, you would have no knowledge of it. It has come to our attention that this non-violent sect you so eloquently plead for has a leader, someone called Veregin. Exiled, I believe, in Siberia. We have reliable information that, over the past two years, this Veregin has been in constant communication with Tolstoy. Even you, my friend, should know what that portends."

"Tolstoy? You mean the Count Lev Tolstoy?"

"The same."

"But, Governor, I fail to see any danger in that. After all, he has been in England for years."

"The government does not share your view. They consider him a dangerous radical. A heretic. And he is now in Moscow."

Opening the door, both men disappeared into the dim, cool interior.

In peaceful little Orlovka,
On a sunny summer's day,
The villagers held a Sobranya,
To their God they came to pray.
The might of the Tsar
Encircled them,
Filling all with fear.
Their day of reckoning
Close at hand,
"Exile" they would hear.

2

Black July

This was their church, their Sobranya. Blue, cloud-etched sky above, Mother Earth below, earth worn and packed by the shuffling of many feet, over many years, and, all around, row upon row, stately golden sunflowers. A massive, twisted apple tree, seeming as old as time itself, sent out branches unifying earth and sky. This the focal point where, for so many years, the villagers had gathered to pray and to communicate with their God.

The warm July breeze rippled first one then another of the tortured heavy branches, ruffling the dry leaves, stirring them to a gently soft whisper, and seeming to blend in with the harmonious chanting of the villagers.

In the dappled shade cast by the gnarled tree, sat a rough wooden table, covered by a snow-white cloth, on which there stood the jug of water, the loaf of dark rye bread, and the dish of salt, the symbols of the basic elements of life. As ever, the women and young girls had gathered to one side of the table, facing their menfold who were grouped on the other side, behind the Elders of the village.

This was their Sobranya. A place of meeting. Not so much a meeting of bodies, but, rather, a settling down into the past. Here the legends, the story psalms, the prayers, were handed down by word-of-mouth, from one generation to the next. Here was perpetuated the Living Book, the only Bible they knew.

Small children ran in and about the adults, completely oblivious to the sonorous words of the old patriarch, Ivan

Lebenoff, who, despite his ninety-odd years, could still recite the ancient prayers in a clear, resonant voice. Quietly attentive, the Brethren listened as he recounted the oft-told history and sad demise of the wise old diplomat, Lukeria Vasilivna Kalmokova. She, during her reign some forty years ago, that far-off time when the sect were as one, farming the rich soil around Goreloye, had managed to successfully meet the demands of the government. By supplying much-needed wheat, corn, and horses to the army, they were given a pledge that no member of the Doukhobor faith would be called upon to take up arms in the war against Turkey, thus pleasing and placating the non-violent ethics of her people. Nevertheless, despite the fact that this bargain led to an enrichment of the sect materially, and an easing of government persecution for a time, there were those who still felt that this had been an unwise move. The basic tenets of their faith had been violated for the first and only time in their long history.

Now, the leadership had passed to the young man, who for many years had been groomed for this post by Lukeria Kalmkova; he, whose origin and birth remained a mystery. Some claimed that he had been Lukeria's lover; others that he was her son. The majority, however, accepted him as the true leader in Christ, Peter Vasilovich Veregin. That the authorities took him seriously was evident. The moment he had been proclaimed and acknowledged as leader, he was arrested and shipped off to a camp for political exiles in far-off Siberia, where he still languished.

Quietly, another of the Elders took over with an announcement that couriers had been dispatched to the far north to inform their leader that his strict edict regarding the burning of weapons had been carried out. A short prayer for his early return was then offered by the Elder.

One of the women then led off with the opening notes of a psalm, praising the deceased Lukeria Kalmkova, and extolling her virtues. Others picked up the chant, and soon gave full voice to the sad, poignant hymn.

Nickolai, his attention wandering, glanced around him. Despite the serenity of this day, he could not shake off a sense of unease and foreboding. Full well, he understood that the heavy fist of the government must soon descend, and demand retribution for the burning on St. Peter's Day. His eyes came to rest on Elizabeth, noting the small bare patch on her head, gleaming whitely amidst the dark hair. That she had recovered from her ordeal was apparent. Where, he wondered, did she find the strength to carry on? To retain and nurture her deep abiding faith in God, a strength and a faith that gave him many pangs of guilt. Never had she displayed the slightest trace of rancor against those who so brutally inflicted pain on her body, and on the bodies of her Sisters and Brethren. Would she, he wondered, really be prepared to die for her faith? He knew the answer, even as he broached the question. Yes, She was fully capable of giving up life itself, rather than weaken her fervent beliefs.

God, he prayed, why am I so weak? Can it be so wrong, that my only interest lies with my family, with my home? Why is it that I must so completely resent any force that threatens the security of either?

Could it be his little daughter, Nastasia? Her deep-seated shock? Her obvious terror at any sudden noise? Her fright, that even now, three weeks after the tearing lash had scarred her slight body, would awaken her in the dark of night, screaming in a frenzy of fear? Was it her open display of her very real need to be near him at all times? Her silence, the reproach that crept unguarded into the once-smiling eyes? Was it this that made the difference in his beliefs? In his faith? He could not know. Only he knew that, for the first time in nearly thirty years of living the Doukhobor faith, he knew hatred, bitterness, and a violent need to strike back. Even in his reverie, he was conscious of her tiny body crouched at his feet, uncaring of the activities going on around her, as if in physical contact with the father she loved, she found her one haven from a world she could not comprehend.

Tenderly, instinctively, Nickolai reached down and gently teased Nastasia's long braided hair. Rubbing her cheek against his leg in response to his gesture, she raised her solemn face to gaze up at him. For a short moment a fleeting smile crinkled the corners of her eyes. Then, for no apparent cause, sheer panic contorted the small features, twisting the eyes and mouth into a mask of pure terror. Moaning, gasping, white-faced, she dropped to the ground, her arms wrapped protectively around her head. Mystified, Nickolai glanced around, to find Captain Praga and his sergeant grimly surveying the worshippers. Unnoticed, the troop had ridden into the meadow, and, deploying on all sides, had effectively blocked any escape.

The menace of the encircling troops set up an uneasy shifting and shuffling amongst the assembled villagers. All eyes were on the captain. Slowly, he removed an official looking document from a side pouch, lazily glanced from it to the silent people. Even more deliberately, he unfolded the document and commenced reading. It was evident that he thoroughly enjoyed the suspense.

"His Highness, the Tsar, Nicholas Two, sends his royal greetings to the townsfolk of Orlovka. He requests, nay demands, that this troop under my command be quartered on your esteemable village, and that you, the villagers, will provide food and bed for the troopers, and fodder for the mounts. Further to the above, you will supply any other needs as might be deemed necessary to the health and well-being of this troop."

Audible groans met his demand. Someone deep in the assemblage cried out: "No, no, it cannot be."

Amused, the captain let his eyes slowly roam over the gathering. Then, pretending amazement, he exclaimed:

"Can it be that we are not welcome? I had been given to understand that this sect were ever willing to extend the hand of friendship to the homeless wanderer. Ah, well. Never mind. It will not be for long. Now pay attention. I have not yet finished reading. Here is the portion of the proclamation I know you are going to relish."

Unrolling the document once again, he paused, cleared his throat, let his eyes move again over the waiting throng, then read: "It is also decreed that, within three days from this date, every citizen of the village of Orlovka will gather on the high road at six o'clock in the morning, carrying only the possessions you will require on your journey to the Province of Georgia. You hereby forfeit, and will leave behind, all livestock, all furnishings, all equipment, and all of your crops, both in the ground and in storage. This decree has been adjudged necessary for the good of the State, by your continued refusal to serve the Tsar, and by your recent demonstration, wherein you all, collectively and foolishly decided, and did in fact, set the torch to all of your weapons. Now..." Deliberate in every action, the captain rerolled the document, returned it to his pouch, then allowed his eyes, hard and set, to survey the aghast people. Satisfied that the impact of these words were having their desired effect, the captain signalled the troop into line. Stunned, the villagers could only stare. Nickolai, shaking his head in rage, blurted out violently:

"No, no. You cannot do this evil thing. It is...it is wrong."

For a moment, the captain studied Nickolai, then ordered his sergeant: "Arrest this man. I will see what he has to say in the morning. And as for the rest of you, return to your homes and start packing. Now go."

Slowly, their faces mirroring disbelief and shock, the villagers began to set off for their homes. Elizabeth hurried to where Nastasia had remained, cowering on the ground, gathered her up in her arms, and strode away, her eyes on Nickolai being led in the direction of an old barn by two troopers.

Other than the shouts and calls of the troop, unsaddling and leading their mounts towards nearby pastures and barns, no sound could be heard. Not a murmur escaped the lips of the villagers, as, a people without hope, without a future, they stumbled away.

*   *   *

All that sunny afternoon, Elizabeth sat staring out the small opening that served for a window, her eyes on the busy troopers, and on the barn that had so completely engulfed her husband. She watched with apprehension as each male of the village was marched to join Nickolai in his temporary prison. At least, she thought, the children were out of harm's way. She had sent both up to the sleeping loft with her stern admonitions to remain there until she called them down.

The arrival of a corporal and two troopers, loud and raucous as they set about spreading their straw pallets on the kitchen floor, scarcely broke into her spell. Only when the corporal, a large, perspiring, dark-featured bear of a man peremptorily ordered her to get some food on the table did she move, draggingly, to the stove. While they were busy gulping down the evening meal, she saw to it that the children were fed and made comfortable for the night.

Again, she resumed her seat by the window. From her attitude, it was obvious she was determined to ignore, as much as possible, the presence of these intruders in her home. Darkness she knew, would not fall till around ten o'clock. Her mind could take her no further. There was no escape. Even if she would leave her children, where could she go? She sensed that the stage was being set for a night of terror in her little village. Already, the odor of vodka permeated the hot, sticky evening air. Voices, loud, harsh, and drunken, seemed to issue from every corner, and from each house. In her numb shock and desperation, she prayed, "God, let my Nickolai sleep this night. Numb his tortured mind. Still the hatred that would destroy him. Let him sleep, oh Lord. Let him sleep."

Almost unnoticed, twilight filtered down on the village.

"Queer," thought Elizabeth, "how, with the coming of dusk, sounds seemed to decrease." She noted with a sense of relief, that, at this moment, the village had assumed a normalcy usual for this time of day, despite the rude invasion. It was as if each of the villagers, each of the intruders, was busily, quietly engaged in the final tasks of the day.

But peace was short-lived. A sudden high-pitched scream tore through the hush, followed by a man's coarse, loud laugh. From around one of the houses further up the street, the form of a young girl appeared. Her upper garment had been torn to shreds, revealing the full, firm breasts. Close behind the darting, running youngster, the sergeant was in full pursuit, laughing and cursing with excitement. Clutching her underskirt in both hands, the frightened girl stumbled and fell to the dust. Gleefully, the sergeant was on top of the struggling girl and with brutal zest, tore away the underskirt, leaving her body startlingly white against the dirt of the street.

"Poor little Anna," mused Elizabeth, "so young to have to endure this indignity. Only fourteen." With a strange sense of detachment, she watched the struggling girl being dragged, kicking and screaming, into one of the nearby houses.

In this detached, bemused mood, she was barely conscious of her visitors standing in the open doorway, howling bawdy encouragement to their sergeant. Laughingly, one of them remarked: "That sergeant, always after the young ones."

Turning from the door, the corporal laughed, "He can have them. Give me the plump hens. Like this one."

Standing directly behind her, he thrust both rough, calloused hands down the front of Elizabeth's dress. Other than an involuntary shudder, she made no move.

"What say, little hen? You're not much company sitting there by yourself, watching the fun. Come, join your guests."

Forcing her to her feet, he half-dragged the frightened, resisting woman to the table. Pushing her down onto the bench, he poured and offered her a full mug of vodka. Shaking her head in mute refusal, Elizabeth remained silent, watchful, wondering.

"Hey, men. Our little hen needs persuasion. Let's help her."

Willingly, the others grabbed her by the hair, pulling her head back, at the same time forcing her mouth open. The mug of vodka was then poured down her throat, to the accompaniment of shouts and gleeful giggles. Sputtering, choking and retching, the tortured woman struggled to release her head from their grip. Again, the mug was filled, and again poured down her throat.

"My, this little hen is a greedy one. No more for her. Let her go. Don't want her falling asleep on us. Right, boys?"

Releasing her, the men stood back, howling with glee, as Elizabeth, confused and shaken, attempted to rise and leave the table. Rough hands tore at her as she slipped, unable to stand, from bench to floor. Raw vodka sent a course of fire from lips to groin. Her senses reeled, her vision distorted, and became a blur of leering, sardonic faces — evil, lustful. Hands pulled at her clothing, fumbled over her defenseless body. Her mind in a sick turmoil, she felt only relief to find herself lying in her bed. Mercifully, gratefully, she slipped into semi-consciousness. The last thing she knew, was a voice shouting at her. "Where is your

God now? Why does he not help you?"

Although she thought that she answered audibly, it was only in her mind that any reply manifested itself. In the gathering confusion and darkness she believed that she shouted, "I suffer with Christ. Though my body might be harmed, my spirit remains invulnerable."

Then, the night closed in.

The sharp, insistent barking of a nearby dog forced a passage into her fogged mind. Somewhere, close at hand, a rooster's crow, loud and demanding, followed by the rapid slap of his wings, penetrated her cloudy bewilderment, beating her senses into a full awareness of her surroundings. The first faint glimmering of a new day outlined the small window. Then, as wave after wave of nausea swept through her tortured, wracked body, full realization of the past night flooded her mind. No clear images. Nothing concrete. Not yet. Vague, unformed sensations. But so real. Innumerable men, many of them, one after the other, thrusting their forceful way into her passive, unresisting body. Faint recollections of threats and curses. Slaps, hard, hurting. Vicious slaps, taunting her to show some life, to at least acknowledge by some struggle the fact that she was in the process of being raped. There had been no response. Not once had she moved a muscle. And now in drunken, snoring stupor, her violators lay around her, supine, limp as rag dolls. One hairy muscular arm weighed heavily down upon her bare breast, a leg thrust between hers.

The dark, choking, everbeating wings of total insanity began to close in around her. In her delirium, images, thoughts, words of prayer swept through her nearly deranged mind.

"Even you, Christ. Even you could not know the agony of this night. Then, would my suffering be your suffering? What was it You cried, nailed to the cross? Forgive them Father, for they know not what they do? But, then...Dear Christ, these men know. They know what they do. These beasts. These swine. NO...NO...Stop. Must stop. No hate, no hate. But then, how do you learn to love your violators? Those who would rob me of my dignity, of my humanity, of my very womanhood? Oh, Lord. Help me, help me to understand. Show me the way. In your divine mercy, let me endure this night without hatred. For are not even such as these your creatures also?"

Somewhere, in the sod roof above her head, a meadow lark burst into song. Sweet, melodious song, proclaiming to the world the sheer joy of living. Forcing her eyes open, Elizabeth found the interior of the hut filled with the soft glow of the rising sun. Dust motes danced and hovered in the golden rays. She had her answer. Life must go on. Wearily, carefully, she disengaged herself from the tangle of bodies, dressed and busied herself with preparing breakfast. Soon, bugle notes echoed throughout the village. Loud, commanding voices forced sleeping men to their feet. The day had begun.

Unlike Nature's gift, a morning of pristine beauty, man brought misery. This was the day that saw all young men of conscript age marched off to join penal battalions in Siberia, most of them never to be seen again.

For Elizabeth, it was a day when, withdrawn into an agony of spirit, she could only sit by the window, a silent witness to the unfolding of one callous horror after the other. First, there was the capture of young Gregory Lebenoff, grandson of the old patriarch. Rather than be marched off to Siberia, the young lad had taken refuge in the communal chicken house, only to be flushed out by troopers searching for fresh eggs. Flanked by his grinning captors, he faced a very calm Captain Praga, who, resplendent in the morning sunshine, idly tapped a riding crop against highly polished cavalry boots, and pondered the punishment. Elizabeth, though unable to hear any of the words, was soon made aware of the cruelty of his decision. Indicating a nearby wagon, the youth was roughly hauled to it, and tied, spread-eagled, to the large rear wheel, in such a manner that both hands and feet extended beyond the rim. A team of coal-black horses were harnessed and hitched to the wagon.

It was then that the old grandfather stepped forward to protest. His pleading words came faintly to Elizabeth.

"Please, Captain. Do not do this. He is only a boy. Let my hands and feet be shattered. Only let me suffer for him."

The captain made no reply. Merely signalled two men, pointed to the wagon seat, and watched as the old man was hoisted up, then handed the lines and a whip. Captain Praga's voice came to Elizabeth, startingly loud and clear. "Now, old man. I give you a choice. Whip up the horses, and drive this rebel into hell quickly. Otherwise, we will walk them so slowly, you will hear the bones crunch and break."

Ramrod stiff, the old man stared straight ahead, the lines in one hand, the whip in the other. Face grey and set, not a muscle flinched. To the wide-eyed, stricken Elizabeth, it seemed that time itself had ceased to exist. Unable to contain herself, she moaned in pain, praying, the words tumbling from her throat.

"Oh, God in Your mercy. Do not let this thing happen. Show young Gregory Your compassion. Let a lightning bolt strike. God, help him."

Something about the eerie, long drawn-out silence, halted her words, opened her eyes. The wagon remained as before, the boy suspended head down, the old man rigid in his seat. A new element had been added to the scene. The carriage she had seen at the burning now stood to the rear of the wagon. The tall, well-dressed nobleman who had prevented the massacre now had placed himself in front of the captain, remonstrating violently. Fascinated, she watched as the captain shrugged, motioned to his sergeant, who directed the untying of the boy. He was then led to stand, facing his tormentors.

That the captain had lost his calm, was evident. Loudly, he exclaimed, "Very well, Count. I shall accede to your wishes. Yet, this rebel has defied us, and punish him, I must."

Scarcely pausing for breath, angrily, vindictively, he spat out: "Twenty lashes. Sergeant, carry out the sentence."

All eyes were on the unfortunate lad, as he was led back to the wheel and tied by the wrists, face against the spokes. A large trooper, having removed his coat, administered the lashing. Other than an odd low moan, the boy made no whisper, as his back was peeled raw. By the count of ten, he was unconscious.

Standing to one side, the Count, his face mirroring revulsion at the severity of this sentence, counted out each stroke. When the trooper would have administered one extra lash, he placed his hand forcibly on the whip, and prevented the final stroke.

This was also a day that was to see their own Brethren from Gorelyoe and from Horlovka — those who once had been friends and neighbors — descend on the village, like vultures, thought Elizabeth. Because of their willingness to co-operate with the Tsarist regime, they would now take possession of all property and holdings in this village. She watched with resignation as they moved through the buildings, accompanied by the captain, who decided who would get which parcel of land, which plow, which of the livestock. This was the price the government would pay for their continued subservience. She watched drearily, as the nobleman followed the others around, then, as if frustrated and sick at the injustice he had to witness, moved quickly to his carriage, jumped in and drove rapidly out of sight.

Somehow, the morning passed. Wearily, numbly, Elizabeth fed the children, reiterating her command to stay out of sight. Occasionally, her eyes would stray to the barn, where, by now, most of the men not sent out on the long march north had been incarcerated for questioning. At least, she thought, Nickolai has company.

Nickolai. Somehow, very soon, she would stand in front of him. She would look into his eyes, and he would know. Inwardly, she shuddered. This man she loved, how well did she really know him? Her revery was interrupted by the notes of a bugle. Noon. Draggingly, uncaring, she set up the table, ladling out large servings of borscht. By the time she had completed her task, the three men stamped in. Despite dust-streaked perspiration on hands and faces, they were in a jovial mood. The corporal, in a teasing mood, playfully slapped her across the rump.

"Maybe no good in bed. But you sure good cook."

Ignoring them by her very silence, Elizabeth retired to a corner, sat down, and stared into emptiness. The emptiness of uncaring, the emptiness of the days and years ahead, days and years she must somehow learn to live through, with the bitter new-found knowledge that her God was not always just, that He was capable of inflicting the harshest sufferings even on the innocent. Conflict raged within her. For the first time in her twenty-nine years, she now had to balance the grim realities of life against the teachings of her forefathers. At this moment, like one in shock, no ray of light could penetrate her deep gloom, her aura of depression. Where, she wondered, could she now find the strength, the hope, and the courage that would be so necessary to carry her through the future hardships of life?

Deep in her misery, she was barely aware of the entrance of the sergeant. Brusquely, he ordered the men to finish eating, pack and be saddled up within fifteen minutes. Even as he spoke, the bugle sounded assembly. Rapidly, the men finished eating, struggled into military coats, and moved out the door. Stepping over the doorsill, the corporal paused and turned. His fingers fumbled with the brass buttons of his jacket. He stared at the woman, half hidden in the corner. Silently, he raised an arm towards her. About to form a word, he stopped. Something in her eyes, the desperation, the naked hatred hit him. With a light shrug, he turned and rapidly disappeared out into the noon sunlit street.

Strident commands, the neighing of a restless horse, the jingle of chain and bit, all sounds of the troop moving out, reached her ears. Still she sat unmoving, waiting, listening to the receding hoofbeats. The moment she dreaded was close at hand. And then it was upon her. A shadow darkened the door. A figure moved in. Nickolai. His eyes squinted in the gloom, features hard and set. This was a face she had never before seen. Moaning as an animal in pain, she was at his feet, kneeling in an attitude of abject suppliance, head on the dirt floor, hands and arms outstretched. Incoherently, she jabbered words that made no sense.

For a moment, Nickolai stood, stiff, shocked, gazing down at the rolling head, the quivering arms. Reaching down, he gently lifted the sobbing woman to her feet, placed one hand under her chin, forcing her eyes to meet his.

"Is this how you would greet your husband, my Elizabeth? after a cursed night out in that shed? Come, I am famished. See to my food."

Releasing her chin, in a sudden rush of emotion, he placed both arms around her, pulling the shaking body to his. Tightly, he held her.

"There, now, my wife. Whatever occurred these past hours, will be forgotten in the mist of time. Whatever hurt you suffered will ease. Whatever bitter memories you hold will wash away. Is this not what you have been taught? Is not God forgiving? Should we be less so? Elizabeth, Elizabeth... Do you not believe that He lives within each of us? That if we suffer hurt, He also hurts?"

The soft voice, the gentle tone, stilled the quivering of the tortured woman. Slowly, gradually, she relaxed, and leaned against his strong firm body. Raising her head from his shoulders for a long moment, tear-dimmed eyes stared into his. Then she released herself from his arms, moved towards the stove.

"Sit down, my husband. There is borscht."

And so life began again.

Dark of night descends from high;
Courage, Hope, all taken flight.
Wings of death flutter near;
How escape our nightmare plight?
You, my Brothers from afar,
Heard our mournful plea,
In mercy, offered loving hands,
Drew us cross the restless sea.

3

Georgian Nightmare

Three winters and three summers had passed. Each a year of torture. The physical torture of watching loved one's suffer and weaken, day by day, as malnutrition, dysentery, and malaria took their grim toll.

Worst of all was the mental torture: rumours that, even bizzare and unfounded, nevertheless gave the Brethren the strength to carry on. That first winter, the hope, the promise whispered about. The Tsar had relented. They would be returned to Orlovka. Later, a persistent rumour of an early release from their penurious bondage reached the exiles. They were to sail across a strange ocean to a strange land, where they would find a paradise flowing with milk and honey. Many acres of virgin land were to be had for the asking. The sun was warm and shone all year round. Most intriguing of all, there would be no government to interfere with, or dicta*e to them.

Nickolai, sitting with his back against a wall of the sod shanty they had so laboriously built, reflected on these rumours. The promise of a new land had given hope to all for a while. Now even these had ceased. All hope had gone. His eyes on the last rays of an autumn sun, he knew full well that another winter in this bleak forbidding place, and they must surely perish.

So many had already gone. Of the more than two thousand peasants expelled from around Orlovka, and the surrounding villages, less than fourteen hundred now lived. Many had not even survived the brutal six-weeks-long march to these Georgian marshes. Most of the Elders had been buried by the side of the road, unable to stand the rigors of this new life. Others had perished miserably in the grim, futile attempt to keep body and soul together against insurmountable odds. They had, thought Nickolai, just given up. What with the government's cruel edict, condemning to exile any Georgian citizen who dared to assist these homeless, broken refugees, together with a total ban on the ownership or leasing of any land or livestock, life had become unbearable, almost impossible to sustain.

Even their spiritual strength had been weakened and sapped. No more than three families had been allowed to settle in any given village, thus thinly spreading the Brethren over a large and desolate area. Somehow, though, furtively and in secret, in all kinds of weather, they had managed to occasionally gather together for the odd Sobranya. Had they been discovered, the penalty would have been flogging or death.

Maybe, he pondered, that would have been the easy way out. More than his Brothers, he knew that this was no punishment handed down by a wrathful God. Rather, this was a policy of total, deliberate extermination by a vengeful government, assisted and condoned by the Orthodox Church of Russia whose members and clergy constituted an ever-present threat, spying and probing, ever-ready to report on their struggle to survive. The possibility of release from this degradation had often been presented by various Bishops, and higher clergy, if they would but recant their fanatical ways, renounce their beliefs, and publicly declare the Orthodox Church the only viable religion. None had weakened, nor taken this way out. Even now, with the war long over, there could be no forgiveness, no relenting of the harsh policies of the Tsar.

In the gathering dusk, chilled by the raw night air, Nickolai rose and stiffly pushed aside the burlap that served as a door, and entered the dimly-lit smoky interior of the shanty. Elizabeth, on her knees by a small stone fireplace, busy with her cooking, turned to him.

"Sit, Nickolai. Time for eating."

Grunting in reply, he sat down at a table built from an old birch log. Tonight, turnip and carrots. Last night, a frozen cabbage and some small wormy potatoes. All had been filched from a neighboring field, dug furtively from the hard earth, while the Georgian farmer had looked the other way. One had to survive somehow.

Silently, Paul and Nastasia crept to the table to join their father. They looked, thought Nickolai, like undernourished, mute ghosts. When was the last time they had laughed, or shouted, or even played as children? He could not remember.

Their silence cast a pall over every living minute. Only Elizabeth seemed determined to live and, with an inner strength founded on her renewed faith in her God, was able to carry on in some manner. The wasted frame, the early greying hair, testified to the rigors of her struggle. Glancing across the crude table to his morose face, she paused in her eating.

"Tonight, my husband, a Sobranya. All must go. There is news. Good news, We soon will leave this accursed place."

Elizabeth's animated features only served to deepen his frown.

"We have heard such news before."

"You do not believe?"

Nickolai shrugged.

"Believe? There is nothing to believe. We will die here."

Perturbed by his defeatist attitude, Elizabeth stared at him. Seriously, determined, she proclaimed, "Nickolai, we leave this place. It is so. Tonight, some very important person is to attend. He has papers."

Nickolai did not allow her to finish. He rose abruptly, and stumbled to the door. Pausing, one hand pushing aside the burlap, he yelled at her, "I will go. But when we return, lay out your dead clothes."

Then, with an inarticulate cry of agony and despair, he fled. How could he find the strength to impart to this wife he loved so dearly and yet was so powerless to protect that only this day he learned the Tsarist regime in a final, sadistic decree, had ordered that all children of the Doukhobor faith be separated from their parents, and placed in the custody and care of the Orthodox church? This, he knew, could well be the hammer blow that would kill Elizabeth.

On the verge of insanity, overflowing with the futility of living, and filled with fear and desperation, he fled out into the night. And the night engulfed him in its anonymity.

*   *   *

The melodious strains of a popular Strauss waltz echoed throughout the immense luxurious ballroom of the Winter Palace in St. Petersburg. The whispering shuffle of many well-shod feet, the quiet laughter, the muted conversations of highly-place government officials and their wives, created an atmosphere of dignified, subdued merriment. This, the final of many State balls held during the winter of Eighteen Ninety-Eight, heralded the advent of spring, the slow, sure exit of harsh winter.

Here were gathered, this one night, the cream of Russian society — the nobility, the judical, the military, and the church; all combined in a vivid display of the awesome power that regulated and ran the nation. Here, too, scandals were whispered about, marriages arranged, and, behind closed doors, policies, rules and laws formulated — laws generally aimed at repression of any freedom and liberty that might endanger or threaten the status quo. A forcible statement, a wavering indecision could alter the lives and welfare of millions of people.

High in the dark-panelled ceiling, light from numerous, elaborate chandeliers illuminated the jewelled costumes of the ladies, and cast reflections from the highly polished breast plates sitting so magnificently over the white tail coats of the Cuirassier's Guard of His Majesty the Emperor, scintillated and glinted from the gilded sword scabbards worn by the sides of the many dress uniforms of the General Chiefs of Staff officers, in stark contrast to the dark blue and gray uniforms of the few Cossack officers present.

At the far end of this gigantic room, on a raised dias, and enthroned in royal loneliness, sat the Tsar Nicholas, his wife, the Tsarina Alexandra. Behind them, the Dowager Empress Maria sat in shadow — silent, watchful, her face expressionless.

To the right of this dias, in a curtained alcove partially removing them from the activities on the main floor, the Count Kripinski, and the dapper, well-groomed Minister of the Interior, Sergius Witte, sat, ensconced in comfortable leather chairs, engrossed in conversation, and oblivious to their surroundings. With a quiet smile, Witte rose from his chair, about to leave, then, pausing beside the Count, placed a friendly arm about his shoulders.

"You can be so stubborn, Count."

"Stubborn? Not really. Persistent, perhaps. And, Sergius, persistent I shall remain until I find a way to assist this Sect."

"But, Count, why are you so concerned? Surely, you know that the government looks on them with a jaundiced eye?"

"It is our government that deserves the jaundiced eye. After what I have witnessed in the past few weeks, the horror and the shame of our treatment of these people will remain with me to the end of my days."

The sigh was audible as Witte stiffened, and moved back to his chair.

"They have only themselves to blame. All they have to do, Count, is to obey the laws of the land."

"Sergius, that's just it. They are quite willing to obey any law, as long as it does not run contrary to the dictates of their conscience or teachings."

"They refuse military service."

"Only because they follow and live by the teachings of Christ.

And, surely, Sergius, you will be the first to admit He would never sanction the killing of our fellow man."

For a long moment, the Minister remained silent, his eyes on the sober, thoughtful Count.

"Tell me, Count. If we all felt the same way, how could we defend ourselves against the aggressor?"

"Throughout the ages, Sergius, men have sought the answer to that. They sought in vain."

It was a thinking, questioning Sergius that replied, "Fanatics. So willing to die for their faith, but never for their country."

The Count was quick to earnestly counter, "But it is their own lives they give. They do not, and cannot, take another's life."

"Why Count? Why? Where do they find the faith that allows them to suffer torture and death, rather than follow the ways of their neighbors? After all, are we not all Russians?

"They place their faith before nationality, Sergius. These people honestly regard Man as the Temple of the living God. In no case can they even prepare themselves to kill."

Softly, without rancor, Sergius replied.

"And He made Man in His own image. Very well Count, I will support you in getting these people out of Russia. They have been a thorn in our side for too long. But I must warn you. There is little I can do."

"I know you are close to the Tsar, Sergius. That is why I have come to you. Surely, he will listen?"

"Hah. He may listen. But I doubt if he will act. It will be dificult.

I cannot offer much hope, my friend."

Before he again moved away, the Count saw him nod to a man across the room.

"There is your man. Durnova. As Minister of Internal Security, he could do your cause a world of good. That is, if you could interest him in it."

"Durnova? Never," the Count protested. "I detest that man. I had thought we might approach the State Council, and possibly..."

Witte's derisive laugh cut him short.

"Waste of time. A lion without teeth or claws. No Count, they would be useless. I am afraid you must seek the assistance of Durnova. And, anyway, as head of the police, you will have to obtain his sanction to allow these people to emigrate."

For a few moments, both men studied the full-bearded, glowering, stocky Minister of the Interior, who was in heated conversation with several members of the state Council. That he dominated and overpowered the group was evident from the manner in which he spoke. His forcible words were accented by violent motions of the large hands, and punctuated by voracious gulps from a long-stemmed glass clutched in his fist. His features, mottled red with anger, thrust first at one, then another, of the intimidated group. His eyes still on Dornova, Witte murmured, "I do not envy you, Count."

On that note, he would have departed, had not the Count, clutching his arm, said; "Sergius, wait. You know I cannot approach Durnova. Surely, there must be another way?"

The urgency of voice and action impressed Witte. Yet, still undecided, he stood quietly, his eyes on the Count. Thoughtfully, he turned his gaze towards the Tsar. "Another way? Possibly. Yes, there just might be another way."

Suddenly, brusquely, almost roughly, as if inspired, he again moved his chair and sat down quickly.

"Sit down, Count. In a few minutes, I go to pay my respects to the Tsar."

Excited by this new and unexpected turn, the Count eagerly sat down, leaned forward. "But, you just said..."

"I know. The Tsar would be difficult. However, there is one other. The Dowager Empress. She, at least, has some sympathy for these people."

The Count eyed the shadowy face of the Empress.

"Did she not just return from a visit to the Caucasias?"

"Yes. And I understand she has received a petition from this Doukhobor sect."

"A petition? Have you any knowledge of the contents?"

"Something to do with exemption from military service, which, of course, they cannot have, or on the other hand, permission to emigrate."

"Two alternatives," the Count retorted bitterly, "they are not likely ever to see."

A little taken aback by his friend's defeatist remark, Witte calmly ignored it and continued. "The time may never be more favorable to rid ourselves of these fanatics. It is common knowledge, Count, that the Tsar is furious over the lurid news items appearing in the British and American press about our treatment of religious minorities."

"Tolstoy?"

"Probably. At least, that is what we suspect. We do know he has set up a committee in England to gather funds to aid these people. Chertkov, I believe is in charge of that end."

"I am aware of some of this Sergius. I understand that they have a sum of twenty thousand pounds to be used to assist in their emigration."

"All foreign monies, Count?"

"I believe so. Mostly. I do know that some of it has come from our own people. I am not alone in feeling repugnance on this subject. And by the way, Tolstoy has donated the entire royalties from his last book to this fund."

Musing, Witte extracted a cigar from his case, lit it, watched as the smoke curled upwards.

"That would be his Resurrection? Ironic. He tears down the fabric of our society in print, then uses the proceeds to break us up. Ah, well, if somehow we do obtain permission for these people to emigrate, will this be enough to get them out of Russia?"

"I believe so. Those that wish to leave."

"And are you sure they would be willing to leave Russia and sail to a foreign land, Count?"

The Count jumped to answer the question. Assuredly, but sadly, he replied, "I am very sure. Unfortunately, many will be too weak to move. These will die."

"Hmmm. And this foreign land. It is somewhere in the Americas?"

"I hear it is a British colony, north of the United States. A place called Canada."

"Canada? Yes, I have heard of it. You have contacted their government, Count? Are they really willing to accept these troublemakers?"

"More than willing. It seems they have millions of fine arable acres just waiting for the hand of settlers. and, one thing, you will admit. These Doukhobors make the best farmers."

"Then, how are you going to find the monies to purchase these fine lands?"

"The land is free, Sergius. One hundred and sixty acres to a family. Something they call a homestead. Also, once they disembark, I understand the Canadian Government will allot funds to take care of them throughout the first year."

"Very generous, I must say. I hope the Canadians never have cause to regret their generosity."

"From these people, Sergius, never."

"Count, are you positive this information you have given me is, well, accurate?"

"Absolutely. I have been in constant touch with Aylmer Maude. He is working with Tolstoy on this."

"Ah, Maude. The Quaker fellow. That reminds me, Count. I have reason to believe that this leader of theirs, this Peter Veregin, has written to the Empress. Must have been a moving, well-written letter, as I hear she has been deeply impressed with it."

"Then, surely, Sergius, your task should not be too difficult. We have in our favor, the foreign press, Tolstoy, Maude, and many others, including the nephew of the Empress, Prince Hilkov, working together to get these people out of Russia."

"Maybe. But a word of caution, Count. You could be treading on dangerous ground. If the Tsar should become belligerent..."

His slight shrug depicted clearly what meaning lay behind the unfinished sentence.

The Count retorted to this quickly, determinedly: "If assisting my fellow man to escape torture and death is dangerous ground, then Sergius, I will take the risk."

"Maybe so. Nevertheless, it would seem to me that we have an intolerable interference in our internal affairs by many foreigners and by some nationals. I can only trust that the Tsar does not feel the same way."

"Would you rather we exterminate a minority, Sergius? Men, women, children, babes in arms? That is the alternative."

"I would rather they might act like other citizens and obey the laws of the land. But then, you have made it abundantly clear that they would rather die."

Witte momentarily studied a small gold watch he had taken from his vest pocket. "Time to go. I shall do what I can, Count. At least, the Dowager Empress will listen to me."

The Count rose quickly. Eagerly, thankfully, he clasped the outstretched hand Witte offered.

"I will be eternally grateful, my friend. Release me from my nightmares. They haunt me so."

His tone was wistful, almost pleading.

Though having already overstayed his time, Witte could not resist a parting comment.

"It is unfortunate, Count, that you never married, and raised a large family. Then you would be so busy with family affairs you would have little time for other matters."

Smiling, he turned to leave. The Count watched as the swiftly moving Witte made his way round the dancing couples, to disappear through a door near the dias, which, he noticed, was now empty.

"And so," he pondered, "the lives, the fate, the future of so many hang by such a precarious thread."

*   *   *

Low, speeding clouds alternately obscured and revealed the moon at its full. Across the icy marshes, a cold northern wind howled its melancholy protest. Winter was fast squeezing the land in its frozen grip. Stumbling to the centre of a small field surrounding the shanty, Nickolai stood gazing up at the lowering sky. Raising his arms, as if he would reach to the scuffing clouds, he cried out, "God, if you can hear your humble servant, then hear me. Let them inflict their devilish tortures on my body. Only on me. Take my beloved Elizabeth, my son Paul, my little Nastasia. Take them, Oh Lord. No more. No more. Let me in my sorrow suffer for them. Scourge me. Burn me in hell if you must. But only leave my loved ones in peace. If only in death there be release for them. Then, Lord, I beseech you, take them. Release them for this misery."

Sinking to his knees, he remained quiet, waiting. There was no answer. Only the sighing of the wind, the rustle of dried vegetation, and, somewhere far off, the faint lowing of cattle. And then, the tender, comforting arms of his wife were around him, rocking him as a mother would a sick child.

"Oh, Nickolai. My husband. Do not despair so. We have suffered. But only believe me this time. It is over. I know. I know. The good Lord in His wisdom has decreed. No more. Listen, my husband. Tonight, this important man carries papers. We are to leave, Nickolai."

Roughly, she shook his unresisting form.

"Listen to me. Anna Maharikoff has seen him. Has talked to him. Some Count Kripinski has arranged it all. Now come."

Dragging him to his feet, she led him, dazed and unbelieving, back to the house.

*   *   *

And so it came about. A meeting such as had been undreamt of in the last three years. From every corner of the District of Signak they came: two hundred families packed into an old barn. They were furtive, secretive, even when it seemed that the need for secrecy had passed, as evidenced by the presence of two minor government officials, accompanied by a well-dressed stranger, and the Count Kripinski.

After the customary deep bowing to the God within each other, and to the guests, after the psalm singing, the prayers, both of which, tonight, seemed to echo an unaccustomed jubilation and thanksgiving, a paper was read by the stranger, who was introduced by the Count as a man from far-off England, Arthur St. John, one of the many who had struggled for so long to have the Doukhobor sect released from their bondage. He informed them that it was now the government's desire to rid themselves of these peoples once and for all. Even now, a ship lay in wait at the port of Batum, ready to take them across a large ocean to some strange land called Canada. On the next morning, they were to gather their belongings and trek to the railway, to be transported to the ship. In return, the Tsar had decreed that never again might any of the sect return to their homeland. This release from their miseries had been attained by monies contributed by the Quaker Society of Friends in America, and by Tolstoy's committee in England. Here, the Count paused, his voice rising, as he emphasized the assistance of several of the more liberal moderate of the Russian nobility; those who had been sickened and revolted at the treatment religious minorities had received in their attempt to abide by the dictates of Christ. All this, the Count patiently explained to the silent, astounded gathering. Nickolai listened, dazed, bemused, almost unbelieving. He heard the joyful cries of "Slava Bohu" echoing again and again throughout the large barn. Only when Elizabeth threw her arms around him, pressed her tear-wet face to his, and cried, "Now, my Nickolai, you see? The compassionate hand of God has reached down, even to the least of His kind. Oh, Nickolai, it is over. It is over."

Only then did he believe.

*   *   *

Dawn came late to the sickly Georgian marshes. Long before its wan light had penetrated the small shack, the Obedkoff family were packing. Not that there was much to pack — a few meagre blankets, little treasured possessions of the children, hoarded over the years, and only one thing of bulk. It was the one thing Elizabeth had shown any real interest in: goose feathers. These, she had diligently collected and saved, as no Russian housewife would ever discard these products, so necessary in the warming of a bed on chilly nights. Although light in weight, they made an enormous bundle, carried as they were on top of her head, as they finally set out to walk the twelve miles to the railroad. Not one of the family felt any regret at leaving this abode. Even so, the mother had insisted on a thorough cleaning of the interior, and, as a last gesture, had placed on the table the symbolic salt, water and a moldy crust of long-saved bread.

Waiting by the small shed of a station for the noon train, the children huddled together, their wondering eyes on the rapidly approaching coaches. There was no excitement. That would come. Rather, they were awestruck by the suddenness of events. Quietly, they watched as the locomotive, pulling a long string of cars, moved into view. The piercing wail of the steam whistle sounded frightenly loud. For three years, the whistle had been part of their meaningless, empty, barren days. Now it seemed to awaken them — to send the warm blood coursing through their wasted bodies in an unaccustomed rush. It seemed to call to them: You are free. You are free.

Not until they had safely boarded the rusty old freighter, the

S.S. *Lake Huron* (hastily converted into a passenger liner, by the cramming of wooden bunks into every available nook and cranny) — not until the lights of Batum faded into the night — did a sense of freedom finally settle over Nickolai. As the more than twelve hundred emigrants made their way below to retire for the night, Nickolai's last thoughts, upon turning away from the rail, were a mixture of relief and nostalgia for the receding past, which had become so strangely perverted, and an awakening hope that this new land would welcome these defeated and beaten exiles, and would offer a chance to rebuild life on their own terms.

BOOK
II

Cross a storm lashed
Devil sea,
Twelve hundred souls
Now set free
From Tsarist might,
Vengeful lust.
Their faith in God
A solemn trust,
Carried to this
Adopted land.
Peace and love,
A Brotherly hand.

4

The Awakening

The storm had subsided. Across the restless water of the North Atlantic, a brassy midmorning sun sent rays of light darting over the tips of white-capped waves. Laboriously, the *Lake Huron* reeled her drunken way through the limitless expanse.

Would they ever reach land? Elizabeth paused in her task of hanging out bedclothes too long unaired, and glanced anxiously ahead. Despite the past twenty-two days of sickening, close confinement, there was now a renewed sense of expectancy and excitement in the chatter of the busy women, mingling with the regular pulse and throb of the ship's engine, the swish-slap of waves against her rusty side, and the occasional clang of the watch bell.

In the cold January air, a sudden, loud shout rang out. All talk and movement ceased.

"Land Ho!"

"Where away, Lookout?"

"Dead ahead, Sir. Across the bow."

Voice and movement rose to a crescendo. A long piercing blast of the ship's whistle added to the turmoil. With the others, Elizabeth ran to join Paul and Nastasia at the rail. All eyes strained eagerly ahead, towards the horizon.

"Where, Paul? Where? I don't see any land."

"In a moment, Mother. Soon, we shall see it."

"That dark line. There, where the sea and sky join." Nastasia, standing by her mother, pointed. "See? That would be land."

Of all the excited faces peering ahead, she was the only one who reflected no emotion. Calm, quiet, her little girl features remained unperturbed, as if in wonder at the excitement around her.

Exhilarated by the nearness of this new land, Elizabeth turned to Paul, one hand lightly pushing at his shoulder.

"Your father. He would not wish to miss this. Go fetch him, Paul. Quickly now."

Unwilling to lose any part of this moment, Paul protested vehemently. "He's probably asleep, Mother. I want to watch for the land."

Before the mother could remonstrate further, Nastasia moved away.

"I'll go get him."

Her eyes on the retreating girl, Elizabeth murmured, "That sister of yours. Can nothing stir her?"

Paul, unheeding, his eyes fixed on the horizon, called out, "Look, Mother, look. The land. It's rising right up out of the water."

"Those low foreboding hills?" One hand shading her eyes, she peered anxiously ahead. "Can that be Canada? It is as I said all along: this ship lost its way in the great storm."

"Big ships like this never get lost." Paul was quietly confident. "They have a thing called a compass. Even at night, in the darkness, it can point the way."

Elizabeth remained unconvinced.

"Huh. Probably got turned right around. You will see. Siberia, it looks like."

Paul shrugged and smiled. Somewhere, a woman's voice commenced to sing. She was joined by others. Hymns of thanksgiving, joy and hope floated across the ocean. Snow-mantled, green-timbered hills rose up out of the horizon.

Making her way round the innumerable wooden bunks filling the dimly-lit hold, Nastasia paused by her sleeping father, and gently shook him.

"Father, wake up. Poppa."

Only half-awake, Nickolai struggled to a sitting position, glanced wildly around.

"Huh? Oh, 'tis you Nastasia. What is wrong? Tell me girl. The ship, it is sinking?"

"No, Poppa. The ship, it is not sinking."

Swinging his feet to the steel floor, he hurriedly searched under the bunk for his boots.

"My boots. Never can find them in this mess." Dragging one boot out from under the bunk, he looked around in surprise and smiled, "Why, the ship, it no longer heaves and rocks."

"Here, Father. Here is your other boot. Lift your foot up, I'll help you." Busily fitting the shoe to his outstretched foot, she glanced up at his wondering face. "The ship does not rock and heave. The sun shines, and the water is as glass."

"Then why am I awakened so rudely?"

"There is land."

"Land? Thank the good God. Now, my poor stomach can cease this devilish retching." Excited at this news, he jumped up and attempted to move away. Nastasia still busy with the lace held onto his leg, stubbornly. "Come, girl. Never mind the laces. Let us go."

Rising to her feet, Nastasia impeded any further progress, by placing both arms around his waist.

"Father, wait. This new land. This Canada. It is a great land?"

Impatient, but puzzled, he stared down at the little girl.

"Great enough to open its heart and allow us to make our homes there."

"There would be government and soldiers?"

Hesitant, wary, he continued to stare down into his daughter's eyes. He knew what was in her mind, but hoped against hope that she would not utter the words.

"All lands have government and soldiers."

"These soldiers, they will have guns and carry the lash?"

Very quiet, very hurting, the father tried to push past the distressed girl.

"Why, why, yes. All soldiers carry them. Please, my pet. No more."

Stubbornly, Nastasia continued to cling to him.

"Then, they would use them."

"Well, only if they must."

In rising, uncontrollable frenzy verging on hysteria, she shook him violently. "Then, why did we come here? Tell me, my Father. Would it not have been better to stay home and be beaten by our own Cossacks?"

The words tumbled out. Tears streamed down her face. Troubled, perplexed, the father groped for some answer.

"Nasta, Nasta. My baby. Please, let us wait. We will see. Remember, my little One, we are all in God's hands."

Scarcely listening to the fumbling words, her face hidden against his chest, the slight body rocked in agony.

"Let us hide, Poppa. On this great ship. Maybe it will take us to some land where there not any guns, no lash. Please, my Poppa. Just you and I?"

In sudden frustration and anger, the father roughly pushed her away from him.

"There is no such place. Now stop this nonsense."

"Maybe there is. Mayber there is, Poppa. I would be such a good girl. From dawn to dark, on my knees, would I slave for you."

Unable any longer to take his daughter's hysteria, hurt and confused, he slapped her across the face, yelling, "There can be no such place. Do you hear me? Now stop this. Let us join your mother. Come."

Then, shocked by his use of force, he quickly enveloped the trembling girl in his arms. Never once had he raised a hand in anger against anyone. In his mind's eye, he recalled the time, when as a young boy, he had come upon a tiny baby rabbit caught in a metal trap. Cruelly ensnared, it had still been alive. Shame and remorse raged within him. Picking his daughter up in his arms, he tenderly cradled the sobbing child, as he moved to the exit, and soothingly, he murmured: "We are in God's hands, my pet. It will be good. You will see."

On the stairwell leading to the upper decks, they passed groups of women, laughing, chattering excitedly about this new land. They were on their way to clean and tidy up the holds in preparation for landing.

* * *

The warm heart of this great land reached out and enfolded these refugees with love, with compassion, but with little or no understanding. As they left the ship and set foot on the snow-covered dock, they responded to greetings in the only way they knew. Each bowed low and deeply to the crowd of officials and onlookers. From somewhere in the crowd, a voice commented, "Look. They kneel and bow to us. Can these by the people who defied the might of the Tsar?"

Only Vasa Popoff, the interpreter, understood the remark, and retorted in English, "We do not kneel to you. Only do we bow to the spirit of God that lives within your heart, the spirit which caused you to take us unto yourselves as Brothers, in this your homeland."

Nickolai, unaware of this exchange, turned to Elizabeth. "Look well, wife. There are our good neighbors."

"So many of them."

Awed by the tumultuous welcoming cries and cheerful loud greetings, she had drawn behind her husband, as if to hide herself from sight.

Paul, eagerly eyeing the crowd, cried out, "Listen. They call greetings to us. They do seem happy to see us."

Through all this, Nastasia had remained silent, withdrawn, her eyes moving over the crowd, and then beyond the low long sheds that stood at the far side of the railway tracks. She was wary and uncertain, peering out from behind her father.

Once the long line of immigrants had disembarked and stood huddled on the dock, the crowd again broke into loud shouts of greetings, and welcome to Canada. The travellers quickly felt their friendliness and openness. Silence descended as a tall, well-dressed individual stepped forward and addressed the Douk-hobors in their own language. Beside him, the Canadian government agent, a Mr. Smart, deputy minister for the reigning Liberals, intently observed the proceedings. Elizabeth, gratified by the warm welcome accorded them, attempted to hush the still-chattering Paul.

"Hush, Paul. That man, he is talking to us. Listen."

"That is Prince Hilkov. He has come to welcome us."

Paul's attentiveness to, and understanding, of the proceedings had been keen, despite his chatterings. In their wonder and awe at finding themselves finally standing on Canadian soil, most had failed to pay much attention to the words of the speakers.

Nickolai, suddenly uneasy, glanced around.

"Nastasia. Where is that girl?"

"Here, Father, right behind you."

Lovingly, he drew her to his side, an arm encircling her thin shoulders.

"Come, Daughter. Stand here by me. See. There are no soldiers. And look. That is the government man. He does not even wear a uniform."

"Behind those large sheds, Father. Maybe the soldiers wait for us there."

His tone fervent, firm, Nickolai attempted to assure her. "No. That I cannot believe. Behind those sheds lies this great land. Mile upon mile. So many miles. Land rich and fertile. Just waiting. That Mr. Smart, Nastasia, he says wheat will grow high as a man's head. Grass reaches to the cows' bellies. All any man could wish for. Just wait, my pet, you will see."

"I hope so, Father. Here in my heart, I do want it so. For you and for all our Brethren."

The mother's voice, quiet and dreamlike, broke in.

"And in all that great emptiness, we will be alone. Not even the government will trouble us so far out."

Unable to contain himself, Paul hugged his little sister. "We are free, little sister. Don't you understand? We are free."

Unable to cope with the exuberance in her brother's voice, Nastasia, for the first time, felt a sense of wonderment, a touch of hope. Softly, she replied. "How can I understand? First we must learn the meaning of this new word."

Intent now on the speech making, Nickolai hushed the children. "Mr. Vasa Popoff speaks. Quiet, children. Listen."

"May God bless you for your kind words and deeds. For taking us into your hearts, into your country. We give thanks to you, and to God. May He never forsake you. Slava Bohu."

Finished his greeting, the interpreter led the Brethren to the waiting train — a train that would carry them up the shores of the mighty St. Lawrence, around the Great Lakes, through the icy wastes of northern Ontario, to finally deposit them in the midst of a bustling, new metropolis, the City of Winnipeg.

In the last week of January, dusk came early to the rugged, hilly terrain that comprised the border countries of Nova Scotia and of New Brunswick. Once in a long while, the tree-blanketed void was punctuated by lights of small scattered settlements, which flashed past and were lost to the darkness — a darkness relieved only by the passing of the many colonist trains that raced westwards in this year Eighteen Ninety-Eight. For this was a vast, empty, waiting land — waiting for the plow, and for the seed, that would, in time to come, help feed the hungry millions of this earth.

In their warm, steamy, comfortable coach, the Obedkoffs sat gazing out at the gathering dusk. A large, coal burning stove at one end, served to both heat the coach and to provide warm food. At the other end, a white-coated porter demonstrated to some of the mothers the mechanics of pulling down and making up the berths, so that the younger children might be put to bed. The others, exhilarated by the day's events, had no thoughts of sleep. Excited voices filled the car. As with all immigrants, their talk dwelt mostly with the land they journeyed to, the land they passed, and the land from which they had so recently been exiled.

One voice in particular, that of a woman, dominated the others.

"Christians? How can you say these Canadians are Christians? They even spit the dirty tabac on the clean snow. Ugh."

"But, their welcome was warm, Olga, straight from the heart."

The speaker's voice retorted kindly, and yet with inquiry. "And, anyway, how do you tell a Christian in a strange land?"

As if to settle any contention, a male voice, quiet and intoning, interjected, "By their scent, you know the flowers; by their calls, you know the birds; and by their deeds do you know a Christian."

Again, the kindly female voice broke in, laughing.

"Then, these were truly Christians. See how kind they were to us. Sweets for the children. Lovely white bread, and this delicious cheese to stay our hunger."

Not to be outdone, the first female, still pessimistic,

pronounced, "This land we go to. Could it be as Siberia? Long, dismal nights of ice and cold? Short days so dull and gray? Even Death becomes a welcome friend."

Nickolai noted the unease spreading over Elizabeth's face. Hurriedly, he spoke up.

"What does it matter? Just so long as we are left alone to till the soil, and to worship God. Then we need not worry our heads about these people, nor about their government."

"Pravda. Pravda." A male voice heartily agreed. "They must be a good people, else they would not let us have so much of their rich land."

Paul, who had been listening to all this, turned to his father.

"Do you think they tell the truth? About owning all this land, I mean?"

Before the father could make any reply, the mother countered bitterly, "No government tells the truth. You should know that, Paul."

A little angry, Nickolai spoke.

"We are in a new country, wife. Try and remember that. It will be different here. You will see."

Testily, the mother retorted, "New country. Hah. Rocks, trees and snow." She pointed dramatically out the window. "Siberia! You'll find out. Tomorrow, we will look out that window, and there will be the suffering, struggling chain gangs."

Worried, Nickolai, following the finger, stared out the window, his confidence shaken.

"Maybe. But, Elizabeth," not sure how to reply to this, he stopped, changed the subject by turning to Nastasia, "Nasta? You do not eat your sweets."

He threw his arm about her, pulling her head down onto his shoulder.

"Can it be my pet has lost her appetite?"

Making no reply, other than a sigh of contentment, she closed her eyes and snuggled down.

Angered by her husband's change of tactics, Elizabeth remarked, almost sarcastically, "You act towards that daughter of ours as if she were still a baby. Have you forgotten that only last month she became a young woman of eleven?"

Tenderly, the father stroked her hair. "She is still my pet. And always will she be that."

Visibly annoyed, Elizabeth turned again to the window and doggedly persisted in returning to the former subject. "See? Just like Siberia. Dark so quickly."

Impatient now, Nickolai queried, "How would you know? You have never been there."

The mother replied dreamily. "So long as our beloved Leader in Christ remains there in exile, so there will my heart be."

From somewhere to their rear, a female voice softly proclaimed, "Like Christ, He suffers for us."

As if wearied of talk, the voices dropped off to a sleepy murmur. The people busied themselves making up the berths, distributing sheets and blankets, all in preparation for a night's sleep. Paul, ignoring the others, stood in the aisle, waiting for the berth to be made up. In his hands, he held a small book, and idly turned the pages. Finished her task, Elizabeth moved to stand beside him. Curious, she asked, "What do you have there, Paul?"

Guiltily, with a start, he closed the book and attempted to hide it under his blouse.

"Only a book."

"Only a book." With sarcasm, his mother aped his words. "And what does the book say?"

"I would not know, Mother. It is something called a dictionary."

"Where did you get it?"

"From one of those ladies with the red cross on their blouses. One of those that gave us the food."

Snorting loudly, as if she were the discoverer of some dark secret, Elizabeth announced, "Ah, they give you food for the stomach and in return corrupt the mind."

Nickolai, having placed Nastasia in the upper berth, and drawn the curtain, turned to the mother and son. Mildly, almost scoffingly, he remarked, "Oh, come now wife. Surely, a little book that might help the boy to learn this new tongue, this English, is a far cry from corrupting the mind."

Tartly, his wife answered,

"He would be better off memorizing the Living Book. There, he would learn all he need to know, both for this life and for the next."

Nickolai's reply was firm.

"Maybe so. Yet, some among us are going to have to learn this new tongue. As for now, Son, up you go."

Accompanying his words with a boost, he assisted Paul into the upper berth, eliciting a low protest from the already sleeping sister.

As if determined to get the last word in, Paul poked his head out from between the curtains.

"Anyhow, Mother, it is of little matter. I do not even read the Russian words."

With a slight smile, Nickolai waited for Elizabeth to climb into the lower bunk, then he himself disappeared behind the curtains.

And so, for three nights and four days, they were carried across the vastness that was Canada, this adopted land they would call home. Slowly, the longing for a return to the Caucasias and the old home they had left diminished.

Wild, unbroken,
Prairie lands,
Await the toil
Of human hands.
Buffalo bones
Bleach and dry,
Sad witness to
Times gone by.

5

Toil And A Peaceful Life

As cities go, Winnipeg, in the year Eighteen Ninety-Eight, was a mere stripling. Nevertheless, it had become the gateway to the Canadian West—a sprawling, bustling metropolis, ever spreading out—devouring the fertile prairie land around it—a giant, spotted octopus, writhing in compulsive, acute birth pangs.

In the centre of all this energy, long, low wooden sheds housed the new arrivals. Already, they had attracted a great deal of curiosity. News items had duly reported the imminent debarkation of these refugees, as they fled from the despotic, barbaric Tsarist regime of Imperial Russia. The more lurid details of their past persecutions were graphically emphasized, and with no little exaggeration, all of which served to creat a more than passing wonderment in these new immigrants.

Traversing the short distance from the train station to the immigration sheds, the strange, exotic procession was watched by a small crowd of onlookers. The remarks of these onlookers, although not unkind, expressed some bewilderment. One buxom matron called out, "My God, look at the bundles those women carry on their heads."

In utter disbelief, another replied, "They must weigh a ton. How on earth do they do it?"

Once the gist of these remarks had been interpreted and passed on, Elizabeth and her female neighbors broke into good-natured giggles. Little did these Canadian women know that the bundles in question, though of extreme bulk, containing as they did, only goose feathers, were almost weightless.

Now that the long arduous journey over land and water had come to an end, a restlessness set in. Here, in this hive of a city, the Brethren were to wait until the severity of the Canadian winter had moderated. The men spent the first days wandering through the streets, gaping, wondering at all the activities going on around them. At every corner, new buildings sprouted from the raw earth. Electric tramcars clanged their way up and down the main avenues. Horse-drawn sleighs were constantly on the move, loaded with produce, building materials, and other assorted cargo so necessary to the maintenance of a growing city.

Despite the language barrier, many of the Brethren quickly found work, cutting wood, shovelling snow, and other odd jobs. Some, Nickolai amongst them, had been hired by a large business contractor to peel logs suitable for poles; a difficult, back-breaking task, in the sometimes sub-zero weather.

At the day's end, they would receive two pieces of silver, which was dutifully turned over to the common fund, administered by Vasa Popoff, a dedicated disciple of Peter Veregin who had taken over the leadership of the Winnipeg group. Loyal and devoted to the principles of the Doukhobor faith, he had cheerfully and without hesitation turned over his monies and property to assist in the migration of his Brethren. His grasp of the English language, and his understanding of Canadian ways gleaned on previous visits to Canada as one of the committee who had set out to select the land and deal with the government, now proved invaluable.

After his first week at this new job, Nickolai, chilled and weary, made his way through the icy darkening streets, his mind troubled by the day's strange events. Before this day, his co-workers had always smiled, and seemed to welcome his efforts, even to showing him in pantomime how to use the peeler on the logs, so that he would not injure himself, and often inviting him to join in their lunches. Today had been so different. Rather than smiles, he had been greeted by scowls, and what he had taken to be curses. One man had gone so far as to yell and shake an angry fist at him. Unable to understand and completely mystified, Nickolai had gone about his tasks doggedly, relieved when at last the whistle had blown, and he could return to the warmth of the sheds.

Even then, it appeared his troubles were not over. Rather than the usual cheerful greetings, Nickolai was surprised to find the Brethren gathered to one side of the large dining hall listening intently to Vasa Popoff, who stood on a chair addressing them urgently. On his entry, he called to Nickolai.

"Ah, here he is. We have been awaiting you, Nickolai. And where are the monies you earned for this day's labour?"

Moving forward quickly, Nickolai handed up the two pieces of silver.

"Here it is. The same as always. There is something wrong, Vasa?"

"Yes. Now, listen, all of you." Holding up the larger piece of the money, he shouted. "This is called a quarter of a dollar, twenty-five cents. Now this," he held up the smaller piece, "this is a nickel. Five cents. Altogether, a total of thirty cents. My Brethren, we are being cheated. The Canadian working men have what is called a union of labour, and this union demands that no man get less than one dollar and fifty cents for one day's honest labor. From now on, you will demand the same. Else, there will be trouble. Much trouble. Only last night, this union hold big meeting. They call us the New Chinese, and accuse the government of bringing us to Canada, just so we will work for less money, and take away their jobs. This must not be."

Confused, Nickolai blurted out, "But how could we know? I had thought that we were doing so good."

Smiling, the speaker assured him, "You could not know. And, Brother Obedkoff, do not feel badly. You have no blame in this. Only tomorrow, you will say, One dollar, fifty cents, or no work." Pausing to allow the murmuring that had broken out to die down, Popoff raised a hand for quiet. "Now. There is one more thing. Here, as elsewhere, there is in existence a powerful Orthodox Church. It seems that their clergy have made complaints to the police and to the magistrates, that we violate their law by working on Sunday, which they call a day of rest. I have assured them that this will not occur again."

Someone called out, partly in jest, "When we go back on our land, then how do we feed our animals on this Sunday?"

Smiling broadly, Popoff answered, "I do not think you will have much worry then. And, by the way, next week some of the Brethren will be called on to travel to our new land and start building shelters."

This news was greeted with welcome cries.

Jumping down from his chair, he glanced around and, spotting Paul in the assembly, motioned to him to come over. Together, they moved off to the small cubicle occupied by Popoff.

Wondering, Elizabeth watched this, and turned to her husband who had joined her as they walked to a table.

"Nickolai, what is it that Vasa has to do with Paul? Each night now, they go into that little room."

Nickolai, tired and hungry, sat down, reached for a bowl of soup, and answered shortly, "'Tis' nothing to worry your head about woman. Vasa simply teaches Paul the English."

"From that little book?"

"Yes, I suppose so. And after today, from what I have seen, some of us had better learn this tongue in a hurry. Now please, my wife. Stop your chatter and let me eat."

Though successful in silencing Elizabeth, the chatter of the others kept up unabated. The general theme of their talk moved rapidly from military service in Canada to the government of the day, then to the fact this land must be one of perpetual ice and snow.

Turning to a companion sitting beside him, Nickolai remarked in bantering tone, "These women. How they do chatter."

Raising his voice, he informed the woman who had been complaining about the weather, "Did you not pay heed to the government man, Mr. Smart, who welcomed us? Did he not assure us that this is a rich land and that the summers are hot and good for growing?"

His companion continued the conversation, though hesitantly.

"I did not understand him too well, Nickolai. What was it he said about army service?"

"Never again do we have to worry about serving in any war. It has been solemnly promised by this government. We will be free. Did not Vasa demand this?"

His companion nodded soberly.

"We settle the land, and grow the wheat. In return, we live as we please?"

Spooning food into his mouth, Nickolai shrugged, "Canada is so big, how else could it be?"

Not to be outdone, one of the women laughingly remarked, "Can you believe these Canadians would allow a Frenchman to rule over them? How could this be? Some man with a queer name."

An older man, who had been listening to this, interjected seriously, "You mean this Laurier? He is not really their ruler. They have a woman, a Queen, who lives far away across the great sea. It would seem these people asked this Laurier to rule over them for her. I do not know why."

Matter of factly, Elizabeth brought the conversation to an end.

"It matters not who rules who. Just so they leave us to live as we please. That is all I ask."

His appetite satisfied. Nickolai straightened up, and stretched his arms to relieve the tension of his day's labor.

Elizabeth regarded him fondly, reached over and tenderly stroked his face.

You must be tired, my husband. This work you do, it is hard?"

"I have worked harder. At least, I get some monies for this

labor. I must remember. One Dollar Fifty cents."

Although he said this with a smile, there was a trace of bitterness in his voice. From now on, he would no longer labor for a mere pittance. He had learned the hard way.

Pursuing a subject that was obviously bothering her, Elizabeth asked, "You will go with the Brethren to our new land?"

"If I am asked, yes."

"You think maybe we could go with you?"

"No. It would be much too cold."

"But Nickolai, in all our lives together, we have yet to be parted."

Thoughtfully, he answered.

"That is so. But then, my wife, we are in a new country. There may be other times in the days to come when it will be necessary for us to part for short times. This is one of them."

"But, what will we do without you?"

"You will be well looked after here, Elizabeth."

"For how long do you think it will be, my husband?"

"For as long as it takes to build the shelters and for the warm spring sun to arrive."

"It will be a dreary time for us."

At this moment, Paul joined them, looking a little disturbed. His father greeted him jocularly.

"And how is our student doing?"

Siting down by his father, the boy glanced away.

"Not too well."

"How is that?"

"These English words. I first must learn something called an alphabet. When I have learned that, then I can maybe understand some of their words."

"For a boy with your brains, that should not be too hard."

"It will take time, father. It is hard. And tonight, Vasa is so upset."

"Why should he be upset? Is it because of the little monies we earn?"

"No, Father. He learned only today that some of our Brethren have been in the town changing rubles for dollars."

Shocked, Elizabeth exclaimed, "But that cannot be. Our Brethren know that any monies must go for the good of all."

Cynically, Nickolai replied, "Not all. It is evident that some of our dear Brethren now put their own welfare before that of the others."

Still unbelieving, Elizabeth cried, "But how can that be? Surely, he has made a mistake?"

With absolute certainty, Paul answered, "There is no mistake.

Anyway, Mother, he is going to speak to them in the morning."

Rising to his feet, Nickolai walked towards the curtained-off bunks that served as family sleeping quarters.

"Time for bed. We have had enough for one day."

Elizabeth called to Nastasia, playing with a group of the younger children, and helped her undress, then tucked her into bed. Lights were extinguished, as, tired from the day's activities, the Brethren retired for the night.

*   *   *

The weather in late February was clear and cold. The worst of the prairie winter was over, though snow still lay in powdery drifts that blocked many of the Indian trails and old buffalo paths cutting across the almost limitless grass lands of the territory that was soon to be proclaimed the Provinces of Manitoba and Saskatchewan.

Disembarking at Cowan, the furthest point to which steel of the Canadian Northern Railway had been laid, they were met by Nickolai Zibarov. He had driven up from Yorkton, bringing with him sleighloads of much-needed provisions pulled by ten horses and six oxen. These would be all the animals that they would have to farm the tough prairie soil in their first year.

A hard two days' journey took them to the banks of the Swan River. Here, thirty miles north of Yorkton, would be established the first Doukhobor village in Canada — the village of Milhailovka — one of thirteen that would be built during the first spring, to house the fourteen hundred Brethren, that even now, were waiting patiently in Winnipeg for the day when they might join their menfolk on this, their own land.

All of these immigrants who would settle in what was known as the North Colony, were lifelong neighbors of Nickolai, those with whom he had tilled the soil of the Treeless Wet Mountain region in the Caucasias and then been exiled to the Georgian marshes. Almost all were penniless and had it not been for the Canadian government granting a subsidy of five dollars per head to assist settlers on to the land, they would have been hard-pressed to eke out of any kind of living, isolated as they were in the midst of these lonely, almost uninhabited plains of the Canadian West.

Arriving at their destination, sleighs were quickly unloaded, tents and stoves erected, and preparations for a first survey of their land grants were soon underway.

Despite the cold, Nickolai felt only exhilaration as he looked around. Here, on this land, he would at last find the peace that for so long had eluded him. Although he had been in Canada only a month or so, he had sensed that this was truly a land of the free. From his fellow workers at the log peeling plant, once the unfortunate business of the daily pay had been settled, he had learned to say please, hello, how are you, and a few other words in English, and, of course, one dollar fifty cents, or not work. This, he thought ruefully, he would never forget.

The days passed rapidly—days of hard grinding labour from dawn to dusk. First the poplar trees that grew in meagre clumps along the river banks had to be cut. Then, it was the toil of hauling them to the site of the new settlement. Deep was the satisfaction and pleasure of all, as five rambling, low log structures rose up from the land. No palaces these, but sufficient to keep out the rain and the cold winds that blew at night.

On a day when the snows had finally melted, the sun's warmth beat down on the earth, and the first wild crocuses had burst through the beaten down yellowed grasses, the voices of women and children were heard throughout the village. The first contingent had arrived.

Then, chattering like magpies, Elizabeth and the children were around him. In the midst of the greetings, crushed in exuberant embraces, his ears assailed by the babble of voices exclaiming and extolling their joy at being reunited after weeks of separation, a transient thought flashed into Nickolai's mind. This wife of his looked as young now as she had on their wedding day more than fifteen years ago. Despite the persecutions, the hardships, and the physical deprivations she had endured, not a line marred the smooth oval face.

He was brought back to the excitement of the moment by Paul tugging at his arm.

"Father. I have learned much English. You wish to hear?"

Amused, and a little proud, Nickolai, one arm around Elizabeth, the other around Nastasia, replied in heavily-accented English, "Hello Paul. How are you? It is good day today."

Both burst into laughter.

Only Elizabeth, soberly and in some consternation drew away; her worried eyes on her husband.

"There is much work to do. Show me where we stay, Nickolai. I will get the beds ready for the night. And soon it will be time to eat."

And so they settled into their new life. Some distance behind the sheds, away from the riverbank, a wide street was marked out, and the frameworks for houses quickly erected. Again, poplar logs formed the walls, the women chinking them with mud gathered from around the homes. Roofs of sod and willow branches made an effective barrier against the heavy spring rains.

With what few plows were available, others broke the soil with an increasing urgency, in tempo with the steady rise in daily temperatures. On a day when the sun shone and the ground was moist and soggy from the rains, all men, women and children gathered in the fields to scatter the seed that would be their first crop; the wheat that would make the bread to keep them alive through the first winter. Many of the older men, impatient with the slow progress, and desirous of planting as great an acreage as possible, broke the prairie earth with hand-made shovels.

Dutch ovens for the baking of the bread were erected in the open. The last building to go up was their communal bath house. In this, rocks were heated and water thrown on them so that whole families might enjoy the pleasures of a cleansing steam bath whenever possible.

Notwithstanding the fact that every waking moment was occupied in the arduous toil of carving homes and crops out of this wilderness, it soon became very evident that, somehow, monies would have to be earned to enable them to carry on through the first winter. More animals and equipment would have to be purchased for the following year.

Heartbreaking though it might be, the decision was made that all able-bodied men would contract to clear the right-of-way for the railroad now reaching out of Cowan and building towards Kamsack. Once more, Nickolai bade goodbye to his family for the summer months. Only the women and children, with a small number of old men, remained behind in the village to carry on as best they could.

Relaxing peacefully after a long, hard day's work chinking the logs of her small home, Elizabeth with some of her neighbors, sat absorbed in the colorful sunset. Silently, their eyes followed the sun as it slowly slipped behind the gentle rolling hills of the prairie. Great red and orange streamers flared across the azure blue of the evening sky, tinging a few lonely drifting clouds to a mosaic of breathtaking loveliness.

Elizabeth's eyes fell on the seemingly meagre patch of seeded ground surrounded by thousands of acres of unbroken, fallow land, covered with a primeval matting of grass and bush. Somehow, she felt, this had to change. Into her mind, an old folk story related by her mother, many years in the past, came to her. Excitedly, she exclaimed, "Olga, Anna. Remember the old tale of the virgins hitching themselves to a plow and drawing a furrow around their village to keep out evil spirits during an epidemic?"

With a laugh, Olga, a woman about the same age as Elizabeth, replied, "I have heard that, yes. But I think it is just another old wives' tale."

Anna, one of the oldest women of the group, chimed in, "No

old wives' tale. It was truth. My old grandmother was one of them."

"You mean your grandmother was a virgin, Anna?"

"I mean when she was a young girl, silly."

Breaking in on the general laughter, Elizabeth vehemently declared, "Listen. I have an idea. Why do we not take those idle plows and break the soil ourselves?"

"But Elizabeth. The horses they are with our men."

"We shall replace the horses. Do you not see? We will pull the plows with our own bodies. After all, what could be more evil than hunger?"

For a moment, the women fell silent. Then Anna replied quietly, thoughtfully. "Yes, it could be done. With enough of us on each plow, we could break the soil. Some of the old men could walk behind and guide the plowshare."

Hesitant, hopeful, Olga glanced around at the unbroken land.

"If only we could. Oh, Elizabeth, if only we could. Why, then we could plant all those vegetable seeds the government gave to us. It would be such hard work, Elizabeth. Could we really do it?"

Firmly, Elizabeth declared, "By noon tomorrow, we shall know. Now, let us tell the others, and early in the morning, we shall give it a try."

Early next morning, once the children had been fed, and the other chores completed, some of the women commenced to put Elizabeth's idea into practice. Although some of the older men snorted in derision when they heard what was afoot, they nevertheless gave a hand. Tying a long length of stout hemp rope to the plow, they then inserted thick sticks into it at intervals, so that twelve pair of women could pull in unison. Breathlessly, with the whole village watching, the plow started to move. With an old man guiding the plowshare so that it bit into the virgin earth, a furrow a full acre in extent was cut without any appreciable exertion on the part of the heaving women. It worked. Before noon, all six plows were engaged in this gigantic task. As one team of women tired, another stepped up to take their place. As if to express their joy in performing this undoubtedly arduous labour, and to help them overcome the aches that eventually crept in as the day wore on, the women gave voice to their beloved psalms and story hymns.

Little did they realize, however, the furore this was to create in the minds of those far removed from the land. The daily newspaper from Winnipeg to Halifax described in headlines accompanied by photographs the slave labour conditions claimed by their reporters to exist in the Doukhobor land holdings. With the mutterings of the labour unions who had not forgotten the unfortunate misunderstanding of the daily pay rate occurring earlier in Brandon and in Winnipeg, the reports gave added fuel to the Opposition party in Ottawa in their severe criticism of the immigration policies of the Liberal party headed by Laurier. No one, apparently, was interested enough to talk to the women involved, nor to show that this was in fact a courageous voluntary act on their part, and could have been as easily classified as a labour of love.

*   *   *

Almost unnoticed by the villagers, the cool temperate days of spring gave way to the dry heat of summer. The wheat, the flax and the vegetables, planted with so much care and toil, seemed to leap from the virgin soil, to grow in stature, day by day. Although it seemed there were never enough hours of daylight to complete the numerous tasks, it was a lonely summer for the women of Mihlailovka. With their menfolk away, they were faced with day to day decisions, sometimes difficult to resolve. Early in the summer months, all could see that, despite all their efforts, there would not be food enough for the winter. Even now, they were forced to live on a limited diet: a soup consisting of boiling water with flour, augmented by an ever-dwindling supply of vegetables and dry bread baked from low-grade flour. Shared too were fish caught in the nearby Swan River and in the many adjacent sloughs. Twice during the hot summer, the women had to haul a wagon the thirty miles to Yorkton to secure much-needed provisions from the communal warehouse.

To compound their miseries, the frosts came early that year. With the frosts came their menfolk. Now, the village settled into a routine — the routine of harvesting and storing whatever they could save from the first icy touches of winter. Long lines of men and boys, armed with scythes, worked doggedly, hour by hour, mowing the ripened grains, followed by the women and girls beating with their flails, the plump heads of wheat and oats. Every grain, every vegetable that could be salvaged was stored in the crude barn built behind the houses in the village. As the work progressed, the chilling reality soon became apparent. There would not be sufficient food to ensure survival through the long, bleak winter days ahead.

And then, a miracle. The great warm heart of a nation reached out and enveloped them in its compassion, its kindness and in its generosity. That no people can rise from destitution to prosperity in a few months was self-evident.

Unknown to the villagers, their plight had been observed and publicized. By November of that year, the Canadian Council of Women had dispatched spinning wheels, looms, stoves, tools and bolts of cloth, along with forty-nine cows and twenty oxen. The American Quaker Society collected the sum of Thirty Thousand Dollars, with which they purchased carloads of sugar, corn meal, rolled oats, potatoes and onions. A further sum of Two Thousand Dollars was loaned to the villagers to be used in the purchase of flour. To their credit, the Doukhobors repaid this loan in full by the next year.

Through all this, Nickolai and Elizabeth, along with their neighbors, toiled from dawn to dusk. They had little or no understanding of the forces at work around them. They were concerned only with the basics of survival — the day to day struggle to apportion out the dwindling, meagre supplies of vegetables and grains, so that all might have enough to at least prevent outright starvation, and also to give them the necessary energy to carry out their daily tasks.

On an evening when the north wind howled around the village, blowing snow in every direction, Nickolai sat watching his wife prepare the children for bed. As was the custom in this weather, the children slept on top of a large clay oven that had been built in the centre of the small house. At least they would be warm through the long night. Something about the way in which Elizabeth moved provoked his curiosity.

"Elizabeth, you do not feel well?"

Without pausing in her activities, she replied, "I am well. Why do you ask?"

"You move so clumsily. And your body..."

"Nickolai."She turned to face him. "I thought you knew."
"Knew what?"

"That I am with child."

For a long moment, Nickolai remained silent, his eyes on the flames visible in the open fireplace. His voice very soft, he replied, "No; I did not know. but then, I should have guessed. When? Do you know when this little one will arrive, Elizabeth?

Moving to his side, she sat down heavily on the bench near him.

"Some time by the end of the year, I figure." Then, wearily, tiredly, she muttered, "Another mouth to feed. I do not rejoice in this."

Confused and hurt, almost unbelieving, Nickolai clasped Elizabeth by the shoulders, forcing her to face him. "Yes. Another mouth to feed. But also, another Servant of God. Where is your faith woman? You should rejoice and give thanks.

Before Elizabeth could reply, a quick, loud rap on the door, followed by the appearance of Vasa Popoff, startled both her and Nickolai. He had travelled far. Snow clung to his eyebrows, mustache and clothing. His greeting was loud in the silence that had descended on his entry.

"Nickolai, good news. Very good news."

Brushing the snow from his heavy coat, he removed it, hung it on a wooden peg by the door, and moved to the stove, rubbing both hands briskly in the warmth.

"Elizabeth, you have some soup, maybe? I am famished. There is food. Much food. At Yorkton. Carloads arrived yesterday."

Placing a large wooden bowl of thin gruel in front of him, Elizabeth exclaimed, "Thank the good God. I was beginning to wonder why we left Georgia."

Noncommitted, Vasa grunted, between spoonfuls.

"There are people in this land who care. Now, Nickolai. Once this snow clears, can you manage with the sleighs?"

"Yes. Gregory has removed the wheels. The runners are on. How many shall we need?"

"All you have ready. And take some extra men. You will have a few cows to bring back with you."

Her interest aroused, Elizabeth remarked, "Vasa. These people have given us cows? How then do we pay for all this?"

A little annoyed at this question, Vasa Popoff answered quickly. "There is nothing to pay back. These good people, the ones who helped us out of the Motherland, have made this a gift."

"Why would they make this gift to us, Vasa? Have they not done enough?"

"They do not wish to see children starve in this land of plenty, Elizabeth."

Breaking into their talk, Nickolai whispered, as if thinking out loud, "It is so difficult to understand."

"What is so difficult, My friend?

"People. Here in this country, they give us free land. They feed us. They even pay our train tickets. Then, they make gifts to assist us in our time of need. Yet in our homeland, they tried so hard to starve us to death. Are not all men Brothers, Vasa? How can this be?"

"Yes, Nickolai. In God's sight, all men are truly Brothers. But then," Vasa shrugged, "as in some families, you have brother against brother. Have you not ever seen the meek one whose only concern is to be left in peace and work for the welfare of the whole family? Is he not usually bullied by the more aggressive brother who desires all for himself.

"And the stronger one generally wins his ends," added Nickolai.

"That is the way it is, Nickolai. It is God's will. That I do not question."

Elizabeth, who had been listening attentively, interrupted, "Truly spoken, Vasa. Truly spoken. God, in His infinite wisdom, has said, 'And the Meek shall inherit the earth'."

Nickolai smiled at his wife's fervor.

"I will be satisfied to inherit merely my one hundred and sixty acres."

Read, write,
Learn a sum,
Goodbye to flowers,
The breeze, the sun.
A child of nature,
You were born,
Goodbye, dear child,
Accept the norm.

6

School Comes To Milhailovka

The hot July sun, brassy in brilliance, beat down on the land, tinging the long-stemmed, plump heads of wheat to a soft golden brown. As if to ensure that no single head would remain untouched by the nourishing sun, a gentle breeze stirred across the fields, bending and twisting each bearded grain, like, thought Nickolai, like a Sea of Paradise. Green, golden-flecked waves rippled gracefully on as far as the eyes could see, hypnotic in beauty, stirring memory to other days and other fields in other lands. How many years had passed? Three? Four? No matter. They had passed so quickly. In the beginning, harsh years, doubts, frustrations and, above all, years of toil. Winter and summer. Dawn till dark. Yet, he reflected, such satisfaction, so much accomplished. He rose each morning with a renewed sense of hope and peace, such as he never before in his life had known. The knowledge that the years ahead ensured, nay, guaranteed a future, not so much only for himself, but for his sons, grew. For the first time in his turbulent life, he knew a sense of continuity, a sureness. The fruits of his labour would now remain in the hands of his heirs.

Resting in the cool shade of Saskatoon bushes lining the large slough near the bottom of his acreage, Nickolai idly scanned the low rolling hills, his eyes coming to rest on the small house and outbuildings so laboriously erected during the winter months, and, which even now, had not really been completed.

This adopted land of the Brethren, this Canada, had lived up to her material promises. But now, like a dark evil shadow from the past, the long arm of the government had reached out and touched them. Quiescent for so long, it seemed they must now sign papers, making an oath to some far-off Queen, and another paper so that they might claim title to this land. In return, this would give government the power and authority to levy and collect taxes each year. Well, mused Nickolai, he had no real objections to any of this. After all, to exist, he supposed the authorities had to have money. And the land was rich. A man really should not expect to be given all this for nothing.

Nevertheless, many of the Brethren, Elizabeth included, vocally and strenuously objected to any interference of any kind from the government. The constant mutterings, the bickerings, the discontent had cast a deep pall of gloom and despair over their last Sobranya. The age-old fear, that by aligning themselves with the authorities, no matter how benevolent, would place their young men in a position of being conscripted into an army, predominated, despite the vehement denials of agents sent out from Ottawa. The very sight of a mounted, uniformed policeman sent many of the villagers into a raging hysteria, even though the visits were always of a friendly, inquiring nature. Only the younger villagers and a few of the more thoughtful elders such as Nickolai and Vasa Popoff would in any way welcome and respond to the advances of these officers. Nastasia, by listening to Paul and her father, had gradually overcome her inborn fear of uniforms. Over the years, she had come to regard these occasional visits with a mixture of curiosity and of apprehension. The urge to run and hide still lurked far back in her mind.

A loud hail broke into his reverie.

"Father. Father. Where are you?"

Glancing up, he noted Nastasia standing on the crest of the nearer hill, one hand to her eyes, shading them from the brightness, as she searched for him. In her other hand, she carried the tin pail he knew contained tea and his afternoon lunch. Spotting him in the shade of the bushes, she waved and ran rapidly towards him. Rising, he unhitched the team from the loaded stoneboat, allowing them to graze freely on the buffalo grass at their feet. Resuming his seat, he watched as Nastasia moved quickly towards him.

Soon, he mused, that one will be on her way to a family of her own. Even now, several of the young men showed more than a casual interest in her. She surely was growing into a beautiful woman.

Panting slightly from her run, Nastasia entered the shade and, removing her kerchief, mopped her perspiring face and arms. Setting out the food on a white cloth, she then poured his tea and handed it to him. Only then did she speak.

"Mother wants you home early. Before the sun goes down."

"Another Sobranya?"

"In the village. It would seem that we have something new in our midst. A school teacher."

Surprised, Nickolai's jaws stilled. He stared at his daughter.

"You mean the government has finally sent a man to learn our little ones reading from books?"

"It's not a man, Father. It's some woman from the Quaker People. The Ones that helped us so much."

For a moment, he chewed away, reflecting on the impact this news would have on the village.

"Your Mother. She would not be too happy about this?"

"No. She vows no child of hers will ever learn to read from any book."

Bitterly, she stared ahead. "I'd say it was a little late."

Nickolai studied Nastasia's sober face. thoughtfully, quietly, he replied, "You would wish to learn these things, my pet?"

"Would it be so wrong, Father?"

Shrugging his shoulders, he rose and moved to the horses.

"You know how they feel."

Her eyes following his movements, Nastasia burst out angrily, "I know. But Father, Paul now speaks this English. Maybe in the Motherland they were right. But here, someone has to figure how much wheat we have. Someone has to know the price we should get. Otherwise, we will always be cheated."

To cover her confusion at her sudden outburst, she busily gathered the dishes and cloth and replaced them in the pail.

Gently brushing the annoying flies and mosquitoes from the necks of the team, Nickolai stood quietly, his eyes on the immense fields of wheat that surrounded him. As if to himself, he murmured, "I have no argument with that, Nasta. Look, girl," he waved his hand around, "do you think all the Brethren working together could harvest all this before the snows fly? Never. The old ways must change."

Reaching down, he gathered a handful of the ripening grain, rubbed it gently in the palms of his hands. For a long moment, he stood staring down at the green-brown kernels. Smiling slightly, he turned to Nastasia.

"I...I have bought one of those new machines. A binder it is called. You drive around the wheat. Round and round. This machine cuts and ties it into bundles. Why, girl, I could have this whole field finished in one day."

Lovingly, Nastasia placed an arm around his waist, and with a gentle, teasing finger, ruffled his beard.

"My Father. Always the rebel. You know what Mother and the others will say."

"Machines and learning are the work of the Devil. Yes, I know."

Ruefully, almost sadly, he disengaged himself from his daughter's encircling arm. Impatiently swatting at the persistent, annoying mosquitoes, his eyes took in a sun now so low in the sky, it cast golden flecks of dancing light throughout the cool shade of the dry rustling leaves.

"Anyway, let us declare a holiday. The stones will be lying there tomorrow. And those mosquitoes would eat one alive. Come, girl. Climb up on Bess, and we shall ride home in style."

Laughing gaily, Nastasia climbed on the back of one of the horses, her father on the other.

"And face the music. Never mind, my Father. I am on your side."

With little urging, the horses were soon in full gallop, headed towards home and a night's rest.

*   *   *

This was no ordinary Sobranya. Owing to the fine weather, it had been decided to hold it in the open, in the large pasture behind the communal barns. Nickolai, glancing around with curiosity, noted the presence of several well-dressed persons standing between Vasa Popoff and Nickolai Zibarov.

During the intoning of the prayers, and the singing of Psalms, Nickolai's mind, as usual, wandered. These communal gatherings had, of late, become almost meaningless to him. Was he, he wondered, irritated by the fact that he would much rather be out in his fields, or completing the necessary chores, than standing here, idly listening to the constant argument and debate on matters he felt were of no importance to him? How many of these had he attended in his lifetime? And, the chill, the sense of unease, as if he would look up, and find the sardonic features of a Captain Praga eyeing him. The encircling menace of the Cossack troop was ever with him. Then, too, there was the knowledge that, by demanding and working his own piece of land, as was his right, under the law of the commune, he had diverged from the beliefs and practice of the majority. Elizabeth in particular had been torn between her duty to her husband and her loyality to the Brethren.

Philosophically, she had accepted her husband's stubborness as just another form of punishment handed out by God for her imagined weakness. As she so often put it, "Another cross to bear."

Something about the way in which the government agent

stepped forward, produced an official document from his side pocket, slowly unrolled it, reinforced Nickolai's sense of unease, the premonition of evil to come. The gruff voice of Nicolai Zibarov cut into his thoughts.

"And now, Brothers and Sisters, we have with us this evening a Miss Nelly Baker, sent to us by the Quakers, and a Mr. Hartley from government, who has something to say to us. Vasa will interpret the words."

With a slight nod of greeting to the assembly, the Agent commenced to read, slowly and forcefully; his tone of voice and his manner of speech, clearly bespoke no good news for the Brethren. Finished, he brusquely stepped back to allow Vasa to interpret.

Vasa, serious, evidently perturbed, addressed the gathering. "The government has decided that, as we have not yet registered nor made entry for our lands, and as we have refused to take this oath of allegiance, that henceforth our lands will revert back to the Crown, and be made available to the public under the Homestead Act. Fifteen acres per head, we will be allowed to keep."

The seriousness of this announcement caused a stir and a murmuring throughout the Brethren. Angrily, Nickolai Zibarov took up the task of replying.

"It is not sufficient that we have paid the ten dollars per entry as demanded by the government? Why is it we now make this paper entry and swear this oath?"

Vasa relayed Zibarov's question to the Agent, who vigorously shook his head, and again read from the document, stabbing it forcefully with his finger for emphasis. On a further question in English from Vasa, the Agent shook the paper angrily in his face, then waved it around, as if to encompass the assembly in its meaning, and in its purpose. From the violence of his actions, there could be little doubt remaining in any mind, that, whatever the argument, they would have no chance of succeeding.

Shrugging in defeat, Vasa turned to the watching crowd, his voice restrained, echoing the hopelessness of a lost cause.

"No. The ten dollars is only a land entry fee. We must also, he says, immediately swear this oath. But he carries a promise from the government that no one of our young men will ever have to serve in their army. This oath is only so that we may own the land, and no one can take it away from us. It is necessary, he says, and must be done by the end of this month."

Now, Elizabeth spoke up.

"Can his government not wait for our Leader to come to us? He will be here soon, will he not?"

Elizabeth's question, relayed to the Agent, brought only another vehement reply, followed by the Agent turning abruptly and leaving the group, moving to a small buggy awaiting him. Without another word, nor a glance at the surprised people, he whipped up the horses and disappeared in the direction of Yorkton.

For a moment, Vasa watched the retreating buggy, then turned and said: "He has no more to say." His voice dropped almost to a murmur. "We would have had him stay the night. Oh, well." Then, in a voice more commanding than informative, he announced, "Those papers he carried make the instructions final, and they must be acceded to. He says also the information the government has is that Peter Veregin is still in Russia and that it will be some months before he is free to join with us here in Canada."

Several voices spoke up at the same time, creating a jumble of sound. Vasa raised his hand. The voices died away.

"We will decide on this issue at a later time. Now I would have you meet Miss Baker, who has journeyed far to speak with us."

Taking her by the arm, he politely led the small smiling woman to face the assembly.

Quietly, he informed the group, "I have already spoken to this little lady, and to save time..."

He was interrupted by a loud voice demanding:

"Of what use learning, Vasa. It would seem we are now about to suffer persecution and lose our lands."

Again, a hubbub broke out, everyone talking and shouting angrily, and at once. Obviously, the land question had not yet been settled. The outburst was hushed by Zibarov, who stepped forward, raised both hands and shouted.

"Still your angry tongues. Have we not a guest in our midst? Let us make her welcome and hear what it is she has to say."

Subdued by his passionate outcry, the others quieted, their eyes on Miss Baker. For some time, she spoke in English, then with a slight shrug, and a wave of her hand, she turned to Vasa.

Quickly, he interpreted her remarks.

"Miss Baker has been sent to us by the Quaker Society. As you well know, we owe this Society a great debt. They ask only that we build a small room for use as a school, so that she may have a place to teach our little ones to read and write this English. Also she says that if we wish, she will help us in our dealings with government. She says that she is not happy with what she has heard here tonight, and prays that we will come to some amicable conclusion."

In the deepening twilight, the discussion became muted and

less intense. It was decided that there could be no harm in the building of a school, and that in the morning, a start on this would be made. In the meantime, she would use a tent. Despite the general unease the subject of education raised in the minds of many, there was an air of agreement and a liking for this small determined woman. Her willingness to assist them in their struggle with the government endeared her to them almost immediately.

One of the Brethren remarked:

"After all, did not our Leader write that if God should grant to our people to settle in America, then learning to read and write is necessary?"

This seemed to settle any further talk, and, after a closing prayer for guidance on these thorny subjects, the Brethren drifted homeward. From the chatter and murmur of the departing men and women, it was apparent there would be many heated and prolonged discussions on these matters within the confines of the communal homes.

*   *   *

School had come to Milhailovka. On a bright Monday morning, six scrubbed, timid children entered and took their allotted seats on the rough wooden benches that lined the hand-hewn log tables. Miss Baker, smiling cheerfully, exuding confidence, greeted each in turn with an emphatic "Good morning." She moved to a small blackboard set up on an easel, deliberately picked up a stick of chalk, and wrote, "Miss Baker." Turning to the watchful children she pointed to the words, then to herself repeating over and over, "Miss Baker, me. Me, Miss Baker."

One little girl, sitting near the front, giggled and pointed to the teacher. "Me. Miz Baker. Me, Miz Baker," then pointing to herself, said, "Me Anna, me, Anna."

In a flood of gratitude at this seemingly rapid breakthrough in communication, Miss Baker rushed over to the little girl and hugged her, then, whirling, she quickly pointed at a larger boy nearby who, startled, exclaimed, "Michael," then with a broad grin repeated, "Michael. Me, Michael."

In an excess of exuberance, Miss Baker danced from one to another of the children pointing at each in turn. She was greeted with silence and stony stares. Sensing that her show of relief had only caused an unease and withdrawal in these children, she moved quietly to her desk. For a moment, she stood studying these bewildered pupils. Picking up a pencil, she enunciated slowly and clearly, "One." She was greeted only with blank uncomprehending stares. Now, two pencils were held up and the word "Two." repeated over and over. Then, the same with the books. The eyes of the children never wavered from the objects she held up in turn, yet their puzzlement was only too obvious. Baffled, she realized that she was not getting anywhere with this lesson.

So engrossed were teacher and pupils, they had failed to note the unobtrusive entrance of Paul, who had quietly taken a seat close to the flap of the tent. For a while, he studied the motions of the teacher, then impulsively cried out, "One." It had come to him in a flash of insight that the word she so determinedly repeated over and over related not to the name of the object, but to the number.

The desperation that had begun to show in Miss Baker's eyes gave way to relief. Withing the hour, the children were repeating after her the magical words "One, two, three, four, five," and besides this, related these words to the number of objects she held in her hand. Once the idea had caught on, they were quick to learn. Enthusiastically, they shouted each of the numbers.

Around noon, the heat within the little tent became stifling, bringing with it one more problem. How to let the pupils know that school was over for this day? Pointing first to the children, then to the tent flap, Miss Baker said, "Home," then, again, "We now go home." With great interest, all the little heads swivelled to the flap as if expecting something exciting to occur. Nothing did. They turned to stare at her inquiringly. Nonplussed, she stared back. Then, an idea. Picking up her pencils, pens, books, and a ruler, she deliberately opened her desk top and deposited them inside. Next she walked to the blackboard and thoroughly wiped off the morning's work. This done, she once more pointed to the flap, and with a shooing motion of her hands, moved towards the watching little ones. The children caught on. Giggling and laughing, they ran for the exit, a few of them pausing to wave goodbye before fleeing into the open air. Only Paul remained seated.

Inquiringly, she moved to where he sat, and stood looking down at his upturned, sober face.

"You must be the boy Mr. Popoff told me about? Paul Obedkoff?"

Not fully understanding the words, catching only the names, Paul smiled and answered.

"Yes. I Paul. Vasa Popoff learn me much English. See?"

Eagerly, he extended the well-worn dictionary to her.

Taking the book in her hands, Miss Baker absently ruffled the pages. In the presence of this boy, she sensed a desire, an urgency to learn in his very enthusiasm. In the days to come, this would serve as a challenge to her teaching abilities, invading every one of her waking moments. With his lack of background, she envisioned the feat that would be the taking of an illiterate boy of fifteen years of age and in the short time at her disposal, keep alive in him the incentive and the drive to master not only the written language but the mathematics and other subjects she knew would become so important to his future.

She felt a womanly intuition that made her dimly aware this was a boy with a native intelligence far beyond his years, which, coupled to an active, inquiring mind, could in the end result in a force capable of exerting a meaningful influence on the outcome of any future events in which he might be involved. Little did she realize the stubborn resistance her plan would meet with, both from a zealous mother and from the majority of the Brethren.

The entrance of Vasa Popoff, bustling and perspiring, brought her back to the present. Moving to Paul, and placing a kindly arm about his shoulders, he said:

"Ah. I see you two have met. This is the boy I mentioned. Paul Obedkoff."

"Yes. We have been having a little talk."

"And how was your first morning, Miss Baker? The little ones behave themselves?"

"Like angels. Really, they do so want to learn. But, Mr. Popoff, I was given to understand you had more than forty children of school age in this village."

Vasa Popoff answered slowly, carefully.

"Ah, yes. Well, now. That is true. However, a strong feeling exists amongst us that learning of any kind only makes young minds dissatisfied with the land. And the land, Miss Baker, is our life."

"But, surely, now that you are residing in a Western culture, you can see the need for the children to be educated?"

"Not all of them, Miss Baker. Not all of them. That is the reason it was decided to select only six. These, if they continue to study, will be able to conduct all necessary business for the villagers with those on the outside."

"And what about Paul, Mr. Popoff?"

"Ah. He is a special case. I think, Miss Baker, you can understand why. But here also, you must somehow convince his mother of his need to learn.

The father is already in agreement."

Miss Baker enthusiastically exclaimed, "I will convince her. If Paul has the desire to learn, why then, Mr. Popoff, he will be taught. And if I have the opportunity to assist him through the winter, why, maybe next year, we could send him to our school in

Philadelphia. Would that not be wonderful?"

Shocked at this disclosure, Vasa urgently replied, "I must warn you, Miss Baker, never repeat nor broach that idea to anyone in this village. It has been difficult enough to get my people to even agree to going this far. Please, Miss Baker. Take my warning to heart."

Quietly, determinedly, Miss Baker replied, "With God's help, I shall yet see him at our school."

Smiling a little at her determination, Vasa turned to leave.

"If it is God's will, Miss Baker. Then so be it. And, by the way, you will join us for lunch in the communal dining hall?"

"Thank you. I shall be there."

Turning away from his departing figure, she seated herself near Paul, opened his dictionary, and soon both were lost in the intricacies of the English language.

Heigh Ho,
Away we run,
Off on a trek
To the land of sun.
Where milk and honey
Flow in streams.
We'll live with God,
In a temple of dreams.

7

Pilgrimage To Nowhere

The harvest had been abundant. The sun, the wind and the rain had apportioned themselves so that the wheat ripened and swelled to bursting, forty bushels to the acre. Hay plugged the many barns. Kitchen gardens thrived. There were carrots and turnips, potatoes and cabbage in such quantities as ensured a winter of plenty.

Yet, despite this magnificent bounty, a deep pall of gloom pervaded every village. The government seemed determined that this would be the last year in which the villagers might harvest and work these acres. Land commissioners had nosed about, assessing and enumerating the various holdings, listing the acres cultivated, the buildings erected, and other improvements. The fact that they based their findings on individual entries rather than on the enblock acreage granted originally by the government gave a totally false picture. On their recommendations, the government had declared their intention of taking away from the Doukhobors more than one hundred thousand acres located in the Swan River and South Yorkton areas. Each of the individual landholders would be left with only fifteen acres for use as gardens, and would be considered as tenants at will, which in fact meant they could never own even this fractional acreage. A few of the Brethren, those who had decided to take the oath of allegiance and sign the entry papers were granted title to their homesteads. Nickolai was one of these.

Although he knew a deep satisfaction in the ownership of his land, Elizabeth's constant acrimonious remarks never ceased.

Day and night, she would lament and decry his apparent falling away from the dictates of his forefathers. She refused to listen as he patiently attempted to explain to her that, with the help of Miss Baker, they had been able to convince the Land Agent to strike out the offending clause, affirming, rather than swearing to, this oath of allegiance so feared by the others. Many of his neighbors referred to him as a No Doukhobor, accompanied by veiled threats of punishment and chastisement once their Leader arrived in Canada, and learned of these divergences. Through it all, Nickolai stubbornly clung to his land.

In mid-October, the blow fell. For weeks prior to this, as the intentions of the government had become ever more clear, cries of oppression and persecution had echoed at every Sobranya. Zealots wandered through every village, exhorting and calling the Faithful to leave this accursed land. They released their domestic animals to fend as they could on the open prairie, calling them Brother Ox and Brother Horse. Those that survived were rounded up by the Mounted Police and eventually sold by public auction, the monies from these sales going into a trust fund in favor of the Doukhobors. Everything made of leather or animal skins was burnt in ritual fires reminiscent of the Burning of the Guns. Sheepskin coats, boots, shoes, belts, all were given to the flame. Metal objects were discarded since these could only have come from the sweat of man engaged in pitiless labor deep underground. All articles that it was felt might interfere with spiritual well-being were tossed away.

With the help of Paul and Nastasia, Nickolai had managed to prevent Elizabeth from turning loose any of his animals or destroying the equipment, in her desperate bid to bring him back to the fold.

Angered and frustrated, she would plead with him, "Our own Leader has written, 'No man need work. There is corn aplenty for all mankind on this earth, if only avarice could be diminished'!"

Bewildered by these events, yet maintaining a firm hold in his beliefs, Nickolai could only reply to her reasonings by expressing his doubts. "Where are these writings? Why is it only our Elders claim to have seen these? How do you even know Peter Veregin wrote these words?"

Shocked at this apparent heresy, Elizabeth exclaimed, "Only our Leader could write about Humanity regaining the spiritual stature lost by Adam and Eve, and that we, the Chosen Ones, will go to seek an Earthly Paradise."

Paul, sitting quietly, writing on a small slate, spoke for the first time.

"Mother is right. Miss Baker explained some of this to me. It would seem these were letters written by our Leader while in Siberia, to his Mother here in Canada. She passed them on to our Elders."

Surprised by the boy's knowledge, Nickolai inquired, "Since you know so much, my son, what else do these letters say?"

In a struggle to recall the words, Paul closed his eyes, and quietly recited, "Something about the earth, freed from the violence of man's human hands, would begin to abound with all that is ordained for it, and also that, in a hundred years, she would have time to clothe herself completely and return to primitive conditions."

Perplexed by all this, and not too sure of himself, Nickolai enquired, "And you perhaps know where this earthly paradise is?"

"No, Father. But he does say that it must be place where there is an abundance of sunshine, and that man would live on the tender fruits and berries, so that his organism will be formed of energy itself. In consequence of this, man should be wiser, since he would no longer labor with his hands. I must admit, Father, I do not really understand all this."

Still skeptical, Nickolai murmured, "Ah, well, I think that we will be around these parts for some time yet. Maybe such a land does exist, but I do not think that we will ever find it."

Alive with interest, Elizabeth loudly announced a development she had withheld.

"You do not think so, my husband? Then you have not heard the news. We go to find this land. Tomorrow."

Unbelieving, Nickolai said, "What? What do you mean we go to find this land tomorrow?"

Looking him straight in the eye, she confidently answered, "Even now, the Brethren gather. At first light, we start."

Confounded, Nickolai spluttered, "But...but we cannot go. And...and how can the Brethren know where this land is?"

Their voices, increasingly loud, awakened the sleeping baby, suspended in a hanging cradle near the stove. Elizabeth moved to it and gently picked the baby up.

"We do go. With or without you, Nickolai, I and the baby go. The others," she shrugged expressively, "they make up their own minds." Hushing the baby, she turned to Paul and Nastasia, and asked very softly, "You will go? Paul? Nastasia?"

Fearful of having to make such a decision, they both mutely shook their heads. Nastasia shrank into her corner, as if in an attempt to become invisible. Then, not knowing what action to take, and to avoid her mother's pleading eyes, she rose and moved to her father's side. Noting this action, Elizabeth again shrugged and, with resignation, said:

"Then stay with your Father, if that is what you wish. But come first light, I shall be gone. So, make up your minds."

Silence reigned supreme in the little house. Even the baby, soothed by the mother's cradling arms had gone back to sleep. Wearily, Nickolai announced, "Enough of this for tonight. Let us get to bed. Maybe in the morning, why then, some sanity will come to our befuddled heads."

Reaching for the hanging oil lamp, he blew it out. In the darkness, the family quietly prepared for bed, in an attempt to get some sleep. But, for Nickolai, it was a sleepless night.

*   *   *

Seventeen hundred of them, plodding across the frozen prairie, men, women and children, forming a line of humans stretching as far north as the eye could see. And on the fringes, the non-participating relatives, mounted on horseback or in wagons, pleaded for their return home. One of these was Nickolai, riding as close to his wife as he could get, constantly asking her to abandon this folly, at least for the sake of the child she carried in her arms. His pleas fell on deaf ears. Doggedly, she stared ahead, stumbling along, refusing even to look at him. His only reply came from others of the Brethren, cajoling him to abandon his horses and join with them in this march to Paradise. Stubbornly, he followed along as the line of tiring people moved from village to village, exhorting the Faithful to seek this land of Eden with them. Whole villages emptied as the frenzy took hold. Turning southwards, they passed through the village of Poterpevshee, where they paused and asked to see the mother of Peter Veregin. Coming out of her house, she smiled upon them, after which they departed in the direction of Yorkton.

Once the news of this strange pilgrimage reached the larger centres, the daily papers had a field day, most of them quoting grossly exaggerated accounts of the march. Some took a more sane and responsible approach to the proceedings, one of which, the Manitoba *Free Press,* wrote: "They are showing signs that hunger, fatigue, and emaciation have weakened their stalwart frames. Every man's face is an index, silent and eloquent of what he has been, and is, enduring. A drizzling rain is falling adding to the self-inflicted miseries of these martyrs to mistaken ideals of right. Ever and anon will rise their plaintive psalm, its weird minor cadences rising and falling with varying strength, now swelling higher on the breeze like martial music, and again sinking into a mournful dirge of sorrow. Nearly all are barefoot and hatless. All their outer clothing, their heavy felted cloaks and overcoats have been thrown away.

"The trail over which these thousand feet have travelled is worn level as the floor of a dancing pavilion. Their tired feet are cut and bruised, some of them bleeding. Whenever the way lies near a ploughed field, the weary concourse walk across it to ease their tired feet, and the path they have travelled looks as if it had been pressed by a gigantic roller. All who have seen it say it is like a dreadful dream, that it is incredible, unrealizable — hundreds of men, with the light of insanity in their eyes, roaming whither and for what they know not, and animated by a belief that brings the dark ages into the dawning twentieth century."

Darkness fell early on this October day. The scudding clouds that had brought the cold rains disappeared far to the east. The skies cleared. A hard, chilling frost whitened the prairie stubble to a ghostly phantasy.

Within sight of the glow emanating from the street lights of Yorkton, the pilgrims halted. Dropping to the bare earth, they huddled together like sheep exposed to a sudden storm, seeking whatever warmth they could find from the bodies of each other. This would be a long, dreary night. The singing, the praying had ceased, hushed by the bitter knowledge that religious crusades could be lost to the hostile elements.

Elizabeth lay in the press of bodies, fighting for sleep that refused to come, the baby clutched close to her breast. He slept fitfully. These nights away from his warm, comfortable cradle, knowing for the first time hunger and cold, set up a resentment in him. Spasmodic fits of coughing wracked his small body. His little fists beat weakly and ineffectually against the yielding body of his mother. Now, for the first time, Elizabeth knew a deep, soul-tearing fear. Her baby was sick. The realization of this had been growing all through the day. Only in fatigue, in cold, in hunger, could she now admit this to herself. In her fear, her total exhaustion, she shivered uncontrollably. Every muscle in her frame quivered. As if in the torment of a debilitating fever, she felt as if she were about to be torn apart.

"Oh, God," silently she prayed, "let my Nickolai come to us. Let me feel again his strong arms about us. His warm body cover and shield us. Oh, Lord. Let him come this night."

But Nickolai did not come. Desperate and frightened at this display of excess zealotry, against which he was powerless, he had ridden into Yorkton with some vague idea of seeking help. At the Co-op store, operated by the Brethren, he found Vasa Popoff and a policeman in earnest discussion. As he neared, words came to him.

"They are breaking no law, my friend. What do you suggest I do?"

At Nickolai's entrance, the sergeant turned towards him.

"Ah, one of the farmers from the North Colony. What do you suggest?"

Taken aback at the unexpected inclusion of himself into this conversation, Nickolai shook his head and passionately replied. "They must be stopped. Many are ill, and near to death."

Slowly, as if thinking out loud, Vasa remarked, "Ah, yes. So true. Very well. They will enter Yorkton in the morning. Early. I shall get the Brethren to talk with them. With God's help, we may convince them of the folly of this march."

Nodding in agreement, the sergeant replied, "If you can do this, I shall see to it that the immigration hall is made ready for them. Possibly, your womenfolk might have hot soup prepared for them, Vasa?"

"Yes. I will see to that. But, Sergeant. You may have to assist us in this."

"I shall give you all the help I can. Only I cannot use force. As I said, they break no law."

"Very well." Vasa spoke now to Nickolai. "And you, Nickolai. Ride to the South Colony and say that I wish as many of our people as are available to gather here early tomorrow morning. We will stop them."

Nickolai hurried away. Cold and tired, with a long ride ahead of him in the darkness, he was glad of any task that might aid in getting Elizabeth and the baby to return home.

As he made his exit, the sergeant asked Vasa, "What exactly is it that drives your people to commit such folly?"

"Many things. You must remember, Sergeant, we have only lately escaped torture and death in upholding our beliefs. For this, and this only, we were feared and hated by a despotic regime in our homeland."

"But, surely, Vasa, they must know that such treatment in this country is impossible."

"They know that. Yes. But you do not wipe out centuries of oppression, of persecution overnight, Sergeant. There is still the fear, the mistrust of government. It will take time."

"I wonder if you will be given the time. This is a very young country, Vasa. Still, it suffers from growing pains. And mistakes will be made. You must keep in mind, Vasa, all over the world, there are many people hungry for land. People who will go to almost any lengths to secure for themselves a homestead. Oath swearing, paper signing, would be of no consequence to them. To the contrary, they would only feel more secure."

"What you are really saying is that if we do not fall in line and abide by your rules, why then we will be dispossessed and our land given to others?"

"Something like that, Vasa. It has been talked about in our Parliament. It has also been said that your real intentions are to embarrass the government so that you may be able to settle without any oath swearing or paper signing." As Vasa began to interrupt him, he raised his hand. "Wait, there is more. It has also been argued, and in Parliament, that you are working to set up an autocratic society within the framework of Canadian society, so that you may make your own rules and law, as distinct from ours."

Somewhat puzzled, but vehement, Vasa declared: "That is all nonsense. We obey willingly all laws of this country, just so as they are not contrary to the Law of God."

The discussion came to an abrupt end with the entrance of a young constable, red-faced from cold, muffled to the ears in a heavy, bulky buffalo coat. Nodding to the two men, he removed his gauntlets and stood by the stove vigorously rubbing his hands together.

"What a night. Must be down to thirty degrees. McGregor's still out there, keeping an eye on them, Sergeant."

"What is the situation, Constable?"

"They just lie there. I can't understand any of it. Poor blighters must be freezing. I tried talking to some of them."

"Your orders, Constable, were to leave them alone, unless they made any kind of trouble."

"I know, Sergeant. And I'm sorry. But I just had to. I only asked them why they did this, and where they were going."

"Did they give you any reasons, or say anything about their destination?"

"All that they would say was that God was in their hearts, and that He tells them what they must do. I said they would freeze to death out there, but they only answered that God would not let them suffer and that if He did, why then, they were willing to suffer for Him. It's the children I'm afeared for. They were crying, some of them."

For a moment, the sergeant studied the sober face of his constable. Suddenly, mind made up, he said, "Ah, yes. Very well. We must see to it that this nonsense ends tomorrow. Get some sleep, Constable. You will be up early. And I think that might be a good idea for the rest of us. Vasa, I shall drop in on the immigration people on my way home and make the arrangements."

Vasa, who had been sitting silently, listening to the policemen, rose and followed the constable to the door.

"Good. My people should be here by dawn. We will talk to our misguided Brethren."

Ready to open the door, the voice of the sergeant reached him. He paused and turned inquiringly.

"Yes, Sergeant?"

"That man, Obedkoff, the one who came in earlier, looking so worried. He did not go on the march?"

"No. He believes in going the independent way. He is one of the few who have made their peace with the government. But his wife and child are out there. Tonight." Dramatically, he waved his arm around, indicating the outdoors, then in voice expressing his perplexity, he stated with conviction, "Never before in our history has an event of this nature occurred. Believe me, Sergeant, I am as bewildered by this as anyone."

Both men moved through the door, Vasa turning to lock it. The sergeant, shaking his head, watched.

"There is no way I shall ever understand you people. Anyway, Goodnight, Vasa. Try and get some sleep."

"You too, Sergeant. And a goodnight to you."

Both men went their separate ways. Vasa's thoughts on his Brethren in their misery, the sergeant's mind pondering the problem of a possible conflict, and the most expeditious method of handling it.

As dawn cast its fitful light across the icy prairies, the weary pilgrims struggled stiffly to their feet, and were on their way. Most shivered in the raw morning air. Some coughed, spat out phlegm from congested lungs, others banged their arms together to restore circulation. Little children cried ceaselessly. Those too ill to walk were carried along in crudely made litters of blankets and poplar branches. The blind were led gently by the hand. They had been hoping for a miracle and, though none of them considered it such, it had happened. Not one of them suffered any frostbite in the freezing temperatures of the past night, despite weakened bodies and hungry bellies.

Straggling in to the outskirts of Yorkton, they began their sad poignant psalms. Raggedly at first, from voices weakened by exhaustion, the cadence and volume increased until, by the time they had reached the main street, nearly seventeen hundred voices united in a hymn of joy and of glory to God. The many spectators, some of whom had ridden miles to witness this spectacle, were held speechless and awed at this moving harmony of voices.

Once the procession had passed into the outskirts of the town, the police had joined the front ranks, riding alongside, gently but firmly guiding them towards the immigration hall located by the railroad station. Here, they could go no further. They were faced by a number of citizens, police and the Brethren from the South Colonies, forming a solid block across the street. Urgently, the Elders in the opposing group appealed to the marchers to break off and return to their homes.

Someone in the crowd replied loudly but firmly that their home lay far to the south in the land of perpetual sunshine, and that was where they intended going.

After considerable argument and haranguing, when it seemed the marchers were fully determined to continue, despite their fatigue, the sergeant stepped forward and announced, "Although it is true that you have broken no law, nevertheless, for strictly humanitarian reasons, I cannot, and will not allow the women and children to proceed. The men, if they wish, are free to go."

They had no choice. Slowly, the women and children, the sick and the blind, moved into the warm steamy hall, where odors of fresh-baked bread, hot soups, and other cooking foods were strong in the nostrils of those in the front ranks.

Meanwhile, Nickolai had walked up and down the long impeded lines, seeking his wife and baby. Not until they had begun to move through the open doors of the hall did he finally locate her, stumbling along as if in a trance, cradling in her arms a very quiet baby, covered by her shawl. Stepping in front of her, Nickolai forced her to halt. Cupping her bowed face in his two hands, he raised it till their eyes met. Unbelieving, he stared. She had aged ten years in a single night. Deep furrows channeled her features — lines he had never seen before. Her eyes, as she stared into his, were without light, unseeing, uncaring — the eyes of a human in shock. Gently, firmly, he guided her unresisting form away from the multitude, and into the hall.

"You will come home with me, my Elizabeth?"

Listlessly, she replied, "Home? My home is with God. With my little son."

Roughly, he pulled back the shawl to reveal the stilled form of his son. Incredulous, fearful, his voice shook.

"What do you mean, wife? The little one. He is only asleep?"

"He passed over. While he slept. This morning, early. Oh, Nickolai. I would go with him."

Her tearing cry of despair and loss calmed him.

Grief-stricken, he replaced the shawl. Closing his eyes, he uttered a quiet prayer.

"Oh, God. If in your eyes I have sinned, then I now have paid for it. Take this little Soul, this little One, who suffered so, and let him sit by your side. Let him bask in your warmth and in your glory, that he may never again suffer. I ask no more."

In her own torment, Elizabeth reached out to him. With her free arm, she encircled his neck, drawing his head to hers. Hoarsely, she whispered, "No, my husband. The fault and the blame are mine. Better you would have left me with the Cossacks."

Breaking roughly into her lamentations, Nickolai retorted, "Of what matter is it, who is to blame? Our little One is gone, yet there are two others eagerly waiting our return. We go home, Elizabeth."

Nodding her head in agreement, Elizabeth and Nickolai moved to the tables loaded with food. Slowly, she commenced to eat.

Welcome, dear Petrovka,
You've come at last,
Our bulwark 'gainst injustice,
Woeful days now past.
We'll build for you an empire,
For you our chosen King,
And labor hard, from dawn to dark,
Your praises, we will sing.

8

Peter The Lordly

The land lay at rest, wrapped in the frozen grip of sub-zero temperatures. A fiery red ball, deep in the southwest, marked the passage of a cold and distant sun across the hard, blue vault of a January sky. Not a puff of wind blew to disturb the powdery, sparkling blanket of snow.

Despite the bitter cold, the village of Milhailovka was in a festive mood. The long-awaited day had arrived; that day which was to see their leader, Peter Veregin, make his first visit to their village.

For days, every household had been preparing for this event, cleaning, scrubbing, and rescrubbing. Every pot, every pan shone with an added lustre. Wooden floors had been scoured white, window glass wiped clean of every speck, curtains frilled and whitened. Some of the more zealous of the women had attempted to wash down the outer walls of their homes, only to be defeated by freezing water. The men had seen to it that not a fence slat surrounding the many kitchen gardens was out of place. Not a board hung awry. The walks leading to the numerous buildings had been swept clean of snow, and in the street, not a blemish marred the crystal whiteness. Women and children were dressed in their finest skirts, blouses and kerchiefs, colorful and clean. To the eye of a stranger, this village on this day resembled nothing more than a picture postcard.

Some of the older boys had been sent out to watch for the approach of the visitors, but before they could rush in breathless with the news that the sleighs had been sighted, the chiming of many bells, hung on the harness of fast-moving horses, reached the villagers.

Assembling themselves into a large V, the villagers, as was their custom, gave voice to their psalm of welcome. As the lead sleigh, lustre-black, and drawn by six purebred, matched horses, drew to a halt in front of the assemblage, they bowed their heads to the ground, a mark of respect for this man whom they considered to be the living Christ. Rising to their feet, they looked for the first time into the eyes of this leader who, for so long, had been separated from them.

To Elizabeth, this was a moment of ecstasy, of pure joy. Hungrily, she gazed upon the tall, graceful figure. Jet black, luxuriant and gleaming were his hair and beard. Eyes dark and thoughtful, seemed to probe into hers. He looked, she thought, like a man who had suffered much, yet had triumphed over all, through the force of his courage and of his beliefs. She was amazed at his dress: expensive, short blue gabardine coat, trousers encased in grey leggings, piped in black. From a silken cord around his neck dangled a large silver watch and a gold fountainpen.

In a state of bliss, she watched as one of the Elders stepped forward, clasped the outstretched hand of the leader and said:

"Welcome to the village of Milhailovka, Peter Vaselivich Veregin. Many years have we awaited your release. Welcome, and be pleased to accept of our hospitality."

"My thanks to you, my Brother. And to the Brothers and Sisters of Milhailovka, I extend to you also my gratitude for your warm welcome. Now, let us move indoors. There is much to talk about."

Wending his way through the throng, Peter Veregin moved towards the open doors of the large communal dining hall, followed by the others.

On the many long tables, food simmered and bubbled. The air in the hall was redolent with the odors of fresh-baked bread, cabbage, soup, pyrohees, lapshe, and borsch. During the meal, little talk was heard. It was as if all were content to wait for the Sobranya. This would be the time for the airing of problems, and for questions to be asked and to be answered.

At the head of the table, Vasa Popoff and the Elders sat with the visitors, deep in earnest conversation. Only the harsh voice of Nickolai Zibarov penetrated to the diners. Occasionally, he would pound on the table with his closed fist as if to emphasize a point. Suddenly, as if to put an end to this discussion, the leader rose to his feet, signifying the end of the meal.

And then, the Sobranya. Now, it would be settled. Who was in the wrong — those who had clung tenaciously to the faith, defying the government, even to the extent of marching off to settle in some other country, or those who, it was said, had so selfishly given in and signed the hated papers so they might keep their land.

But all were confounded. As was his privilege, the leader was given the last word. He asserted that those who had signed for their lands had done the right thing, as this would secure a needed base for their food growing, in the event the government did indeed carry out their threat to take away the extensive holdings granted to the sect. And after all, it was not the act of registering for the land that was important, but that the lands should be regarded not as individual property but as owned by all.

Of those who had taken part in the pilgrimage, he reasoned that a cold and healthy climate had. its advantages that counter-balanced those of a hot country, where sickness was always a danger. Much better it was to settle down where they were and live as brothers and sisters. As for those other brothers and sisters, the animals, he remarked that to use them was not necessarily to enslave them. Men and horses worked together for their mutual benefit. And did not the horses receive hay and oats, and live in buildings constructed by man? Better to live in harmony, with what they had, than to seek greener fields that may not exist.

After the Sobranya had concluded, Peter Veregin moved around the hall, stopping to speak to many of those he had known in his earlier days, those who had gathered around the gravesite of their departed leader, Lukeria Vasilivna Kalmokova, six weeks after she had passed over, and, as custom dictated, chose her successor. Despite some heated wrangling between opposing factions, Peter Veregin, he who had been the choice of the deceased leader, was chosen to lead the sect. Within days of this move, he had been arrested and shipped off to exile in Siberia. There, he had remained for over fifteen years. Now, thanks to the prodding of the Canadian government, who believed that his presence in Canada could be a solution to the troubles already brewing, and of Tolstoy's influential friends in Russia, together with the pleas of the Quakers, he had been released.

Elizabeth listened and watched all that went on around her with a sense of deep satisfaction; her feelings that of a child whose dearly beloved father has returned to the home after a prolonged absence. Moving to assist the other women in the task of clearing dishes, and washing up, she could not keep her eyes from following her leader as he moved around. With some misgiving, she observed Peter Veregin move to where her husband sat quietly, patiently waiting for the proceedings to end so that he might leave for home.

Nickolai had been troubled. In contrast to the increasing exultation of his wife, as this day had neared, he had become only more and more sombre. Worry that his actions in claiming his land and in encouraging Paul to study with Miss Baker might be misconstrued had haunted him for days. Now that he had been publicly exonerated, Nickolai knew only a weariness, a desire to be away from here. Though he was aware that Paul and Nastasia would faithfully perform the daily chores in his absence, there was one task he loved to do by himself.

Each day, after the supper meal had been concluded, he would hurry the short distance from house to barn. There, he would pause for a moment, standing just inside the closed door, inhaling the warmth, the pungent animal odors. For that moment, he would stand, at peace with himself, listening as the horses, sensing his presence, neighed and nickered their soft welcome. It was a time of renewed hope and of contentment.

So immersed was he in his daydream, he failed to notice that Peter Veregin, Vasa Popoff, and Nickolai Zibarov had stopped in front of where he sat, and were regarding him with some amusement. Breaking the silence, Veregin said:

"Well now, Vasa. Can this be the Brother you spoke of? He who would rather act than dream?"

Startled by this attention, Nickolai rose to his feet, his eyes on Veregin, who laughed quietly and stretched out his hand in welcome.

"I am sorry. We startled you. You are Nickolai Obedkoff?"

Taking the proferred hand, Nickolai's eyes searched those of the leader.

"Yes, that I am."

Nickolai liked what he saw: sincerity of purpose, determination to succeed. Above all, he sensed that here was a man capable of instilling trust in others and of respecting any trust given to him in return.

"I am one of those whose only wish is to live in peace and to till the soil."

His manner changing abruptly, Veregin stared hard at him, his eyes serious.

"What manner of person art thou?"

Without hesitation, Nickolai answered, "I am a person of God." This was a catechism he knew by heart.

Continuing his questioning, Veregin, asked, "Why, then, art

thou a person of God?"

"God created man in order to give His spirit a body on earth."

Here, Zibarov interjected, proclaiming:

"Ah, yes. Is it not also true that man can only realize the presence of God through a clear conscience and good deeds? Have you a clear conscience, Brother Obedkoff?"

"My conscience is clear, Brother Zibarov."

Satisfied now, Veregin stated: "You, Nickolai, are truly a man of deeds. You have proved your wisdom and forethought in signing and in claiming title to the land. We will have need of it. And Vasa," placing a friendly arm about Nickolai's shoulders, he turned to Vasa, "this is one man I would like to see in your village council. You might arrange this?"

"If Brother Obedkoff is willing, yes."

Removing his arm from Nickolai's shoulders, Veregin asked him:

"Are you, My Brother? Would you be willing to represent the village of Mihlailovka at our conventions?"

Despite his misgivings at the thought of the extra load this would place on his shoulders, Nickolai, influenced by Peter Veregin's magnetic, confident personality, could find no way to refuse.

"Yes. It would be an honor."

Gratified by Nickolai's reply, and sensing something of his inner struggle, Veregin replied, "Well spoken, My Brother. I will have need of men such as you in the coming struggle."

Terminating the discussion, Veregin, followed by Zibarov, moved away. Vasa, before following the two men, quickly informed Nickolai, "There will be a council meeting tomorrow noon. You will come, Nickolai?"

"Yes. I will be there."

"Then, goodnight. And, by the way, I am very pleased with the impression you made on our leader."

Pausing to allow Vasa to catch up to them, Veregin said, "I would like to meet with this school teacher. Is she here?"

Zibarov remarked with some bitterness:

"She is here. Over by the stove, talking to some of the women. Probably interfering as usual."

"Ah, yes. But then, Brother Zibarov, is she not here by God's will? We must show more charity. And I am sure that with her limited knowledge of our language, and our women understanding no English, why, her interference must be slight."

Vasa joined them as they moved towards Miss Baker.

"Ah, Vasa. We go to meet the school teacher. You will as usual act as our interpreter?"

With a nod of agreement, Vasa introduced them. The polish that Veregin had acquired in his European travels now stood him in good stead. In his greetings, he was courteous and gentlemanly, and both were soon engaged in lively conversation. In Miss Baker's mind, one thought predominated over all others. Here was the man with the authority and the power to override the objections she had met with in her plan to send Paul to school in Philadelphia.

With genuine interest and his customary warmth, Veregin inquired: "Tell me, Miss Baker. How do our children take to this studying of the English language?"

"Very well, indeed. In the three months that I have instructed them, they are now able to both read and write simple words, and I am confident that, given another three months, they will be accomplished students."

"And what about you, yourself, Miss Baker? Are you comfortable? Do my people see that you are well looked after?"

"Mr. Veregin, I have never been so well looked after in my life. Why, if I keep eating as I have, by spring, I shall be as fat as a little pig."

Laughing heartily, Veregin jokingly quipped, "Then, may I say, Miss Baker, that you will be the prettiest little pig I have ever seen?" Then, changing the subject quickly, becoming again serious, he continued: "Now, my dear Miss Baker, I believe that you have a problem. I am referring to young Paul Obedkoff. I would like to hear of this."

Surprised at his knowledge of this, and of the fact that he would bring the subject up so quickly, she replied, "A problem that can easily be resolved, Mr. Veregin. All we have to do is to overcome the Mother's objections. And Paul deserves the chance. He has a brilliant mind, and will one day, if given the opportunity to learn, be a credit to your people."

"But, Miss Baker. You are by now surely aware of our objections to schooling. You must realize the difficulties in overriding a Mother's objections regarding her own son's future."

Decisively, Miss Baker replied, "You yourself wrote a letter to your Mother, from, I believe, Siberia. In that letter, Mr. Veregin, you stated that since, here in North America, education was compulsory, it would be all to the good. And did you not say that simple literacy is a necessary aid to life, that to learn to read and to write would be a good thing?"

Unperturbed, Veregin retorted, "My very words. Yes, Miss Baker, I admit that I wrote those very words. But then, I did not at the time know that they would be taken so seriously by such a persistent little school teacher. Believe me, I am fully aware of this necessity. But, only for a few, just so that it will be possible to conduct our business with those on the outside. The others, Miss Baker, must be content to till the soil and to live in God's light."

Insistent now, Miss Baker continued: "I have no argument with any of that. But, what about Paul? Can we make arrangements for him to attend our school in Philadelphia next fall?"

"I can only say I shall do what I can for him. It may be that your idea has much merit. His Mother, however, must agree. In any event, I shall have a talk with her."

Sensing that she had attained some success in enlisting the Leader's aid, but still skeptical, she laughed lightly and retorted, "I do hope that you have greater success with her than I have had. In fact, I think the Mother looks upon me as a kind of Satan's agent."

"To some of my people, Miss Baker, you may very well be just that. But, is that not one of the hazards you assumed in coming here to teach?"

"It is one hazard I had not foreseen. But, then, Mr. Veregin, is not all life a hazard?"

Smiling at her evident acceptance of life as it was, he said in an attempt to console her:

"Ah, well. You have my gratitude for the work you are attempting here. Now. Let us forget all this serious business, Miss Baker. I see that we are about to have some choir singing. You will enjoy this."

Now that the dishes had been washed, and the tables cleared and scrubbed, benches had been set up at one end of the room. Here, the villagers congregated. The hall resonated with a harmony of voices, male and female. Her tasks finished, Elizabeth moved to Nickolai's side, and, as darkness fell and lamps were lit, they sat together, lost in the choral renditions of well-known and loved hymns and psalms.

The next morning, Nickolai sat listening intently, as Vasa Popoff outlined plans for the coming year. The more he heard, the more he felt a growing pride in being selected as a village representative. From what he heard, it was obvious that Peter Veregin had not been idle since his arrival in Canada. He had already met with government officials, and, from them, had obtained an agreement that the three years' grace allowed settlers before swearing the oath of allegiance, making them naturalized citizens, would commence from the day of that meeting. Thus, as Vasa carefully explained, it gave them until the year Nineteen Hundred and Five before they would be called upon to make the crucial decision.

For the coming spring, it had been decided that all able-bodied young men would work as before for the railroad, and on the new highways being built nearby. The wages accrued from this labor would go to the central treasury to be used in the purchase of both land and machinery. Nickolai was particularly pleased to learn that the purchase of steam engines was contemplated with which to haul the plows and power the threshing machines that even now were on order for the various colonies. No more would the back-breaking labor of man be all that would be used in the seeding and harvesting of this harsh prairie land.

Discussing all this with Elizabeth, later that evening, while she finished up the supper dishes, he radiated a confidence that the future would be more in line with his ideas. As he explained to her:

"There is no way we can plow and then harvest these immense tracts of land without the use of machines."

Cautious, not wishing to start an argument, Elizabeth replied to his enthusiasm: "Huh. Very soon, my husband, with all these machines you talk about, you will be able to lie around the house all day, talking instead of working."

With some acerbity, Nickolai retorted, "You are being silly, my wife. Man will still have to work with these machines."

"My grandfather, and yours Nickolai, had no machines. Yet, they were able to seed and harvest the crops."

"Yes. By laboring, on their knees, from dawn to dark. And never did they have so much land to till as this."

Unwilling to continue in this vein, Elizabeth snorted her derision, then switched the subject. "There is much talk that this devil, this school teacher, has some thought of getting our Paul to go to some school far away. This, I will not have, Nickolai."

Forced into a subject he would rather have avoided, Nickolai replied heavily:

"You would have the boy always underfoot?"

Shortly, she replied; "Yes. I would have him where he belongs. Here, at home."

"But, Elizabeth. Can't you see? The boy wants to learn. Why, the teacher says that he is exceptionally bright, and that, someday, he could become a doctor, or a lawyer, or something like that."

Exasperated, Elizabeth banged a pan down forcibly, and turned on Nickolai.

"That teacher. She is the one putting ideas into his empty head. If I had my way, he would stop this nonsense tomorrow. Is it not enough to have lost one son?"

Confused by her outburst, she stopped. This was one wound that had not as yet healed. Although she had come to believe that her baby was better off in the hands of God, she still carried a sense of guilt that was hard to shake off.

Knowing her hurt, and wishing to end this talk, Nickolai moved to the door, put on his coat, and turned to the silent, grieving wife.

"I go to the barn now. The children should be about finished. When I return, Elizabeth, we will talk some more. But, Paul must be allowed to decide for himself."

With these words, he opened the door and stepped out into the night.

*   *   *

Serene and quiet, the winter months flowed by. It was as if man had attuned himself to nature, resting, hardly breathing, awaiting the advent of spring, when the earth would burst forth in all her greenery, and man again become active.

Once the plowing, the discing, the seeding got under way, Nickolai found himself too busy to pay much attention to outside affairs. A great, firebreathing steam tractor had been introduced in time to commence the plowing. All lands, Nickolai's included, had been worked communally, the machine wending its way day by day from one holding to the next. Although he missed the personal touch of his horses, he knew that to get this acreage planted, they must, from now on, rely on these mechanical monsters. Work commenced at five in the morning, and, for five hours, the first crew labored, to be relieved by the next crew who also carried on for five hours. And so it went, for fifteen hours each day.

Despite the visible speed with which the work was carried out, Elizabeth continued to decry the use of these devil tools.

"God," she would assert, "did not intend that man should give himself body and soul to any machine. Someday, they would be sorry. Someday, He would punish these foolish men." Ignoring the illogic of her statements, she persisted in denigrating the use of these new machines.

This constant reiteration on the subject of God and machine tired Nickolai, and he began to retire morosely into himself. He refused to be drawn into any further discussion on the subject, until one evening, coming in from the fields, he was dumbfounded to find his kitchen occupied by Alex Makhortov and several of the Brothers and Sisters from the furthest villages. What shocked him was that all had discarded their clothing and sat around in the nude. At his entrance, their eyes had moved to him, as silently they regarded his tired, dusty figure. Nickolai, in shock and confusion, burst out:

"Brother Makhortov. What are you doing? Where are your clothes?"

Solemnly rising from his seat, Makhortov moved towards him.

"We go as Adam and Eve. As they would show Nature to humanity, how man should return to his fatherland, return the ripened fruit and its seed, so do we."

Bewildered, Nickolai backed away, then looked at Elizabeth.

"I do not understand. What is it you wish?"

"That you go with us, Brother Obedkoff. We go to find the Promised Land."

Shaking his head in disbelief, Nickolai could only stutter, "But...but why? This is folly."

Puzzled by this bizzare happening, yet attracted by the zeal and hope of another crusade, Elizabeth cried out, "They say as I do: Physical work is sinful. And our animal Brethren must be liberated."

His hands extended in mute appeal, Makhortov turned to Elizabeth and intoned, "Ah, Sister Obedkoff. You say right. Join with us. Remove your clothing and show the world how Eve went about in Paradise."

Thoroughly aroused, Nickolai thundered, "She'll do no such thing. And now, Brother Makhortov. It would please me if you would leave us in peace."

Calmly, ignoring Nickolai's fury, Makhortov enquired:

"I had thought that you would let us remain here for the night."

Fearful of the results of any prolonged exposure to this misguided zealotry might have on his wife, Nickolai sought desperately to avoid this suggestion.

"I...I...There is little room. Would you not be better off in the village?"

Unaware of any of this, Paul and Nastasia, as children do, had left the barn, and playfully raced each other to the house, in the expectation that supper would be ready. Bursting into the over-crowded kitchen, they stumbled to a halt, to stare in utter disbelief at the scene that met their startled eyes. Nastasia, flushing to the roots of her hair, turned and ran into the bedroom, her eyes averted from the naked bodies. Paul could only stand, his mouth open, gaping, one hand holding to the partly opened door, the other waving around in disbelief. Recovering from his surprise, he gently closed the door, then walked to his father's side.

The boy's discomfort needed no wording. The women moved to the door, one of them suggesting, "Let us then go to the village. Our Brethren will surely welcome us, and we can stay that night. Come, Brothers."

At the open door, Makhortov, his eyes on Elizabeth, delivered a parting shot:

"If you decide to join with us, Sister Obedkoff, we will be in the village till dawn. You too, Nickolai. You too would be welcome."

Before Nickolai could make any reply, he had closed the door and gone his way.

Nickolai sat down at the table.

"Now, if you please Elizabeth. Now that this nonsense has ended, I would eat."

His fury subsiding, he fought to regain some semblance of normalcy in his home.

Elizabeth plodded slowly to the stove, brought to the table a large bowl of soup, spoons and wooden plates. Sitting down opposite her husband, her arms folded on the table, she stared hard at him.

"How can you know that this is nonsense, Nickolai? Who is to say what is right and what is wrong?"

Glancing over at his wife, Nickolai, for the first time in his life, witnessed tears rolling down her face.

"Oh, Nickolai. I can no longer tell right from wrong. It seems, lately, since we came here, that everything is so changed. Before, in the Motherland, it was so simple. We lived in the faith and in God. Now, even our leader has nothing on his mind but the making of money. Why..."

She could go no further. Sobs wracked her body, echoing through the house. Nastasia, who had run in, now stood gazing at her mother in amazement. Paul placed a consoling arm about the quivering shoulders, an arm Elizabeth rejected with a determined push.

"Even my son. My own son. All day and into the night. Books, books and more books. What has happened to our Living Book? The Book that served our fathers through the centuries?"

In her confusion and in her fear, her voice broke.

"Nickolai, my husband. Help me. Help me to know right from wrong. Help me to understand this new way. I am so afraid."

At her side in an instant, Nickolai encircled her shoulders with his arms, drawing her desperate, pleading face so close to his breast.

"There, now. There, now. Do not carry on so. There is nothing to fear. Please, my Elizabeth. Dry your tears. We do the best we can. All I know is that I must plant the wheat."

Tenderly, lightly stroking the grey-black hair, his voice dropped to a whisper. "It is hard. I know, but, Elizabeth, can we not be good farmers, and still love God? Oh, Elizabeth. Elizabeth. Do we not live for each other?"

Pulling away from his embrace, Elizabeth vigorously dried her eyes on the edge of her apron. Rising, she walked briskly to the stove, her voice controlled and quiet.

"Forgive me, my husband. Yet, sometimes, I think that maybe God has deserted us in this strange land."

Within days, the village was buzzing with news of this latest march. Elizabeth could hardly wait to get home from her trip to the communal store to give Nickolai the latest word. Finding him at home on her return, she burst out:

"Nickolai. I have been talking with Olga. There is much news. The policeman have Alex in prison. And all the other Brethren."

Not too interested, Nickolai replied:

"I have heard. Vasa came by today. He told me of their doings."

"But, Nickolai. Are we not going to do something to help?"

"According to Vasa, they attacked Peter Veregin, demanding he let his horse go, and that he join with them. When he refused, they forcibly seized his horse and turned him loose. They also said that they were on their way to Otradnoe to burn down his house. Called it the throne of Satan."

Stunned, Elizabeth blurted out, "I had not heard of any of this. Could it be true?"

"Oh, it is true. Had it not been for our Brethren at Nadezhda, they might very well have succeeded in their bad works. Luckily, our Leader was able to enlist their aid in seizing the women and children and holding them in the village. But Alex and the others went on to Yorkton, and were taken by the police."

"But Nickolai. They did no wrong."

"If they did no wrong, they would not be in prison, now would they?"

Soberly, Elizabeth thought of this for a moment, then asked, "Could this be the beginning of more persecutions?"

"I do not see how. No one has troubled us."

"But, my husband. Maybe it is only the beginning. Maybe they will come here and..."

Impatiently, Nickolai cut her off.

"Foolish woman. Why would they trouble us? Only now, the papers in their big cities say that we all march naked and carry on."

"How can they say such things about us? They were so few."

"Ah, well. It would seem that we are fast becoming news for these people to read about. I would wish it were otherwise."

And news it became. Daily papers in every city across Canada carried headlines proclaiming the fact that the Doukhobor immigrants were now marching naked across the prairies; this despite the fact that only fifty-two out of an estimated four thousand participated in this pilgrimage, and, of these, only twenty-eight men reached the town of Yorkton and were arrested. It was another field-day for reporters. Coupled to the previous march, and to the unfortunate labor troubles occurring during their first few weeks in Canada, the Opposition party in Ottawa had gained, again, ammunition in their constant attacks on Sifton and the Liberal government for what they proclaimed to be their very lax immigration policies.

The twenty-eight men were given three months for indecent exposure. Although given a chance of release if they would promise to keep the peace, they even spurned the efforts of Peter Veregin, and were shipped off to jail in Regina.

Here, all but three refused to work, and insisted on living on a diet of raw potatoes, vegetables and grass. Accusations of brutal treatment while incarcerated, though never substantiated, were to resound through the succeeding years, adding in no little measure to the troubles that were yet to come.

What is fact is that two of the prisoners were certified as insane and sent to the asylum, where one of them died.

Out of all this came mystification that the sight of a naked body could cause such an uproar. For the first time, the term, Sons of Freedom, came into being.. And, in nudity, they had a weapon they were to use to great effect in the years to come.

We toiled for years,
Broke your land,
Worked together,
Hand in hand.
Then, these papers
You brought to us,
The law says sign,
What a fuss,
The only law
We can obey,
Is that of God's,
Our Destiny.

9

The Law Is An Ass

Striding purposefully along the wooden sidewalk that bordered the broad, tree-lined street bisecting the town of Veregin, Paul, on this his twenty-first birthday, knew a deep sense of happiness and contentment. The long, challenging years at the school in Philadelphia were finally over, as were the painful separation from family and friends, and the daily, often bitter, struggles to master subjects so alien to his way of life. Now, the warm friendly greetings he received from and returned to many of the passing villagers and farmers reinforced his feelings of contentment. It was good to be home.

In the short two weeks since his return, he had found himself elevated to the position of business manager for the community, and placed in charge of the many and varied enterprises initiated by Peter Veregin so as to ensure the survival of the Doukhobors in Canada. Paul's skill in speaking English, together with his training in business practices, ideally suited him for the difficult tasks he had been empowered to handle.

With an awed sense of wonder and amazement, Paul had noted the many tangible developments that marked the progress of his people, in the past five years, all of which, he knew, were the creation of an agile, clever mind. To the Brethren and to government officials alike, Peter Veregin had quickly proven his shrewdness and capabilities. Realizing that the obdurate refusal of his followers to the taking of any oath would soon see them homeless, and foreseeing the necessity to gain a rail outlet for the shipping and the receiving of produce, he had bought up thirteen

square miles of farm land on either side of the Canadian
Northern railroad, whose right of way ran between the North and
the South colonies. On this land, the town of Veregin had arisen,
like some mushroom growth spawned by the steel rails that
stretched from Winnipeg in the east to the new Province of
Alberta.

In Paul's thoughts, the town assumed the properties of a
monument — a monument to Man's love, toil, and faith: love for
this Leader who was looked upon by the Brethren as the Living
Christ on earth; toil that somehow had assumed the form of an
art, visible in the beautiful ornate hand-crafted woodwork that
adorned the two-storied, whitely-gleaming, octagonal building
that served both as home and as administration headquarters for
the sect; faith in a way of life that had withstood the ravages of
centuries of persecution and official censure, and that could yet
find the strength to industriously build for the future.

The high, keening whine of a large circular saw biting through
a log, rising in crescendo as its speed increased, signalled the
beginnings of this new day. That, thought Paul, would be his
next task — computing the board feet of lumber available for sale,
and for community use. But, first, he had to check out and
supervise the unloading of the boxcars that arrived overnight
from Winnipeg. From there to the sawmill, and then on to the
brickyard, located a few miles from town. After this, he was
scheduled to meet with Peter Veregin and some of the Elders. He
faced a busy, demanding day.

*   *   *

"The law, Mr. Veregin, is very clear. Each man must make his
own individual entry for his land, and take the Oath of
Allegiance. You, Sir, must be aware of this."

Paul, his eyes fixed on the speaker, wondered at his lack of
understanding and of compassion. This was the Reverend John
McDougal, a Methodist minister appointed by the government to
head a special commission empowered to enforce the law, or, if
this failed, to dispossess them of their land. His recommendations, which were the subject of this meeting, seemed to the
Doukhobors to be unduly harsh and unjust.

Breaking the uneasy silence that had fallen over the group,
Peter Veregin turned to Paul.

"Tell him, Paul, that our people do not wish to own the land —
all they wish is to be permitted to make a living from it."

Upon his repeating this to McDougal, in English, the minister
gave a vigorous shake of his head and replied:

"No. Either you obey the law as it is written, or you lose your
land."

There was no need for Paul to repeat any of this. McDougal's actions had said it all. Baffled, Peter Veregin raised both hands as if in defeat and turned to Paul.

"You carry on Paul. See what you can make of all this." Then, bitterly: "The law is an ass."

Nodding in agreement, Paul continued the discussion with McDougal.

"Are we to understand, Sir, that this is the final word of the government?"

Firmly, quietly, McDougal replied, "That is the final word. You may assure Mr. Veregin and the others that I have full authority to act and that, commencing immediately, I shall enforce the recommendations of this commission."

"But, Sir, you are surely aware that this action will leave many of our people homeless?"

"Not quite, young man. In its generosity, the government will leave each of those dispossessed of their land a minimum of fifteen acres per head so that they may carry on with their gardens. None at least will starve."

Quietly, Paul relayed these words to the Elders, then turned again to McDougal.

"You have figures on these recommendations?"

"Yes." Referring to sheets of notes he carried, McDougal read out: "You have two hundred and thirty-five Independents who have registered and will receive 59,360 acres. A further 122,880 acres have been reserved for your community people in the villages, those who refuse to take the oath. This is the fifteen acres per head mentioned previously. You must also understand that this land cannot be owned by you. Now, on June the first of this year, 258,880 acres that you refused to make entry for will be made available to the public as homestead lands."

Cries of "Persecution! Thievery! Oppression! resounded through the room on receipt of these figures. Raising his hand commandingly, Peter Veregin stilled the babble of voices.

"Ask him, Paul, about the solemn promises made to our people on their arrival in this land."

Questioning the watchful McDougal, Paul asked him:

"Did not your government make a promise to our people when we emigrated to these lands, that we would be allowed to live in the communal way if we so desired? Is that, Sir, not correct?"

Again, reading from his notes, McDougal intoned:

"If any man who resides in a village cultivates land more than three miles from the village in which he lives, his entry will be protected for a period of six months. If he does not build and live on that land within that time, the entry will be cancelled. That,

Sir, is the extent of this government's promises. That, and no more."

About to retort angrily, Paul was silenced by Peter Veregin.

"Wait, Paul. I would have him know that, when I spoke to Clifford Sifton, the Minister of Interior, while in Ottawa, these were not the words I heard."

McDougal's reply to this was quick and to the point:

"Mr. Sifton is no longer our Minister of the Interior. You are now dealing with a Mr. Oliver who has been appointed to that post. He has little sympathies with idealogists that contravene the laws of Canada. And in any event, you must have been made aware of this when my government issued this circular, both in Russian and in English." Waving a large printed form around he continued, "This was circulated to each of your villages last summer. Surely, Mr. Veregin, you have seen this? It clarifies this government's position on these matters."

Reaching out a hand, Peter Veregin gingerly took the pamphlet, and studied it. Handing it back, he said:

"Read it."

Doubtfully, McDougal stared at him.

"All of it?"

"Yes. If you please." Then, changing his mind, he said, "Maybe better if Paul reads it. You go ahead, Paul."

Accepting the paper, Paul cleared his throat and read slowly.

"The government is very sorry to see that after having been in Canada for seven years, the large majority of Doukhobors still cultivate their land in common and refuse to become citizens of the country. They have left large areas of land which government has permitted them to hold in their names without cultivation and improvement. The law is that a man must cultivate his own land or he cannot hold it. The people who are not Doukhobors now demand that Doukhobors be no longer allowed to hold land without cultivating it and becoming citizens of the country."

Smiling, Peter Veregin asked, "Do you agree with this document, Mr. McDougal?"

"Whether I agree or not is of little consequence. I am here to carry out the law. That is what I intend doing, Mr. Veregin."

Rising to his feet, Peter Veregin placed both hands firmly on the table, and angrily stared into McDougal's eyes.

"Tell him, Paul. I have nothing more to say. It would appear that, if we are to be masters of our own land, and on our own terms, why then, it will not be on this land."

Informed of this by Paul, McDougal quietly, politely wished the gathering a pleasant good-day and departed. He left little doubt in any man's mind that he was determined to carry out the government's intentions and take away the land they had so laboriously tilled for the past eight years.

Surveying the dour faces around him, Peter Veregin resumed his seat, his eyes moving from one man to the other. Smiling, half-amused, he asked:

"Why so glum, my Brothers? All is not lost. Have we not suffered even more severely in the past? And have we not always survived?"

Bitterly, Elder Malakoff replied, "But this is, we were told, a free country. Then, how can they take our land away from us?"

Soberly, thoughtfully, Peter Veregin answered:

"Freedom in any country has its price. In this country, the price is the taking of an oath, which, despite all their assurances to the contrary, could see our young men in battle with other young men. This, I assure you, Brother Malakoff, is too high a price."

Murmurs of assent greeted his statements. Waiting calmly for this to die down, he continued, "However, there is one way in which we might yet overcome these objections and gain some freedom. Brother Reibin, would you be so kind as to detail for our Brothers your recent trip west of the mountains?"

Enthusiastically, Elder Reibin rose and addressed the group.

"I and Brother Zibarov have recently returned from a journey west of the Rocky Mountains to the Province of British Columbia. There, we found much land for sale, cheap. Good land. Much of it covered with forest. In the valleys, orchards and berries, and fields for the growing of vegetables. All a man could ever want. The climate, we were told, is mild, both in summer and in the winter. We feel that in this land, we could settle and live our lives without the signing of any oaths, or even bothering with government. We would like to go there."

Zibarov added:

"I agree with my Brother. It is a good land. Only, how can we buy this land? What will we use for money? It will take much money."

Confidently, Peter Veregin informed them: "I have already been at work on that problem. By using our land as collateral, I have secured a large loan at good terms of repayment, from a bank in Winnipeg. Also from Winnipeg, I have a fair offer to purchase the brickyard. By the way, Paul, what is our daily output?"

"According to my calculations, about 50,000 bricks per day. This makes it the largest operation of its kind west of Winnipeg."

"Thank you, Paul. Now, taking into account the wages earned by our men on the outside, and the revenue from the sales of last year's wheat, I have already purchased 2,800 acres at a place called Waterloo and a further 2,700 acres at Grand Forks."

One of the Elders broke in.

"Huh. Even their town names remind one of battle and killing."

Puzzled, Paul asked: "What do you mean?" Then, he caught on, "Oh, I know. You are referring to the Battle of Waterloo. I studied some of that at school."

Cutting in on this conversation, Peter Veregin dryly remarked, "It is of no consequence. Once we settle there, the name can be changed. In the meantime, there are more important matters to discuss." Pausing to gain the full attention of the Brothers, he announced: "My Brothers, we leave for British Columbia within the next month. Those who must finish the harvest will follow us in October. We have found a new home."

It took a moment for the full impact of this announcement to sink in. Paul reflected on the reaction of this news to the independents like his father. How, he wondered, would they feel about giving up all they had worked for over the years and moving to a strange country?

As if in answer to his unspoken question, Peter Veregin said, "Not all our Brothers will wish to go to this new land. Which is to the good, as I wish that some would remain here and grow the wheat. This, they will trade to us for our fruit, berries and lumber. We will be better to have colonies both here and in British Columbia. This is my desire, that we become self-suffi-cient, with no reliance on any outsiders. In this way only can we remain free."

Taking a short-cut across the fields after the meeting, Paul had to admit to himself that the prospect of leaving this land for British Columbia appealed to him. To begin with, the extremes in temperature certainly made life difficult, especially for the old folks. Even he had found the mosquitoes that thrived in the summer intolerable. He had heard that on one of the few nude marches indulged in by the Sons of Freedom some time ago, the police at Yorkton had placed the marchers in an open shed and at night had hung a lit lantern in the entrance. It was rumored that, by morning, all were dressed but scratching vigorously. He laughed a little at the thought, wondering if it were really true. Maybe, he hoped, these zealots would be kept so busy in this new land, they would have no time for defiance and parades; especially since they would have no longer the threat of oath-taking for land hanging over their heads. Youthfully, naively, he visualized a time when his Brethren could look forward to a life of peace, toil and tranquility.

By the next day, news of the impending move had spread like wild fire to each of the sixty-one villages that comprised the North and South colonies, including the independents at Prince Albert. Some of the more ardent silently thanked God, and immediately started packing. Others took time to sort out their thoughts about such a move. They had made their homes here on the prairies, and to leave would, they knew, entail some heartbreak. One of these was Nickolai. At supper that night, after Paul had informed them of the meeting, he sat silent, listening to Elizabeth, Paul and Nastasia chatter away about this new country.

Rising from the table, he moved quietly to the door, opened it, then, pausing, turned to watch his family. After a few moments, he called out:

"Nastasia. It is time to do the milking. And Paul, you would help with the chores tonight?"

"Yes of course, Father. Come, Sis. Enough of this idle talk."

Searching her husband's eyes, Elizabeth asked, "You are not happy, my Husband?"

"We do not leave this place."

Abruptly making his exit, he walked rapidly to the barn, leaving Elizabeth angry and defiant, but with no way to answer. Paul and Nastasia followed quickly, their faces sad and perplexed. On the way to the barn, Nastasia halted and took Paul by the arm.

"Paul. You think Father means it?"

"Yes. He means it, Nastasia. I cannot find fault with him. And I suppose that means you also stay. And Mother."

"Mother, maybe. But not me, Paul." For a moment, she stopped, searching for words, then, "I am getting married." The words rushed out breathlessly. "Mike asked me only today."

"Mike? You mean Mike Popoff?"

"Yes. Oh, Paul. I could not find the words to tell Father."

"I am glad. You have my blessings, little sister." Throwing his arms about her, Paul hugged Nastasia fervently. "Now, you will have the words to tell Father. You will be going to British Columbia. I, also, Nastasia. I, also, will be going."

"Then, I shall not feel so alone. Oh, Paul, I am glad. Come, race me to the barn. Bet I can beat you."

Laughing, they both set out at a dead run. Inside the barn, Nickolai, busy with a large fork, fed hay to his stock. He was worried and depressed, and occasionally glanced towards the door, as if wishing his children would hurry.

Pausing just inside the door, Nastasia peered into the gloom, and called: "Father? Do come over here, please."

Something in the excitement of her voice transmitted itself to Nickolai, who approached expectantly.

"You are going to stay here with me, my Pet?"

"No, Father. But today, Mike Popoff asked me to be his wife, and I said yes."

Unable to hide the disappointment, Nickolai grunted, "So, you will be going with him?"

"Does not a wife follow her husband? This you have taught me."

"Yes, of course, and you have been taught well."

Unable to say more than this, he looked around helplessly, bewildered.

Noting this, Nastasia threw her arms around him, rubbed her face against his.

"Oh, my Father. Please do not look so hurt. Have you no blessing for me?"

Firmly releasing himself from her grasp, Nickolai stepped back, and turned away saying:

"Let us get the chores done. And, of course, you have my blessings. May you both be happy forever." Abruptly, he paused, turned to look at her crest-fallen face, his eyes wistful, his voice a whisper. "You know I would not have it otherwise. Mike is a fine boy. And, I knew this had to happen some day. Let's get to the chores."

As twilight deepened into darkness, Nickolai lit a lamp hanging by the door, and another which he carried with him into the darkening interior. From overhead, in the hayloft, Paul busily sent loads of hay down a chute. He was whistling, loudly and shrilly — a tune that Nickolai had never before heard. Passing Nastasia sitting by the side of a cow, her head pressed deep into its rear flank, hands swiftly moving up and down, sending spurts of milk gushing into a pail held between her knees, Nickolai stood looking down upon her busy form. Bathed in the golden glow of lamplight, she seemed to him to become the little girl he had always loved. As if feeling his eyes on her, she glanced quickly up at his grave features, she smiled, never losing a stroke in her milking. Moving away, Nickolai murmured, "Be happy, little girl. May God be with you always. I shall miss you so."

*   *   *

The days passed quickly. They were busy days of sorting, discarding, and packing; comings and goings from farm to farm, and farm to village; hasty arrangements as to disposal of crops, livestock and equipment to be made with those of the Brethren who would remain behind. From the farthest villages, wagons, loaded with household goods to be taken on the journey, congregated in Veregin days before the day of departure. The communal homes in the town were soon over-crowded, with people sleeping on every available inch of floor space. Latecomers were billeted in the nearby villages, as these also prepared for the long trek.

Already, John Shebinin and Nickolai Zibarov, with a party of young men, had left for British Columbia; there, to arrange for housing and to make ready for the arrival of the settlers. The train that was to carry them across the mountains and down into the Kettle Valley had been chartered from the C.P.R. and was due on the last day of the month.

Through all this bustle and activity, Nickolai remained aloof, going about his daily tasks as if nothing were happening, his face a mask of stoicism and patience. Wistfully, he ignored the furtive manoeuverings of Elizabeth, as she would drag out old trunks and boxes from their storage places in the attic, spending long hours in a pretense of sorting out the contents, as if her only concern was to discard that which she regarded as useless. Busily, she gathered together and moved these trunks and boxes to an old shed close to the house. Not at any time did she mention her aching wish to join with her Brethren and Sisters in this new pilgrimage. And for Nickolai, the same nagging question haunted each waking hour of his daily routine. Would this wife of his, he wondered, go and leave him here alone? He had no way of knowing.

The strained atmosphere, the ill-concealed bitterness of his wife made Nickolai's life a sheer hell. Frenzied activity seemed the only way in which he could cope with this alien situation. Every waking moment of his days would find him in the barn, or out in the fields. Occasionally, he would walk into the village to stand gazing at the unusual hustle and bustle of movement going on around him. Once, as if incapable of believing that this were really happening, he drove into Veregin; moving slowly down the street to the railroad station, his eyes taking in mounds of boxes, machinery and miscellaneous goods being made ready for shipment. Returning home, he went directly to the barn, there to spend the next few hours currying and talking to his beloved horses.

Paul, busy with the myriad details of transport, and of counselling and advising, seldom came home, and then only to eat and throw himself into bed, to sleep in total exhaustion. Nastasia, torn between her love for her parents and her desire to get away to make a life with her husband, wavered between her home and that of Vasa Popoff. Sensing her father's despair, her mother's bitterness, she could only stand by, knowing a deep sense of frustration, a silent witness to this battle of wills. The day of her marriage had been the one bright spot in this month of despair. On that day, the two families with many of their friends, had gathered in a large room in the home of Peter Veregin. With their heads bowed to the floor, the young couple had received the blessing of their Leader, and of the parents.

Later, at the wedding dinner, the talk gravitated to the impending move. Peter Veregin, in an expansive mood, described in glowing terms the valleys and rivers of their new land. With a lively enthusiasm, he spoke of his dream to establish a series of communes, both in British Columbia and there on the prairies, so that, by trading produce back and forth, the Sect might become self-sufficient and free from dealing with outsiders. Fruit, berries, and vegetables in return for wheat and flour. Irrigation in the new land would be no problem, what with the plentiful supply of fresh mountain water. The soil was rich and suitable for all types of mixed farming.

To all of this, Elizabeth listened with rapt attention. Now and then, her eyes would move to Nickolai, her head nodding in agreement, as her Leader continued to outline the advantage of this new move.

For Nickolai, the speech brought only confusion. That Peter Veregin was an intelligent, capable leader no one could doubt. He raidated a confidence and a belief in the future that set eyes agleam with fires of hope and of expectancy. It was with a sense of profound relief that Nickolai greeted the announcement that now was the time for singing. Through their music, the kindness, the heart and the soul of these people were vividly expressed. Backed by a choir of young girls, Peter Veregin filled the house with his clear, resonant voice. Tonight, there were no mournful hymns. Joy and jubilation, faith in the future, and gratitude for past blessings were all expressed in the psalms. Elizabeth joined in with the others, her voice exuberant and exultant. For the first time in many months, Nickolai felt a sense of belonging, as he too gave voice to the hymns he knew so well. These were his Brethren. His Brothers and Sisters, the people with whom he had shared so much. Had Elizabeth, at this moment, urged him to go with his Brethren, he would have agreed. Later, however, on the way home, sanity returned and he felt that no power on earth could willingly make him give up all he had struggled for over the years. This was his land. His home. Here, he vowed, he would stay. Yet, doubts still nagged at him.

On a day when clouds hung low, and drizzling rain made work on the outside uncomfortable, Elizabeth returned from a walk into the village, wet and bedraggled. Finding her husband busily cleaning out stalls in the barn, she confronted him. Quietly, tenderly, she informed him, "I have just returned from the village, My Husband."

Glancing at her, not pausing in his tasks, Nickolai grunted, "You had better get to the house and get out of those wet clothes."

Ignoring his gruff words, Elizabeth continued: "The train that is to carry our Brethren across the far mountains has arrived. It waits at the station in Veregin."

"I shall go tonight and make my farewells." Straightening up from his labors, he leaned on his shovel. "You know, Elizabeth, I shall miss them."

"Nickolai. My Husband. Would it not be so much better if we were to go with them?"

"No. No. I have already said. We stay here. This is our home."

Turning abruptly away from her, he vigorously commenced shovelling at the manure. For a little while, Elizabeth stood, silently watching his movements. Once, about to say something to him, her arm stretched out in mute appeal.

"Nickolai?"

He did not hear her. Silently, determinedly, she turned and walked swiftly back to the house. Darkness, she noted, was not far away. Once she halted, to turn and gaze for a moment back to the barn. The gaping wide doors remained empty. With a slight shrug, she continued on her way.

Entering the kitchen, she closed the door, and stood, letting her eyes roam around the warm, comfortable room. The floor gleamed whitely from the many scrubbings she, herself, had given it. The furnishings, though hand-made, looked sturdy and well-worn. The stairs to the sleeping attic were lost in the gloom. In the centre of this room, a large cast-iron stove glowed in the semi-dark. Moving to it, she opened the door. Flames and hot embers sparked and hissed. For a long moment, she stared into the firebox, then in a fury of motion, she ran to the back of the stove, picked up a metal rake, thrust it into the flames and pulled violently. Burning wood and hot ash cascaded to the wooden floor. With her rake, she vigorously spread the fiery embers about, then moved to the door. Turning to watch, she saw that the floor was soon enveloped in fire. Softly closing the door, she walked to the front of the house and waited. Soon, orange tongues of flame were visible through the glass of the small windows. Sinking to her knees, her head on the ground, she prayed. Here, Nickolai found her. By this time, flames had raced up the walls, and were busily devouring the roof. In a matter of minutes, the entire structure collapsed in a roar of sparks and flame. In the distance, approaching voices, calling excitedly, came to him. He was too numb to understand. Dimly, he was aware of his wife's arms around his waist, holding him, crying.

"Pray with me, my husband. Only pray. Pray that in our new home across the mountains, we will again find the peace and love we have lost."

Sinking slowly to his knees beside her, he pressed his forehead to the wet earth. The earth that had known his footsteps for so many years. And silently, he cried, cried for the dreams that never were.

BOOK
III

Your work on Earth,
Now is done,
With God you sit,
His humble Son.
Forgive our tears,
For we must cry,
Tis hard to see
Our Father die.
Know the flame
We'll keep alight.
Peace and Love,
Our birthright.

10

Passover

Clouds lay like a gray creeping shroud, blanketing the
tree-studded hills, a shroud of clammy dankness reaching down
to obscure the tops of the grain elevator, the jam factory, the
flour mill, the sawmill, and the two-storied brick homes that
made up the town of Brilliant — a town that bore silent witness to
the hand work and to the energies of a great man, Peter, the
Lordly, Veregin.

Tufts of powdery snow, blown about by a raw November wind,
whirled around the legs of the seven thousand mourners who had
gathered to pay homage to their leader, whose life had been so
tragically snuffed out in a bizzare dynamiting of the C.P.R.
coach on which he had been riding. An act, inexplicable,
unreasonable, horrific.

The day for questions had not yet come. Now was the time of
disbelief, of numbness, and the aching certainty that their leader
had passed over and gone from them forever. The bewilderment,
the hurt, the deep love they felt for this man were all expressed in
the tears that rolled down the cheeks of the silent women, and in
the grief-stricken eyes of their men, as they stood by the side of
the road, watching the slow passage of the bier.

As the flower-covered casket carried on the shoulders of the
leader's closest friends wound its way through the streets and up
the hill towards its last resting place, the silent people fell in
behind, so that, by the time the cortege had reached the burial
site, high up on a hill overlooking the town and the spreading
valley, a long, snake-like line almost a mile in length had formed.

In the lead ranks, the family Obedkoff trudged along, oblivious to the cold, to the rough roadway, and even to the mute presence of their neighbors. Under the grief and the bewilderment at this drastic turn of events, Elizabeth knew a fury, a sense of outrage, that very soon must surface, explosively. But now, her eyes were fixed on the casket as it slowly disappeared into the maw of freshly dug earth and clay. Her voice rose in unison with the others, as the funereal, mournful chants of the Doukhobors echoed through this cold winter afternoon of November the Second, Nineteen Hundred and Twenty-Four.

The heartbreak of interment, the soliloquies, the eloquent speeches, the sad chants of farewell were soon over. The long silent walk through the falling darkness, the cooking of the evening meal, the quiet, morose downing of food, that had somehow lost all taste, had at last ended. In desultory, wandering talk, the men huddled round the glowing stove, not so much for warmth, but as if, in their very nearness to one another they might somehow ward off the gloom and the despondency brought on by the day's events.

Meanwhile, Nastasia and her mother busied themselves with clearing the table and the dish washing. In the midst of these tasks, the flood broke. Throwing down her dishrag, Elizabeth whirled and faced the men. Her voice rising to a high-pitched wail, she cried out, "How could this terrible thing happen? Tell me, you clever men. How could this happen?"

Now it was out in the open. The suspicions, the doubts and the horror that haunted each and every mind was, by her cry, brutally exposed. Questions could no longer be ignored by small talk.

The startled eyes of the three men swung to Elizabeth. The ferocity of her outburst discomfited them. Only Paul could murmur, "We do not know, Mother. The police are trying to find out who did this thing."

Sullenly, Mike Popoff remarked, "Hah. The police. Wolves investigating wolves."

Ignoring his remark, Elizabeth addressed Paul, her voice dripping sarcasm:

"Your brains got soft from all those book readings. The government did it. I know."

Quietly, Nickolai interjected, "How could you know, wife? And why would the government do this thing? Tell me that."

"And why not?" Elizabeth raged. "Has not the government always been our persecutors?"

Cajoling, Paul attempted to reason with her.

"Don't be silly, Mother. It could have been anyone."

"Aye. Even our own Brethren."

Nickolai's cynicism shocked Mike, who shouted, "Now it's you who are being silly, Nickolai."

"You think so, Mike? There has been much bad talk lately. Even you have said our Leader talks with the government too much."

"Aye, that is true. Well, he sure as hell won't be talking any more to them."

Nastasia, who had finished the dishes and moved to join the others burst out, "Mike. That is bad talk. You promised me. No more talk like that."

About to reply angrily, Mike was stopped by Paul, who said soothingly, "Why must we go on like this? No one knows who might be responsible. We can only wait."

Nickolai, taking Paul's lead, asked him:

"You think they find out, my Son?"

"They are trying, Father. Some police bomb experts from Vancouver have arrived. Remember, one of their own government ministers was also killed in this blast."

Somewhat mollified, Mike muttered, "Yeah. But maybe they wanted to get rid of him too. Make the plot look good."

"What plot, Mike? Maybe it was all an accident."

Snorting in disbelief, Elizabeth ejaculated, "Accident? Oh, sure. Maybe the Hand of God struck our dear Petrovka down. Maybe He wanted him to sit at His feet. Away from this wicked world."

A threat in his voice, Mike stated, "Anyway, whoever did this vile thing will be sorry. We will be avenged."

"Aye. And all this forcing our children into their schools. Well, now, we'll see." Turning to Nastasia, Elizabeth shouted: "You, my daughter. You will send my grandchildren to these Christian schools?"

Flustered by this sudden attack, Nastasia protested, "I do not know. Maybe they..."

Cutting her off, Mike exclaimed, "Never! No child of mine will go to any government school."

As if recalling her own lost yearnings to learn to read, Nastasia remonstrated gently.

"But maybe, Mike. They would want to learn. I saw little Nick looking at a picture book the other night."

Flatly, Elizabeth remarked, "The only book they need is the Living Book. And if you be a good Mother, you'll learn them that, Nastasia."

"You know I have taught them right, Mother. As I was taught."

For the first time, Paul became bitter and hostile.

"The Living Book. Can you not understand, all of you, that this Book is of no consequence in this land, and in these times? It is of no meaning."

Too angry to retort, Elizabeth could only glare at him. Nickolai, hurt and shocked by this irreverence, intoned, "Without the Living Book, my son, you would be only a stranger in a crowd. No history, no heritage, no sense of belonging. I did not think a son of mine would ever say such words."

Paul's bitter remark, coming as it did on top of all that had happened these last few days, proved too much for Elizabeth. Jumping to her feet, she stumbled to the side of her husband. Kneeling, she placed her head in his lap.

"Nickolai. My Nickolai. Each day, on my knees, I should thank the good God that you are by my side." Her voice broke into a plaintive whisper. "This accursed land. Where are its Cossacks, with their guns and their lash? With their very softness, they break up our families." Dramatically, her outstretched arm pointed to the silent Paul, "And where is that No-Doukhobor wife of yours? Why is she not here to suffer with us?"

Before Paul could reply, Nickolai murmured soothingly, "Come, Mother. Calm yourself. You know Paul's wife is with child, and could not make the trip."

Tears were very close to her eyes as she looked up at his face. Gently, he stroked the almost white hair, as she replied:

"Huh. I was with child, and made many a worse trip, My Husband."

"Mother, please." Paul knew that he had gone too far. Defensively, he looked around. All eyes were on him, shocked, unbelieving. His voice pleading, he asserted: "It is only that I too loved Peter. And now the future is clouded. Without him, I am afraid of what will happen. We are burning schools to the ground. Government schools. 'Tis no wonder these Canadians hate us. That is why Peter had so much talk with the government. And now, without him..." His voice trailed away into silence.

Throughout the winter, the controversy raged. In every home and in every town and village, from Grand Forks in the west, to the Slocan Valley in the east, argument and counter-argument, question and counter-question, accusation and counter-accusation. Schools continued to fall prey to the flames, until, in the spring of nineteen twenty-five, the provincial government decided to take action. School officials and police inspectors visited the community of Brilliant and addressed a mass meeting of Doukhobors. When they were asked if they would obey the school laws of the province, twenty-five hundred voices shouted as one: "No." The loudest voices were those of the many women present. Faced with this defiance, many of the parents were taken to court, and, in Grand Forks, a magistrate fined them the sum of $4,500.00 for refusal to allow their children to attend school. When this fine remained unpaid, the police, assisted by a gang of civilians, forced their way into the warehouses of the community and seized equipment, supplies and lumber, cut and ready for sale. This was then sold at public auction, for a sum of around $3,360 (far below the actual worth of these goods). In the face of this action, and realizing the futility of further resistance, Doukhobor children once again appeared in the classrooms of those schools still in use.

Throughout all this turmoil, the question of leadership remained uppermost in the minds of the Brethren. It had been decided to despatch two of the Elders, the Brothers Plotnikov, and Vereshagin, to Russia, there to intercede with the Soviets for the release of the son of Peter Veregin, and to secure permission for him to travel to Canada, where he would take over the hereditary leadership of the Sect.

Nor had Paul been idle. Working under the trustees who had been appointed by the Elders to handle the affairs of the Doukhobors until the arrival of the new leader, he shuttled busily between Grand Forks and Brilliant, tallying and recording the outputs of the jam factory, the brickyard, and the various small sawmills scattered throughout the Kootenay Valley. One of his most important tasks was that of arranging the shipment of surplus products to dealers in Winnipeg and in Vancouver, where a ready sale was assured for these products.

Returning to the communal offices in Grand Forks, on an evening in the early summer, he heard the news that the two Elders had returned from Russia, and that Peter P. Veregin had agreed to come to Canada, once his affairs had been put in order. The Soviets had placed no bars to his emigrating, and, in fact, seemed rather pleased to have him out of the country. A disturbing rumor that reached Paul's ears and gave him considerable thought and cause for worry was to the effect that this new leader had actually been under arrest for drunkenness and riotous behaviour, and was to be sent to a work camp for incorrigibles in Turkestan.

Sitting in his favorite armchair, tired and contented, Paul idly watched as his wife, Maureen, finished the dishes, and picked up the baby. Carrying him to a rocking chair, she unbuttoned her blouse and commenced feeding the child. His eyes on mother and child, Paul's mind went back to one of the few arguments they had ever had, the naming of the baby. In deference to his slain leader, Paul had insisted that he be named after him. Maureen had countered with an Irish name in honor of her ancestors. So, it had been decided, after much good-natured wrangling, to call him, Peter O'Brien Obedkoff. This memory served to send a smile flickering across his face.

Noting this, Maureen asked him:

"What's so funny, love?"

"I was just thinking. That little one will go through life with quite a name."

"I'm sure it's no worse than some of your Doukhobor names."

That remark, Paul ignored, and asked:

"How's he been, Maury?"

"Well enough, considering as how his Father is only around on the weekends."

"Ah, well. Maybe this next week, I can work around here."

Rising to her feet, Maureen carried the baby back to a cradle hanging from the ceiling, and gently placed him into it. Covering him with a blanket, she stood, slowly swinging the cradle, her head turned to Paul.

"How is the job going? Sometimes, Paul, you look so tired. It worries me."

"I am tired. Our finances are in a mess. Went over the books today. We owe almost a million and a quarter. They've mortgaged everything we own. Even the jam factory. It's all so stupid."

"But, I thought you were doing so well. With all the lumber and bricks you sold, and that jam and even honey. Paul, how could they owe so much?"

"I don't really know, Maury. I do know that we've spent a hundred and fifty thousand on roads and bridges. We had hoped that the govenment would pay some of that back. But they have refused. I wish Peter were still with us. He would know how to handle this."

"Never mind, Love. Maybe when the new leader gets here, why then, he can get things straightened out."

"All I can say is that he'd better get here soon."

"There, now. The wee one's off to sleep."

Moving away from the cradle, she plumped down on Paul's lap. Playfully, she pulled both his ears, forcing his face down to hers. Kissing him lightly, she laughed, "You never said you loved me since you came through that door."

Entering into her mood, he quickly grabbed her and pulled her head down onto his shoulder.

"You know I do, Maury. all the time I'm away, you're never out of my mind."

"I bet. Probably got a sweetheart up there in Brilliant. Maybe that's why you're away so much."

"Oh, sure. Three in Brilliant, and one in every village in between."

"Oh, yeah?" Hugging him tightly, she kissed Paul passionately. "Bet none of them can kiss like that. Tell you what, Love. You go and get the wood in, and I'll get ready for bed. That way, you can earn your keep around here."

Rising abruptly, Paul sent Maureen giggling and sliding to the floor.

"Paul, you're a beast."

"That's what all my girlfriends say."

By the door, Paul removed his slippers and commenced to put on his shoes.

"Seen your folks, Love?"

"Yes. Spent a night with them. Dad seems happier. He's been put in charge of bees. Got some six hundred hives to look after. Keeps him busy. Mother should go to see a doctor, though."

"Her eyes still giving her trouble, Paul?"

"Yes. Some kind of film forming over the eyeball. As usual, she says it's all in God's hands."

Putting on a coat, Paul opened the door, then turned as Maureen called to him.

"Paul, you wish we lived nearer to them?"

"No. Not really. We don't exactly see eye to eye on some matters."

"You mean 'cause you married me?"

"That, for one. There are others. Mother seems to think if a man does not farm the land, why he just wastes his time. Looks on me as a No-Doukhobor."

"Oh, Paul. You do more than most. Can't you make her see that?"

"It is of no consequence."

"Maybe Paul, we should run up and see them soon. Only, she scares me sometimes."

"She scares herself sometimes."

Leaving Maureen sitting comfortably on the floor, arms wrapped around her knees, Paul went out to get the wood. Returning shortly with an armload, he dumped it into a box by the stove. Maury arose and closed the door behind him.

"Let's go up this weekend and see your folks."

"I can't, Maury. Got a committee meeting on Sunday. I was talking with Nastasia. Seems Mike has joined up with the Sons of Freedom."

"You mean the ones as does the burnings?"

"Yes. I kind of worry about Nastasia and the kids. Don't know what they'll do if Mike gets himself put in jail. Oh, well, as you say, maybe our new leader can get them under control."

"Think he'll be here soon, Paul?"

"Who knows? That he is coming is all we can be sure of."

*   *   *

Sunday turned out to be a miserable day. It had commenced to rain, and, on the way to the meeting, Paul had become drenched. On top of this, and to compound his misery, his head ached and pounded. He suffered from a hangover. Despite his better judgement, he and Maury had hired a babysitter the night before and gone down to the local beer parlor. Usually a moderate drinker, he had consumed more beer than had been good for him. Then, he had allowed himself to be drawn into a futile, bitter argument with the other patrons, many of whom were his closest friends and neighbors, over the antics of the Sons of Freedom. He had been shocked and hurt at the expressions of hatred these Canadians felt for his Brethren. It had ended with threats of vigilante action, which must inevitably involve the whole of the Doukhobor community. Ruefully, Paul had to admit to himself there was justification for this anger. It was, after all, their children that were being deprived of schooling. It was their women that were being subjected to the sight of nude bodies on the streets. Behind it all, he knew, was the lurking deep-seated fear that, at any moment, the Sons of Freedom would turn their violence against the Non-Doukhobor community. The result would be mass retaliation. Open warfare, engulfing the Kootenays in bloodshed and flame.

All in all, Paul did not look forward to the wrangling and harsh discussions he knew would take place at the meeting. As he expected, the meeting dragged on well into the evening. The two Elders who had just returned from Russia had delivered a letter from the Leader, requesting that monies be sent to him, to enable him to leave for Canada. It had been voted that a sum of five thousand dollars be dispatched immediately. The trustees had then outlined their reasons for the mortgaging of practically everything of value possessed by the Sect. They had received from the National Trust and the Sun Life, the sum of three hundred and fifty thousand dollars, which would be used to pay off their most pressing debts, and the taxes that had been owing for several years. This brought their total indebtedness to more than a million and a quarter dollars, and made for a grim future. It was the concensus that all they could do now was to hang on till Peter Veregin arrived, and trust that he was as capable a businessman as his father had been.

The Purger decrees,
The time has come,
To leave this land
Of law and gun.
White Horse descend
From the clouds,
Wrap us in your
Heavenly shrouds,
Carry us so
Far away.
We'll live in Peace,
Day after Day.

11

The White Horse

"I shall divide the lies from the truth, the light from the darkness, for I am Peter the Purger."

Listening avidly to these words, a large gathering stood in front of the jam factory at Brilliant, on a sunny, cold October afternoon, to meet, for the first time, their new leader. This was the moment they had so eagerly awaited for almost three years.

To Mike and Nastasia, standing huddled against the chill wind in the midst of the crowd, it was as if, on hearing these words, the hand of God had reached down and enfolded them in light and in warmth. That they were not alone in this was clear from the cries of welcome and joy that greeted each statement.

Again, the words rang out.

"I have come to this strange country to lead you. I have come, not to destroy you, but to strengthen you, to strengthen by purgation if I must, and to bring unity among all Doukhobors. Already, I have met with and spoken to our Brethren in the prairie lands. They welcomed me with joy and with love, as you do now. We shall unite in one great body. Once again, as in the past, Brother and Sister shall be as one, living in the glory and in the service of God. Soon, my Brethren, I shall announce to you the manner in which this is to be done."

Pausing, his eyes moved slowly across the sea of upturned faces, then, inspired by his own eloquence, and by the silent adoration and approval of his words, he shouted:

"And Sons of Freedom cannot be slaves of corruption. You shall be the Ringing Bells of us all. You, Sons of Freedom, you will keep the ears of the Doukhobor always open to the truth."

Mike felt a glow a happiness such as he had seldom known. Now, he thought, Nickolai and the others would stop their constant wrangling and criticism of his actions. But the next words stunned him.

Again changing tactics, the voice of the speaker dropped to a more conversational tone.

"The burning of these schools will stop. Immediately. Your children will attend these schools. Let the Doukhobors become professors. Thus, we will begin the new era. We will take what good this country has to offer and discard that which is bad. Now heed me, and remember well. I am only a man. If my actions seem praiseworthy, do not credit me. Credit only that voice that speaks from within me."

Peter the Purger, as he was to be known from then on, had completely baffled and mystified the Brethren. Later that night, many heated discussions would take place in the communal home occupied by Mike and Nastasia along with several other families. Returning from the meeting, later than usual, they found that supper had been prepared by some of the older sisters, who had decided not to brave the cold to meet the new leader. Among these was Elizabeth, who smilingly greeted her daughter and son-in-law.

"Well, tell me. What is he like? Is he as his father was?"

In her eagerness to hear the news, her words tumbled out. Receiving no immediate reply, she rushed on, "Well? Did he get your tongues?"

Puzzled, she watched Nastasia moving to help serve out the food, as Mike sat down at the table. Raising his spoon to his mouth, Mike paused, and eyed the old lady.

"He got more than our tongues, Mother. I can't understand it. He said so many queer things."

Sitting down by his side, Elizabeth queried: "Like what, Mike? What queer things?"

"Well. He says we must educate our children. Let them be professors. And not to burn down any more schools. It is all a puzzle."

One of the other women, who had been listening to this intently, laughed and said, "Hah. You young ones. You never can understand anything. I know what he does. He speaks with the double tongue. For the law people, he says one thing, but for us it is the opposite. Tell me this, Mike. Was the tie around his neck on very straight?"

Puzzled by this, Mike frowned in thought. Clearly, he recalled how, just as the speaker had begun to talk about the schools, he had reached up and suddenly yanked at his tie, thereby loosening it.

"No. He had it all undone. Why? What has that got to do with what he said?"

"It has everything to do with it. In the old days, when our leaders wished to get a message to us, and because there were soldiers standing around, and they could not say what they wished, why then, they would just wear something backwards."

Smiling in glee, Elizabeth clapped Mike on the shoulder.

"There, you see? We old ones are not so dense. What else did he say, Mike?"

Between mouthfuls of soup, Mike explained, "He said as how the Sons of Freedom would be as Ringing Bells. That we are to keep the truth for our people."

"See? Did I not say all along? What he really means is that we must see to it our Sisters and Brothers live in the eyes of God, and not become so blinded by wealth as to fall into the hands of Satan. He is a wise man."

Joining the group, Nastasia interjected, "I am not so sure, Mother. He sounded like he meant what he said. About the schools, I mean."

Snorting in derision, Elizabeth replied, "A lot you know. Your head has been addled by all this soft living. Well. I have a feeling that will all change. And soon."

"But, Mother. All that means is more trouble. How can we fight this government? Have they not already threatened to take our children away, and send them to their schools. I do not wish to see that."

"Have we not always known trouble, girl? Are we not Sons of Freedom, and does not that mean that we will keep the true path against all government? Or has your heart become as one of those bible readers that pray in their stone church on Sunday, and harass us the rest of the week? They who would steal your children?"

Refusing to be drawn further into this argument, Nastasia picked up a bowl, filled it with hot soup.

"I am going over to see Father. He must be getting hungry."

"That husband of mine. Seems he's always sick these days. Wait, my daughter. I'll go along with you."

Draping a shawl about her shoulders, Elizabeth followed Nastasia out the door.

Busily wiping his bowl with a dark piece of bread, Mike called, "Don't be too long, Nasta. And bring the kids back. Time they were in bed."

About to step through the open door, they moved back to allow

one of the leaders of the Sons of Freedom, Peter Maloff, to enter.
Brushing past them, he murmured, "A good evening to you
Sisters. You are leaving?"

"Just taking some supper over to Nickolai. He does not feel too
good these days."

"His back still giving him trouble, Elizabeth?"

"The same. Maybe those herbs you brought over will help him.
I will give him another poultice tonight."

"I shall come over and see him as soon as I have eaten.
Meanwhile, I must have a talk with Mike. It would seem we have
much work to do."

Walking to the table, he sat down beside Mike, and waited
while one of the women hurried over with a bowl and spoon.

"Mike. What do you think of all this? Peter the Purger, he talks
in a strange tongue. Huh, Doukhobors becoming professors.
Such foolishness."

Smiling, Mike explained:

"Not so strange. Not when you know the signals."

Carefully, he expounded on the explanation given by the old
woman, stressing the disarrangement of clothing that was to be
taken as a signal to do the very opposite of whatever he was
saying.

Chuckling, Maloff said, "I had not thought of that. Good.
Very good. You have looked at this new school at Glade, Mike?"

"Yes. I was up there yesterday. They have made it of concrete
and steel. Very fireproof."

"Hmm. Well, if it will not burn, there are other ways."
Dramatically, he raised both arms into the air, giving out with a
loud "Boom!" and leaving no doubt in any mind of his meaning.

Hesitantly, Mike asked, "You mean, dynamite, Peter? We have
not used this before."

"True." Waving his spoon for emphasis, he continued, "But
then, we have never before had to deal with concrete schools. By
the way, not a word to anyone."

"You know my lips are sealed, Peter. But, still, I wonder how
this Peter the Purger will take this."

"We shall soon find out. He is even now at a meeting with the
Elders. Tomorrow, he goes on to Grand Forks."

"You think he might make his home here in Brilliant, Peter?"

"Hard to say. I feel he would rather stay in his Father's house in
Grand Forks. But then, who knows? I do know he is going to
reorganize the community, and is starting by placing an
assessment on each family. Tomorrow, we should know how
much. You sure about what those old women said, Mike? I mean
about the clothing?"

"Sounds good. Surely, no leader of ours would give in to the government so easily. I mean, he must know what these schools do to our children."

"Hope you're right. Anyway, we will just have to wait and see. You coming over to Nickolai's, Mike?"

"No. Think I'll wander into town and listen to the choir. Maybe I can pick up some news."

* * *

The following days at Grand Forks were to show to the Brethren the true spirit of this new leader. Having being informed that he wished to address them early in the morning, they gathered in front of the meeting house, there to chant and sing all through the long day, and well into the night. When, at midnight, he had still not put in an appearance, the weary, confused Brethren decided to return to their homes. It was at this moment that Peter the Purger appeared. For the next three hours, he harangued and extolled on the future of the Doukhobor community in Canada. He shouted reproaches, accusing them of falling into the trap of Satanism by hoarding their monies and seeking material wealth.

A steady cold drizzle began to fall on the frightened, bewildered people. Standing huddled in the darkness, with only a light bulb illuminating the features of this strange, unpredictable Peter the Purger, not one of the Brethren dared leave the scene. It was as if by the power and eloquence of his voice, he had mesmerized the group into immobility, unable to act of their own will. Finally, when it seemed that the night must go on to eternity, he cried out that they, the Doukhobors, by their faith in their God, would one day act as the jury for all mankind. That day would be the Day of Judgement.

To Paul, the day had been one of frustration and anger. He, along with the trustees and committee members, had met with Peter the Purger, and in a long stormy meeting, had attempted to present a summary of the finances of the Sect. The Leader had been enraged by the debts that had accumulated since the death of his father; going as far as to accuse the trustees of misappropriation of communal funds for their own use. As the meeting wore on, Paul had difficulty in believing his own ears. These trustees and members had worked hard and faithfully in the difficult task of holding the sect together and at least partially solvent. They had succeeded to the best of their abilities and that had been a source of no little satisfaction to Paul. To hear them accused of acts verging on the criminal by this man who had so lately come amongst them infuriated him.

The meeting ended with Peter demanding that a letter be sent to each of the Brethren, both in B.C. and in Saskatchewan, asking for their help and cooperation in reducing the communal debt. In this way, more than $350,000 was collected, and handed over to the central treasury to be used in the liquidation of the more pressing of their debts. Despite his eccentricities, Peter the Purger proved himself as capable and shrewd an administrator as his father. His plan to assess each working member of each family on an increasing annual basis succeeded in paying off at least half of the tremendous liabilities. Still, it was not enough.

In 1929, after two years of constant struggle to pay off loans and interest, Peter the Purger hit on a scheme so extravagant that it would have aroused derision in any other society. Playing upon the ancient, inbred desire for pilgrimage, forever latent in the vision-ridden Doukhobor, he announced that the time had come when they must leave Canada. A great white horse would descend from Heaven and take them to a land where sorrow and persecution would come to an end. In this land, they would live in the innocence of Adam and Eve and as the fruits and berries would be so plentiful, no man would have to work. But, he thundered, whereas other horses ate hay and oats, this horse ate only money, and as they would have no further use for their money in this promised new land, he urged that their savings, carefully hoarded over the years, be given to this white horse. They responded to such an extent that the sum of $525,329 was collected.

Torn between his desire to see the books of the community balanced and debt-free, and his fears of the eventual outcome of this hoax, Paul went about his daily tasks in a constant state of anxiety and of bewilderment. He found it difficult to believe that his people could be so trusting, so naive, as to actually believe in a scheme so far-fetched. He knew that this would have disastrous results, both for the community and for the precarious balance of law and order now being maintained in the Kootenays.

Sitting in the warm spring sunshine, his eyes on the many bee hives, seeming so starkly white against the dark shade of the bloom mantled fruit trees, Paul found, in his father, a confidante always ready to listen and to agree with his fears and distrust of the imminent, and to Paul, threatening changes affecting the Doukhobor community. The hypnotic drone of innumerable bees, awakened from their long winter sleep, the perfumed odour of delicate blossoms, heavy in the evening air, the busy chatter of women and children in the house behind him, all combined to lull him into a deep sense of peace and harmony, so alien to his daily tasks, his job of recording so much produce out, and so many dollars in.

Immersed in the beauty of the scene around him, Paul heard his father speak, his voice gentle, patient, understanding.

"You worry too much, my Son. Have not our people, throughout history, been caught up in this strange urge to be always on the move? As with some other tribes on this earth, Paul, we seem destined to never live in peace in any one place. To me, it will forever remain a curse, and a mystery. But to the others," he shrugged lightly, "it would seem they must forever be on the move towards a Promised Land. A land they can never find. Nevertheless, Paul, it remains a deep-rooted belief, affecting our Brethren in many and wonderful ways."

Paul studied his father. For the first time, he noticed how old he looked. The lined, tired face, and snow-white hair that was thinning and in places showing brown scalp. But the eyes, he noted, were as bright and as alive as when he was a young man. Lovingly, in a rush of emotion, Paul placed an arm about the thin shoulders. Laughingly, he exclaimed, "Never before, my Father, have I heard you talk like this."

"Ah, well. They say, my Son, that with age comes wisdom. I do not know. Maybe it is only that I have much time to ponder these things." For a moment, he fell silent, thinking. "You know, Paul, I do not wish to ever leave this place. So many times have I built, and then said goodbye to it all. Now I would rest."

"You mean this White Horse thing?"

"Yes. Your mother and the other women chatter about this all day long. Some say it will be a great white ship, others that it will come down from the sky. Your Mother spends half the day gazing up into the clouds. With her eyes, I doubt if she could see it five feet in front of her."

"Then, Father, you do not believe any of this?"

"No. I am much too old for that kind of nonsense. Hah, White Horse indeed."

"You have heard of the talk of going to Mexico perhaps?"

"Mexico? Now why would we go there, Paul? Is not that some hot, dry land far to the south?"

"It is a land where the sun shines all day, where fruit and berries grow on every bush, and where as Adam and Eve, we will worship God in our own way." Elizabeth's voice startled both men. Unnoticed, she had come to join them, and now stood gazing fondly down on Paul. "How are you, my Son? I wondered who Nick was talking to."

"I am feeling well, Mother." Rising to his feet, he quickly embraced her, then stood back looking into the seamed, aged face. Worriedly, he noted the gray, whitish film covering both eyes. Soon, he thought, those eyes would see no more. "We were just discussing this White Horse."

"I heard. Why can you not believe, Paul? Has it not been prophesied many times, that in God's good time, we go to a land where we shall be as free as the birds in the air?"

"I cannot believe, Mother. There is no such land. Nowhere in this wide world."

"So. Like your father. Ah, well. That is a cross I should be used to by now. Come, Paul. Brother Maloff would have a word with you. There is much confusion."

Turning, she led the way towards the big house. Anxiously, Paul observed the manner in which she cautiously walked, arms outstretched as if to ward off unseen obstacles. Pausing to allow his father to catch up to him, Paul whispered:

"Can nothing be done, Father? She is almost blind."

Gruffly, Nickolai replied, "Nothing. At least not by any one here. Maybe if you spoke with her, Paul."

"I have. Many times. She keeps saying it is God's will. But I shall try again. If she would just see a doctor."

Helplessly, he shrugged and fell silent.

In the steamy, odour-laden kitchen, Peter Maloff loudly and vehemently aired his views on the latest decrees of Peter the Purger. As Paul followed his mother into the room, crowded to overflowing, Maloff greeted him angrily.

"Ah. Here is the keeper of the books. The right hand of our generous Leader. Maybe you can tell us the truth, Paul. Is it true Peter the Purger has demanded that those of the Brethren who cannot pay their dues be banished from the community?"

Before Paul could make any answer, one of the old women cried out, "That not true. No Leader of Doukhobors could do this evil thing."

Quietly, Paul faced the group, his voice sad.

"I am afraid it is as you say, Peter. He has informed the Central Committee that if any of the Brethren are delinquent in payment of their assessments by St. Peter's Day, why then, they will be made to leave."

One of the Elders, his voice echoing fright, queried:

"But where would we go? Paul, you our friend. You know Peter good. Maybe you tell him this thing bad?"

"I am sorry, but I shall no longer be talking with him."

Sensing that something was wrong, Elizabeth asked: "What do you mean, My Son? You only one can help us."

Loudly, quickly, Paul replied, "I am no longer with the community. Tomorrow, I leave for Vancouver."

"But you come back, Paul. You come back, will you not?"

"No, Mother. I have found work. With a grocery firm. I...I

have come only to say goodbye."

In the silence that followed this announcement, only Mike gave voice to his thoughts. Bitterly, he asked, "You are then running away, Paul?"

"You might say that Mike. There is no way I can go on working for Peter. He..."

Interrupting him, Elizabeth shook him by the shoulders, her voice expressing shock and disbelief.

"How can you say this thing, my Son? You not run away, when we need you so bad. Maybe big trouble come."

Disturbed, yet determined, Paul explained, "I am sorry. But there is no way I can deal with this man. The others may be able to take his abuse, but I cannot do so. He is drunk. Half the time, violent. No matter how hard we work, we are constantly accused of loafing. And what is worse, of taking community funds for our own use. No, Mother. I have made up my mind. I go to Vancouver."

Sensing his son's distress, Nickolai intervened gently.

"You will let us know where you stay, Paul? Maybe, sometime, we come and see you."

His voice was sad, reflecting the acceptance of Paul's decision.

"Of course, Father. As soon as I get settled."

Nastasia, busily stirring food in a large pot on the stove, listened quietly, her eyes moving from one speaker to the other. Suddenly, she dropped her spoon and ran to Paul, hugging him tightly.

"Oh, my Brother, we shall miss you. We shall miss you so." Swinging round, she called to her husband. "Mike. We go to Grand Forks with Paul. I must say goodbye to Maury and the little ones."

"I...I cannot go. Not tonight. You go, Nastasia. I shall pick you up tomorrow morning. Maybe I get there in time to say goodbye."

"Why, Mike? Why can you not go tonight?"

"I must be in Glade. There is a meeting."

"Glade? Then this is the night, Mike?" Worry showed in Nastasia's face as she stared at her husband. The room had become very quiet. All eyes were on Mike.

Puzzled, Paul asked, "What's at Glade, Mike?"

Loudly, Peter Maloff shouted, "Enough. Say no more. Mike goes on an errand for God."

On that night, and for the first time in the long history of the Doukhobors, fire gave way to a much more vicious and dangerous form of protest, that of dynamite. The fireproof school at Glade was blasted apart. The resulting, massive police investigation saw many of the Brethren arrested and jailed, often on the flimsiest of evidence. The children of the Sons of Freedom were forcibly separated from their parents and detained at New Denver, in a futile attempt at compulsory education. The jailings, the break-up of families, coupled to the harshness of Peter the Purger, who publicly and loudly declaimed these acts of violence by the Brethren, gave rise to a startling increase in the ranks of the Sons of Freedom. From a mere handful, the membership escalated to well over fifteen hundred. These, finding themselves homeless, and in conflict with the law and with the community, withdrew to a lonely, barren plain, Krestova, the Place of the Cross.

Krestova, grim
And barren plain,
Our refuge from
A world of pain.
If only you'd
Leave us alone,
To till the soil,
Build a home,
You make us send
Our kids to school,
Why can't they live
By the Golden Rule?

12

The Place Of The Cross

The hungry thirties—a malignant, bitter plague that swept across the land, driving stout men to despair, and to bewilderment: the despair of hunger, the bewilderment of enforced idleness. No less than others, the Christian Community of Doukhobors suffered, when the loans, the mortgages, and the taxes came due. The trust companies, the insurance companies, the banks—those who in the past had accepted the community landholdings as collateral—now demanded their pound of flesh. Unfortunately, with the flesh, went the lifeblood. Even though the total marketable value of community assets had been calculated to be worth between three and four million dollars, to pay off loans of some three hundred and fifty thousand dollars, all was lost.

Eviction notices appeared in profusion. Seizures of equipment, machinery, factories and sawmills were instituted with callous disregard to the very real sufferings imposed on people ill-equipped to deal with the intricate vagaries of modern finance. Compounding their misery was the erratic behaviour of Peter the Purger, who had been sentenced to three years in the Prince Albert penitentiary after criminally perjuring himself in a previous trial involving one of the Independent Doukhobors from Saskatchewan. His arrest and conviction further deepened the fears and governmental mistrust of the ruling Conservatives in Ottawa—fears and mistrust which had become an integral part of the Doukhobor heritage.

The conviction and jailing of Peter the Purger led to one of the most bizzare episodes in the history of Canadian justice. Thinking that, if they could rid the country of this leader of the Doukhobor resistance would cease, the Prime Minister R.B. Bennett had the justice department grant a pardon to Peter—then in complete secrecy, and in the dead of night, had him transported to Halifax, Nova Scotia, there to be taken aboard the Ss. Montcalm, and deported to Russia. But word of this nefarious scheme leaked out, and a reporter for the Saskatoon *Star* informed a Doukhobor lawyer, Peter Makaroff, who immediately telephoned both the Prime Minister, and the Minister of Immigration, to demand that the deportation be stopped. Both of them refused this request. Risking their lives, the lawyer and a number of civil liberties advocates flew, in stormy weather, to Halifax. There, they were able to obtain a writ of *Habeus Corpus* against the captain of the *Montcalm*, thereby preventing the vessel from sailing. The case was then taken to the law courts of Nova Scotia, and the deportation order declared invalid.

Infuriated by the jailing of their leader, and by this clumsy attempt at deportation, the Sons of Freedom became ever more active. In a vain attempt to stamp out nude parades, the government decreed that the minimum sentence be increased to three years. Rather than discourage demonstrations, these repressive measures had the opposite effect. The younger, more rebellious of the Brethren took· to arson and dynamiting. Krestova, the Place of the Cross, was subjected time and again to police raids, often at dawn. Children of school age, whenever they could be found, were forcibly removed from their families and placed in the custody of various governmental agencies. Arrests increased day by day, until more than seven hundred of the Brethren found themselves jailed in make-shift compounds hurriedly erected in Nelson and in Grand Forks.

Caught up in the net of the law, Elizabeth and Nastasia found themselves incarcerated in a compound outside the city of Nelson. With several hundred others, they had taken part in a protest march seeking the release of the children scooped up in the dawn raids. For Nastasia, this experience had been traumatic. Although unwilling to personally expose herself to the harshness of the law, and to public ridicule, she had, at the urging of her father, accompanied her mother who stubbornly insisted on taking part in these protests.

Nickolai, confused and alone, sat on a log in front of his make-shift shanty, staring across the barren plain of Krestova at the setting sun. Wherever he looked, his eyes fell on the many huts so similar to his own. Hastily constructed of tin and salvaged wood, these had become the abode of the dispossessed. True to their lifestyle, almost all had by now tiny patches of garden dug and planted, so that, hopefully, by the next winter, there would be food to eat. No shouts of children at play came to him, no voices of women calling to one another: only a strange, unaccustomed silence. How, he wondered, had he come to this? In his mind, he reviewed the past events: the arrest of Mike and Peter Maloff on charges of arson; their subsequent conviction to six years in the penitentiary at New Westminster. This, he knew, had broken Nastasia. For days, she had sat in her room, mutely staring into space. Only when men had come with papers and, with the aid of sheriffs, had forced them out of their home at Brilliant, had she come to life. With nowhere to go, and at the mother's insistence, they had made the weary trek to this valley, to join with so many others in a like predicament. The winter had been hard and brutal.

Then, the crushing blow. Both of Nastasia's children, Nick and little Anastasia, had been taken by the police. Their terror-stricken screams as they had been hauled out of bed, forcibly dressed, and carried to a waiting police van still haunted him. The memory of Nastasia's broken pleas, that she would send her children to any school they wished, together with Elizabeth's curses, that God would yet punish these child kidnappers, sent a shiver through Nickolai. And yet, he recalled the tears in the eyes of an older police sergeant, as he had thrown his arms around Nickolai to prevent his interfering with the children's seizure.

So immersed was he in these dark thoughts, that Nickolai was scarcely aware of the approach of a small group of women, those who, only an hour before, had brought him the news of his wife and daughter's arrest. Anna, one of Elizabeth's closest friends, stood looking down at his dejected face.

Gently, she murmured, "Come, Nickolai Obedkoff. You will eat with us."

Uncaring, shaking his head, he replied, "I am not so hungry, Anna. You think maybe they come home soon?"

"No. And do not grieve. They suffer for God. The dark times are again upon us. Now you come and eat."

Rising slowly, Nickolai took the proffered hand, his eyes on Anna.

"You think, Anna, maybe if I go to police and say Elizabeth just silly old woman, they let her come home?"

"You know they will not do that, Nickolai. Why, they even use this filthy gas that makes the eyes burn. I think maybe soon now we will see the guns and the lash."

Worriedly, Nickolai enquired as they moved along: "Anna. My Elizabeth. She not get hurt?"

"No. Nasta, she take her Mother and try to run. But they run wrong way. Old Elizabeth, she not run so fast now. Anyway, Nick, she not get hurt."

"I would go see them, Anna."

"Tomorrow. We all go to court in Nelson. Maybe they let your Elizabeth off, Nickolai. She was not one of the ones that took off their clothes."

*   *   *

To Nickolai, sitting uneasily on a hard wooden bench, lost in the crush of spectators, the court proceedings were a complete mystery. Anxiously, he tried to follow the legalistic words of the various speakers, as they outlined the case against the accused Brethren. His eyes followed the groups of prisoners, as, one after the other, they were led into the court, to listen to argument for and against them, then, after the verdict had been announced, to be replaced by others. That very few of the accused understood the proceedings was very evident from their silence, and by the occasional shouted defiant slogans. Finally, after what had seemed an interminable wait, Nickolai watched as his wife and daughter were led into the courtroom, in the midst of about twenty of the Brothers and Sisters who had been arrested with them. In his relief at seeing them, Nickolai rose, and in a vain attempt to push his way forward, called out, "Elizabeth. Nastasia."

At the sound of his voice, Elizabeth's near-blind eyes searched the room.

Questioningly, she asked, "Nickolai?"

"I am here, my wife. I am here."

Struggling to move towards them, he was pulled back to his seat by clutching hands, as the judge, angered by this outburst, repeatedly demanded, "Order. Order in the courtroom. There will be no further disturbance." Authoritatively, he glared down at Nickolai. "Now, let us get on with this."

Confused, Nickolai sat down, his ears recording such words as "Stripping in a public place. Obscenity. Disturbance of the peace. Riotous behaviour." One of the lawyers for the defence went into a lengthly argument concerning the legality of a trial wherein the accused were not given their rights by the fact that they were being tried in groups rather than individually, to which the judge countered that, "Since they had chosen to break the law in groups, then there was no reason why they could not be tried in groups."

Then, the fateful verdict was read out; the same one that all others had received:

"I find each one of you guilty on both charges. The first

charge, that of obscenity, in that you did in fact appear on a public street in the City of Nelson without clothing, and the second charge, that of disturbance of the peace, in that you did in fact refuse to disperse when so ordered by the police, and that you persisted in your unlawful actions. Therefore, I hereby sentence each one of you to a minimum of three years confinement, in a federal penitentiary."

Despite the seriousness of these proceedings, the trial was not without its lighter side. Before these condemned prisoners could be herded out of the court, one of the women stepped forward and addressed the judge.

"You say, we guilty? Then, Judge. I find you guilty. Guilty of defying the Laws of God, and of harassing His children. You say we obscene because we go naked? Did not Adam and Eve go about naked? In Paradise? God did not cry, 'obscene.' He did not close His eyes."

Quietly, the judge looked down upon her upraised face, then remarked:

"Ah yes. But then, I am not God, nor are we in Paradise." Raising his hands slightly, he continued, "And as for my being found guilty, why I think I shall just have to let myself go."

A subdued titter ran through the room at this apparent joking remark, when, recovering judicial dignity, he declared, "That is enough. This is no laughing matter. Now, have you anything else you wish to say?"

Shaking her head in defeat, the woman backed away, to be replaced by a much younger Sister. In her hand, she carried a centrefold cut from some girly magazine. This, she thrust before the judge's nose.

"You say we obscene? How about her? What you give her, eh?"

Glancing at the nude picture, the judge smiled, "If she appeared in my court like that, why, I think I would give her life. But then, young lady, she is not on trial, you are. And now, enough of this. Sergeant, remove these prisoners and bring in the others. We have much work to do this day."

As the little group shuffled out a side door, Nickolai turned to Anna sitting beside him.

"Three years. Anna, can this be true?"

His eyes, frightened, unbelieving, followed his wife as she was led out, leaning on the arm of his daughter.

"Yes. It is true. Now come, Nickolai. I will take you to your Elizabeth."

Pulling him to his feet, she gently guided him through the crowd to the front doors of the courtroom.

"Nickolai." Abruptly, she halted, placed both hands on his

sagging shoulders. "I too love Elizabeth. As girls, we played together in the meadows of Orlovka. As women, we prayed for death in Georgia. Now, do not go to greet her like this. Somehow, you must find the strength to help her through the coming ordeal. Just smile, Nickolai."

With a visible effort to regain his composure, Nickolai raised his shoulders, reached up and took Anna's hands in his.

"Thank you, Sister Anna. You are right. I have been feeling sorry for myself. With God's help, and you beside me, I go to say goodbye to all I hold dear in this life."

*   *   *

The days passed slowly. They were busy days. Nickolai was much in demand, as one of the few able-bodied men not in jail. He wondered, in fact, if the women of Krestova had not plotted together to keep him on the go from dawn to dusk, with innumerable tasks, from cutting and stacking firewood, to patching leaky roofs. All were tasks that left him with little time to brood. But, there was no one to help him through the lonely heartbreak of night. Tossing and turning, his sleepless mind conjured up imagined tortures inflicted on the bodies of his wife and daughter by sadistic, faceless jailers. Predominantly, his mental images were composed of cages of steel bars, back-breaking toil, and the abuse of hunger. He had heard so many tales of how the guards in these jails, knowing that Doukhobors were strict vegetarians, eating no flesh of either animal, bird, nor fish, would slyly slip tiny portions of meat in the soup. Rather than eat of this tainted food, many of the Brethren were said to be near death from starvation. Only too well, Nickolai knew that the intense faith of his wife could well lead her into this predicament, this martyrdom.

Finally, on a night when he could no longer take these hellish nightmares, he rose, dressed, and walked the twenty-three long miles into Nelson, in the hope that he might yet be in time to see Elizabeth.

Weary, dusty, and sick from anxiety, he slowly approached the grim stone building that contained the courthouse, the jail, and a small provincial police office. On this morning, all was quiet. None of the Brethren walked the streets, no uniformed officers patrolled the silent city. Then the melodious chiming of many church bells, reminded him that this was Sunday—the reason for the quiet. Knowing that he was much too tired to attempt the long return journey back to Krestova, Nickolai stared around him. Never before had he felt so completely alone, so cut off from his own people. In his desperation, his eyes fixed on a small sign affixed to a wooden door to one side of the main entrance of the justice building. This was an English word, he knew only too well: Police.

Timidly, with nothing else to do, he moved towards this door. Was it not the police who had so permanently separated him from his Elizabeth? Then surely, they must know where he might find her.

Pushing open the heavy door, Nickolai entered the small office. Sitting alone behind his desk, the same police sergeant who had restrained Nickolai during the seizure of the children, glanced up. Quietly, he studied Nickolai for a moment. Then a slight smile of recognition wrinkled the corners of his eyes. Rising, he advanced to the counter.

"Well. What brings you down from Krestova, Mr. Obedkoff? You see, I remember your name."

Standing stiffly by the half-open door, Nickolai answered, "I only wish to see my womenfolk. They are here?"

"Why, no. They were taken away the day after the trial."

"Taken away? You mean to this jail in New Westminster?"

"No, no. I don't think they would go there. Most probably, they were sent to Pier's Island."

"Pier's Island? I do not know of this place."

"It's somewhere outside of Sidney on Vancouver Island. The government have built a new camp there. But, why don't you come in, Mr. Obedkoff, and close the door?"

So, Nickolai thought, his weary journey through the night had been for nothing. Uncertain, his face pale and drawn, he turned his eyes from the sergeant to the sunlit street, then, with a deep sigh, gently closed the door.

Coming round the counter to his side, the sergeant placed a kindly arm through his.

"Come, old chap. Sit over here. You look all in." Leading Nickolai to a wooden bench lining one side of the room, he enquired, "I suppose you walked all the way in from Krestova?"

"Yes. A long walk. And for nothing."

Striding quickly to a door at the rear, the sergeant called to someone to mind the phone as he was going to lunch early. Returning to Nickolai, he raised him by the arm to his feet, and led him out onto the street.

"You are coming home with me. As it is almost time for dinner, I wish to have you as my guest. Come along now, it is not far."

Unresisting, Nickolai allowed himself to be led the short distance to the sergeant's house. Upon entering the small white painted bungalow, the sergeant called out, "Betty. Set another place. We have a guest."

Ushered into the bright, sunlit kitchen, Nickolai stood gazing around him in amazement. Never before had he been inside a Canadian home. Despite tales of dirt and squalor he had heard whispered about by the women of the sect, this home at least was as neat and tidy as a new pin. Bustling between the large kitchen range, the table, and the sink, the policemen's wife found the time to wish Nickolai a good day, and to welcome him to her home, ending with a suggestion that her husband show their guest to the bathroom, as he might wish to wash up before dinner. The colorful, enamel-tiled bathroom was almost too much for Nickolai. Sensing his unease, the sergeant kindly explained the workings of the toilet pull chain, and, with a final admonishment to be careful of the hot water as it had a habit of scalding the unwary, closed the door, and left Nickolai to himself. Smiling softly, he returned to the kitchen.

"You know, Bett. These people do not eat meat. Can you fix something for him?"

"Sure can, Jimmy. Plenty of cheese and fresh baked bread. There's spuds and carrots on the stove. And look. Peaches. I saved these from last year."

Returning from his toilet, Nickolai stood in the doorway, knowing that he was the subject of this converstaion, yet not too sure of the words.

"I am trouble to you. Maybe better I go."

"No fear. You are not going anywhere till you eat. And it is no trouble. Now sit down here, Nickolai." Pulling out a chair, Betty waved him to it. "Jimmy tells me your wife and daughter are both in jail. Ah, what tragic times we live in. Breaks my heart, it does." Seating Nickolai, and not giving him a chance to reply, she quickly heaped his plate with vegetables. "There. You'll find no meat in that. Now you just dig in, and help yourself to anything you see."

Breaking in on her chatter, the sergeant quietly remarked; "Now Bett. I invited our friend for dinner, not for a sermon."

Turning to Nickolai, he smiled, "This little wife of mine never stops her chatter. Gets tired of being by herself so much, I guess. By the way, you do not mind if she calls you by your first name?"

Munching away, Nickolai glanced over at him. "No. I not mind. I be honored if you call me Nickolai."

"I, too. As you know by now, I am Jimmy. At least when I am away from that office. Nickolai? Your wife, was she not called Elizabeth? That is Bett's first name also."

"Yes. But in our country, we do not have, how you say, nickname?"

Laughing heartily, the sergeant reached over and patted

Nickolai on the shoulder. "Believe me, my friend. That is not nickname. Rather, I would call it a term of endearment." At Nickolai's puzzled stare, he said, "Well, what I mean is, our friends call her Betty rather than the longer Elizabeth, the name by which she was christened, but, as her man, as her husband, why I just got in the habit of calling her Bett. It seemed to kind of fit her. Anyway, no matter. Have some more of these vegetables."

"No. No more, please. I feel that I shall burst."

Unexplainedly, a great warmth seemed to envelop Nickolai. Despite the uniform, with all its dread symbolism, Nickolai sensed that here were two people, a people he had always before regarded as alien and stranger, sharing a similar love that had existed for so long between him and Elizabeth. A love, he felt, that would endure to death and beyond, rising above the pitfalls, the hardships, and the misunderstandings that must inevitably exist in the conflict engendered in the attempt to mix two such diverse cultures. In his simple way, Nickolai understood for the first time that, basically, all peoples are the same. Why then, he wondered, should there be such troubles?

With an effort, he brought his attention back to the voice of his host, who had been having similar thoughts of his own.

"I cannot understand why we have these difficulties with your people. You know, Nickolai, we really have tried to find some way to have your people work along with us. To be...well, Canadians. Oh, I grant you, we have made mistakes. We all do. I am fully aware that we have some foolish men in our government. Men who know only the use of force. Of violence."

Carefully wiping his plate with a piece of bread, Nickolai studied his host attentively, not hearing Betty's request that he have some more bread and cheese. Slowly, he replied, "Although our creed denies violence, we too have men who are foolish. Those who think that only by threats and by the use of dynamite can they attain their ends. But then, Jimmy, they are mostly to be found amongst our younger men. There are times I feel these learn only the bad, the wrong things from you. These are confused, and some blinded by envy. These things, I am sorry to say."

"You would care for some more bread and cheese, Nickolai?" Taking advantage of a moment's silence between the men, Betty's concern for her guest was expressed in her motherly desire that he eat.

"Oh, no. No thank you, Mrs. Betty. I can eat no more. I think, maybe, I talk like old woman."

"Don't be silly, Nickolai. It does my heart good to hear you and Jimmy talk this way. Why, I was beginning to think that all you

people were crazy in the head. Now I know one who isn't."
Laughing, she picked up some dishes and moved to the sink.

Jim also rose to his feet, picked up his cap, moved towards the
door, saying over his shoulder, "Well, time I got back to the
office, Nickolai. Why not stay here for a while and rest?"

Before he could make any reply, Betty intervened. "Haven't
you forgotten something, Jimmy?"

Absently, he replied. "So I did." Moving to her, he put both
arms around her waist and kissed her heartily. "There. And you
keep our Nickolai entertained till I get back. I must run up to
Brilliant this afternoon. I can drop him off by the bridge." As
Nickolai protested, his raised his hand. "Please. It will be no
trouble, and anyway, I would like to chat with you again. You
know, Nickolai, if they would only let people like you and I settle
these problems, why I think they would soon cease to exist. But
then, I guess the experts must earn their pay. So you just rest. I'll
be back soon. And Betty, you can come along if you wish."

With a mock low curtsey, Betty smilingly replied, "Why, thank
you, kind Sir. It is so nice to feel wanted." Noting Nickolai's
consternation at this, she burst out laughing. "Don't mind me,
Nickolai. It's just that sometimes, I feel so neglected. But then,
such is the lot of a policeman's wife." Heaving a loud mock sigh,
she linked arms with her husband and accompanied him to the
door.

*   *   *

Although Jimmy had earlier expressed a desire to continue
their conversation, the journey for the most part had been made
in silence. It was almost as though, immersed in the beauty of the
tree-clad mountains through which they passed, the need for
smalltalk had become unimportant. As the police car, an old
Model A Ford, bounced and jostled along the pot-holed gravel
highway, Nickolai was lost in the wonder of the miles slipping by
so rapidly. Miles he had so laborously trod each step of the way,
through the early morning light of this same day.

Paying full attention to his driving, it was clear from the look
on Jimmy's face that his mind was busy elsewhere. Upon nearing
the road that led to Krestova, he slowed the car and addressed
Nickolai, "If you wish, Nickolai, I could easily run you up to the
valley. You still have three miles to walk." Noting Nickolai's
quick disturbed glance, at this suggestion, he smiled and
murmured: "Ah yes. Better not. It might make things awkward
for you."

Sitting contentedly between the two men, Betty turned to her
husband in surprise.

"Why would that be awkward? The poor man has walked far

enough today."

Quietly, Nickolai replied, "Is okay. Not far to walk. I would not wish to have the Brethren see me come home in police car."

At a fork in the road, where a sign pointed to Krestova, Jimmy pulled over and stopped. Turning to Nickolai, who had opened the door, he enquired, "Wait, my friend. Don't you have a son in Vancouver? Paul, I think his name is?"

"Yes. He work here. Have good family."

"Do you have his address, Nickolai?"

Removing a small, crumpled piece of paper from a breast pocket, Nickolai handed it over to him.

"I do not read too good. But Paul, he send me that."

Quickly copying the address into a notebook, Jimmy handed the paper back to Nickolai, and asked:

"You are alone up there, are you not?"

"Well, there are the Brothers and Sisters."

"What I mean is, you have no family up there. And you would like to visit your wife and daughter?"

"Oh yes. Very much. But, how can I do this? I do not even know where this place is."

"Don't you worry, Nickolai. I will see to it that you get to Vancouver. Now, you just wait until I send someone for you." Reaching across his wife, he proffered a hand to Nickolai. "Goodbye, my friend. I really did enjoy talking with you."

Stepping down to the road, Nickolai paused, ready to close the door.

"I...I thank you, Mrs. Betty. And you, Jimmy. I think now you be my very good friends. Goodbye."

Turning, he strode away from them towards a long wooden bridge spanning the Kootenay River, across which lay his destination.

For a moment, both husband and wife sat watching the retreating figure. Then, putting the car in motion, Jimmy reached out to place a hand over that of his wife. Sadly, he murmured, "I wish, Bett, there were more like him."

Thoughtfully, she replied, "Maybe there are, Jimmy. Maybe we just have to get to know them."

You prisoned us on
This rocky shore,
Loved One's despair,
You'll see us no more.
Oh, government cruel
Can you not see,
We suffer for Christ
To Eternity?
The laws we broke,
God did not make,
We suffer gladly
For His sake.

13

Piers Island

A howling spring gale roared out of the Pacific, buffetting the cedars, the firs, and the pines that so thickly clothed the steep inclines of the hills that dominated Pier's Island, a bleak, desolate place, rising out of Haro Straits, across which the low southernmost tip of Vancouver Island was barely visible through the wind-swept mists that stretched out to the rain-torn horizon. This was the federal government's answer to the ever-increasing number of imprisoned Doukhobors.

Plunging and rolling like some great behemoth, the *Lady Alexander* sailed cumbersomely towards the dock on which waited the guards and matrons who, for the next three years, would have the responsibility of overseeing the daily lives of these prisoners. For the most part, these were people recruited from the many communities on Vancouver Island, who would work under the direction of the assistant warden of the New Westminster penitentiary.

Finally, the lines were paid out, and the ship was made fast to the dock. The slow task of disembarking the more than six hundred passengers took up the greater part of the afternoon. Loud, authoritative commands rang out.

"Okay, now, Start moving. On to the dock with you. Women first. Matrons will lead female prisoners to their compounds. Let's go."

This time, there were no songs, no chants, only the quiet shuffle of uneasy, frightened people moving down the rocking gangplank and onto the dock, urged along through the relentless rain by the busy matrons.

Among the first to leave the ship were Nastasia and her mother. The old lady leaned heavily on her daughter's arm, her near-sightless eyes peering around in apprehension.

"'Tis always so dark. You can see this prison, Nastasia? It is far?"

"No. It is not very far, Mother." Her voice took on a grim note. The prison had come into view. "I can see it. High, barbed wire fences. Dark, evil buildings. Crouching hills crowned by weeping trees. Yes, I can see it."

Sardonically, the mother replied, "True colors of the accursed government." A fatalistic note crept into her voice. "They will beat us now, Nasta. You will see."

"Who knows? It is so lonely here, and so far away." Her fear, induced by her mother's words, gave way to sudden anger. "Do not talk like that. You are a silly old woman. You know that no one beats people in this Canada."

A narrow, rock-strewn pathway led upwards from the dock to a wire gate set into the high fence. Unaware of the change in footing, Elizabeth stumbled and fell to one knee. Seeing her fall, one of the matrons hurried over to assist her. Kindly, she asked, "Can I help? She seems ill."

Pulling her mother to her feet, Nastasia glared at the matron. All the fears, the uncertainties that had haunted her since the trial found voice in anger.

"We need no help from the like of you. Only from God."

Smiling ruefully at this rebuff, the matron replied, "Okay, have it your way." Quietly studying Elizabeth, she waved an open hand in front of her eyes. "I thought so. Blind. Poor soul." Trying to ignore her, Nastasia pulled her mother along as the matron informed her, "There will be a doctor coming over in a few days. We will see what we can do."

As they passed through the gate leading into the compound, another matron stood underneath an umbrella, ticking off the name of each of the inmates, then indicating which of the huts they were to occupy. Nearing a lighted open door, Elizabeth, wearied by the slow progress, whispered, "I see a faint light. It is not far?"

"We are here now, Mother. In this door. Brrrr. It is so damp and chilly in here."

Pushing into the hut, the little group of rain-soaked women paused to survey what was to be their home for the next three years.

Shivering and thoroughly miserable, Elizabeth complained, "How can this be? No fires."

Before she could say any more, the general muttering that had broken out was silenced by the authoritative voice of a matron. All eyes swung towards her as she announced, "Ladies. If you please, give me your attention. This will be your dormitory. I will show you the kitchens later. After you have washed up. Now, on those cots, you will find new warm blankets. Make up your beds. Those are new stoves, the best that money can buy. All they need is wood. That you will find stacked ready for use by the side of the dormitory. In that box is kindling and paper to start the fire."

One of the women interrupted her. In a loud and demanding voice, she called, "Why don't you stop talking and get the fire started? We are chilled to the bone."

Quietly, assuredly, the matron answered, "You will light your own fire. Later, you will cut your own wood. Also, you will cook your food, wash and mend your clothes, make up your beds, and in general look after yourselves."

This was greeted with a chorus of incredulous gasps and cries of outrage.

"No! No, we do not work for government. We are its guests. You work for us. You light fire."

"Very well. Suit yourselves." Turning to the door, the matron opened it, then turned to the wondering women. "If you wish to freeze, or to starve, why no one will stand in your way. Now, goodnight, ladies. I have much to do."

The closing of the door signalled a further rash of comment and indignant cries.

"The cruel government. Going to let us freeze. Let them light our fires. Soon, you will see, they bring the lash."

Standing by one of the unmade cots, Elizabeth, chattering with cold, placed an arm around her daughter.

"Nasta. My daughter, I am so cold. Right to the marrow. I think I will not ever leave this place." Her plaintive cries broke into a loud wail. "And no dead clothes."

Sensing her mother's distress, Nastasia firmly pushed her down onto the cot.

"Lie down, Mother. Here. How you talk. These blankets are warm and soft." Gently covering her mother, she removed her shawl and shoes. "There. Now close your eyes for a little."

The contented sigh of the mother was almost drowned out by an angry voice exclaiming, "For shame, Nastasia. You will do the work of the government?"

Other angry voices joined in condemning her.

Furiously, Nastasia glared at the women.

"My Mother is old and feeble. She shakes with the ague. I will suffer for her."

Silenced and a little ashamed by her fury, the cries died down. Someone coughed. Another sneezed. Others remarked as to how they would surely perish without heat. One voice called out, not very convincingly, "Do not worry. The government will not allow us to freeze. We just wait."

Glancing at Elizabeth snug under her blankets, another timidly suggested, "If we just put the blankets down?"

Busy making up the cot next to her mother, Nastasia declared, "You have made beds all your lives. You did not work for the government then."

A chorus of grunts and assents greeted this remark. Soon, all the women were busy making their beds. One opened the box by the stove and removed paper and kindling. Another came in with an armload of firewood. Soon, a roaring fire was warming up the chilly interior. Gratefully, the women stood around it, briskly rubbing cold hands together and silently enjoying the warmth. No one noticed the matron, who had quietly entered the dormitory, and stood glancing around at the made-up beds and the warm fire. Cheerfully, she called, "Ah. Good. Very good. We have made a fine beginning. Now, ladies, if you will follow me, I shall take you to the kitchen. You must all be hungry by now."

Eagerly, the women crowded through the door after her. Nastasia sat by the side of her mother, her eyes on the hurrying women. Struggling to rise to her feet, Elizabeth was restrained by the firm hand of Nastasia, who pushed her back to the pillow.

"No, Mother. You stay here. I will bring you some nice hot gruel. You just rest."

"You will hurry back, Nasta?" Reaching out she felt for and found her daughter's hand, as if reluctant to let her go.

"I won't be long, Mother."

"Before you go, Nasta, could you not turn on a little light?"

Very quiet, Nastasia studied the old, wrinkled face, then leaning forward, gently stroked both cheeks, tears in her voice. "Soon now, God will send His sunshine. Now hush. In the morning, it will be better. I must go."

Releasing her daughter's hand, Elizabeth lay quietly, listening to the fading footsteps. Despite her previous forebodings, the oft-repeated presentiments of harsh treatment at the hands of the government, she had to admit to herself that she had never been so well off and comfortable. The blankets were so warm, and the pillow, pushing her head deep into its softness, the pillow must be made of feathers. Contentedly, she let out a deep sigh. Maybe, after all, jail was not to be such a bad experience. Only this enforced separation from her husband troubled her. Poor Nickolai. How would he ever get along without her? He could never even find a pair of socks. Three years, she thought. Maybe, just maybe, he would go out and protest and then get himself a nice jail like this. But, deep within her mind, she knew that this husband of hers was incapable of protest. So, all she could hope for was that the Sisters in Krestova might keep an eye on him. Gradually, her thoughts filtered away, and she fell into a light sleep.

Once again, she stood in front of the crude canvas that has served as a door, in the small sod shanty they had called home during their exile in Georgia. As she had so often done at this time of day, just before the supper hour, she again peered across the mist-shrouded marshes, mists which now, by their dreamlike opaqueness, seemed to deepen and intensify her sense of being so all alone on an island of evil, creeping spirits.

Her eyes searched for Nickolai, but could not find him. Yet, she knew he was out there somewhere. His voice, hollow, echoing, all pervading, enveloped every atom of her Being, assailing and hammering every one of her senses, encompassing her from all directions. It was as if Nickolai had become the mist, and the mist, Nickolai. His voice, raised in prayer, reverberated around her. Not a prayer to his God, but rather a prayer directed to his wife. In sheer terror, she clapped her hands to her ears. She must not hear these words, but still they came. The pleading, the accusations, the sorrows — a babble of words that nevertheless came to her as crystal clear sounds. In her horror and revulsion, she staggered blindly to the mist's edge. Somehow, she knew, she must reach her husband, stop this blasphemy, even if it meant killing him. The body must go, so that the Soul might be saved. Again and again, she threw herself into the mist, but, try as she might, the mist remained impenetrable — an impregnable substance, resisting any effort on her part to pierce it. Finally, in her desperation, she beat upon it with clenched fists. Scream after scream tore from her throat. "Nickolai. Stop. No. No. Not to me, Nickolai. I am not God. I am not God. Please. Please. Stop." But it seemed the louder she screamed, the greater the silence around her. This evil mist, in all its perversity, eagerly snatched each word, each scream, so that she was reduced to mouthing her words in pantomine. Beaten, she knew that Nickolai could never hear her pleas. In a last desperate effort, she again threw herself against the mist, only to find herself being slowly, inexorably suffocated by something she could neither see nor feel. When it seemed that her laboring lungs must surely burst from want of air, the voice of Nastasia came to her, calling urgently.

"Mother, wake up. You're screaming. Whatever is the

matter?" At the same time a hand shook her forcefully by the shoulder.

Groggy, and shaking from her nightmare, Elizabeth sat up slowly, her eyes dilated and frightened. "Nastasia? It is you. Thank the good God."

Troubled by her mother's evident distress, Nastasia assured her, "It's all right. You were just having a bad dream. You worry too much."

"Ah. Such a dream. I dreamt of your father. Nasta, it was so bad."

"You're just overtired, Mother. Here, I have brought you some nice hot soup."

Resisting her daughter's efforts to hand her the soup, Elizabeth cried, "But, it was so real. Why, I dreamt of the mist. It almost suffocated me."

Smiling a little now, Nastasia forced her mother to take the bowl and spoon.

"Here, Mother. Start eating. And it was no wonder you had a dream of suffocating. You had the blanket pulled right up over your mouth." Sitting down, she waited while her mother started to eat. "They have very nice kitchens here, Mother. We are to cook our own food. At least that way, we can be sure no meat gets into the soup."

The bustle and chatter of the women returning from their evening meal slowly brought Elizabeth out of her confusion and misery, and back to reality. Nevertheless, between spoonfuls of food, she persisted in relating in detail the dream that seemed to obsess her, in that it foretold some dire difficulty involving Nickolai. Patiently, Nastasia humored her by assurances that she was sure that her father was quite capable of looking after himself, and that, in any event, he would not be alone.

Along with the other women, wearied from a long and trying day, she slowly undressed and climbed into her cot, just as the matron checked in to wish them a pleasant goodnight, and to switch off the lights.

Tired as she was, sleep was a long time in coming. Tossing and turning, Nastasia could not avoid brooding on her mother's dream. Was it, she wondered, an omen? Could it be that her father might really be in some trouble? No. That he would be miserable and lonely without his wife and daughter around, she had to accept. But, she mused, she knew her father too well to believe that he would in any way find himself in trouble. Dismissing her mother's dream as absurd, her thoughts turned to her children. Although during the daylight hours, she could keep busy and force herself not to think of them, now, in the dark of

night, there was no escape. Her aching longing to see them surmounted all other thoughts. If only she could know that they were
all right. As it stood now, she did not even know where they were.
And then, the truth struck her. Three years. Three long, lonely
years before she could even hope to somehow find them. Turning
her head into the pillow, she sobbed for the first time in many years.

                              *   *   *

Despite the monotony of a semi-regimented routine, days
slipped by quickly. Other than a longing for their loved ones, the
women soon became accustomed to, and cheerfully accepted, the
daily life of their prison. A doctor from the mainland had
successfully removed the cataracts from Elizabeth's eyes, and she
could now identify objects close at hand. Eyeglasses, to correct
her near-sightedness, had been prescribed, but she had stead-
fastly refused to wear them, stating that, "If God had intended
her to have the sight of a hawk, why then, He would have given
her eyes of a hawk." No amount of cajoling could alter her
illogical stubbornness. It was as if, in these days of control, when
her every material want came readily to hand, that this was the
only form of protest left to her.

High in an ancient cedar, looming sentinel-like over the camp,
robins chirped and whistled to one another, as they flitted about
from branch to branch, busily occupied in their annual spring
frenzy of nest-building. Far below, in the sunlit yard, the high-
pitched voices of the women mingled with the calls of the birds,
in a cacophony of melodious, cheering sound. The swish and slap
of wet clothes being energetically and heartily washed in large
steaming metal tubs was a sure indication to a knowledgeable
observer that this was Sunday morning. The sudden, startling
clang-clang of an iron rod rotated vigorously inside a metal
triangle, brought all activities to an abrupt halt. Then, with a
rush of feet, and cries of "Dinner. Dinner," the women streamed
towards the dining hall.

Disregarding her age, and moved by the beauty of this spring
day, Elizabeth ran along with the others, giggling like a
schoolgirl. Gleefully, she shouted out, "What a day. This spring
air, and warm sun make of me a young woman."

Striding rapidly by her side, Nastasia glanced at her, and
sourly replied, "You are far from a young woman. Now you get
some sense into that head of yours. Slow down."

As if to accentuate her surly remarks, Nastasia grabbed her
mother by the arm, forcing her to slow to a walk. From the
sombre, gloomy expression on her face, it was evident that
Nastasia, unlike the others, was unaffected by the weather.

Pouring into the large building, the women moved to their

places with accustomed ease gained by nearly a year of constant, daily repetition.Several matrons stood around, their eyes on the diners, and on those whose day it was to serve the food. That these matrons were completely at ease, and in fact bored by all this, could be discerned by the careless attitudes in which they stood around. Their faces plainly mirrored an inner desire to be anywhere but here.

Panting from exertion, Elizabeth commenced to eat. Nastasia, sitting by her side, tasted the soup, then grumbled to no one in particular,

"This soup tastes bitter."

Without looking up, Elizabeth gently replied, "Tastes okay to me."

"Hah. The way you're acting, anything would taste good."

Confused by her daughter's tone of voice, Elizabeth quietly placed her spoon down on the table, and turned to her.

"Nasta. You are so unhappy. How can this be on such a day?"

"The day only serves to remind me of my loss."

For a moment, Elizabeth stared at her, then with a sigh, picked up her spoon and thoughtfully began to eat.

"When you sleep, I hear your cries. I...I know some of what you suffer, my daughter. But please, for now, eat. There is little else we can do."

Lost in her misery, deaf to her mother's words, Nastasia continued to release her hatred for this forced confinement.

"I dream of my little ones. Last night, it was little Nick. Lost. Crying out for me. I think maybe I go crazy, if soon I don't get out of here."

The other women around the table continued eating busily, pretending not to hear any of this. Her mother, disturbed and alarmed by this last statement, retorted, "In God's good time, my daughter. You are so like your Father. Always, no patience."

Before Nastasia could make a reply to this, a matron standing by the door, called out, "Elizabeth Obedkoff. Elizabeth Obedkoff."

Frightened by this summons, Elizabeth grasped her daughter by the arm, and glanced around to the matron.

"What can they want with me?"

Wondering at this unusual break in routine, Nastasia murmured, "Answer her and find out."

Suiting action to her words, she stood up and called, "Over here. What is it you wish?"

Moving over to them, the matron smiled and informed them quietly: "You have a visitor. Your son, Paul. Such a nice young man. He waits outside for you."

Stunned by this unexpected good news, Elizabeth could only sit staring up at the matron. Nastasia, her face breaking into a smile, cried, "Paul. Oh, Mother. Hurry. Come. Paul is here."

In her urgency, she lifted Elizabeth to her feet, and almost dragged her through the door.

Emerging from the dimness of the dining hall into the brilliant sunshine, Nastasia eagerly peered around. Standing near the administration building, a lone figure stood gazing about uncertainly. Unable to contain herself, Nastasia broke away from her mother and ran to Paul, crying over and over, "Paul! Paul!"

Once the greetings, the excitement of meeting after their long separation was over, Nastasia calmed down and asked her brother, "Have you seen Father, Paul? Do you know how he is?"

"He is well. But he misses you both. I think he would die of loneliness."

"Ah. That poor old man. He is still in Krestova?"

"No, Mother. He has been with us for some time."

"You mean in the city? But then how can he be happy in a city?"

"He is contented. Plays with the children. Works around the garden. He's got a job now. I got him into the warehouse with me."

Nastasia stood by, quietly listening, her eyes on Paul. Although his pleasure in this meeting was genuine enough, she sensed a sadness in his eyes, an indefinable something, as though some deep unhappiness cast a shadow over his meeting them. Breaking in on her mother's chatter, she asked, "Paul. You have heard from my children? I dream so often of them."

Flustered by this direct query, Paul turned away.

"I...I...Look. Must we talk here? Can we not go someplace and sit down?"

"Let us walk down to the beach." Quickly, Nastasia linked one arm through that of her brother's, and the other through her mother's. Together, they walked towards the open gate. "The day is warm. Nature smiles upon us. Come."

Doubtfully, Paul glanced at the guards standing idly near them.

"The guards. They would not mind?"

"Mind? Why should they mind? How could we get away? Swim to Sidney maybe?"

Elizabeth laughed gaily at her little joke, happy in the moment, in just being with her son.

"They watch us, Paul. But, as Mother says, how could we get away?"

"Do they treat you kindly here?"

Reaching a small sandy beach, they sat down on a large log washed in by some previous storm. Paul stared out to the mainland, visible as a dark blue smudge on the horizon.

For the first time since their meeting, Elizabeth gave vent to her outrage.

"Treat us kindly? My son. You wouldn't believe it. Make your beds. Cook your food. Cut the wood. Why, even when we strip and appear as God made us, they pay no attention. It's cruel."

Smiling a little at his mother's vehemence, Paul replied, "Ah, yes. I have heard something of this. I have been to see the government about you. It would seem you cost them an awful lot of money. In fact, it's something in the neighborhood of three million dollars, just to keep you all in here."

Beaming, Elizabeth chortled, "My. So much money. We must be of some importance. I had no idea."

Suddenly serious, Nastasia broke in on her mother's glee. Turning to Paul, she asked, "You were going to tell me about the children. You have seen them? Do you know how they are?"

"Anastasia has run away. She is now in Vancouver. Maury was talking with her the other day."

"How is she, Paul?"

"She needs a mother. Anyway, we can take you to her as soon as we get back."

Puzzled, Nastasia stared at him.

"But Paul. That will not be for almost two years yet."

"The government has decided that you are to be released immediately. Nasta. My sister, there is something I must tell you."

"It is about my little Nick?"

With an unexplained sense of dread, she knew that now she was to share in the sadness that lay behind the eyes of her brother.

"Yes. He...he was killed in an accident. It seems that he was riding in a car carrying explosives which went off. I am so sorry. But I wanted to tell you myself."

Unable to make any reply, Nastasia sat with her hands tightly clasped about her knees, her eyes on the waves tumbling gently onto the beach.

Paul's voice, flat, unemotional, seemed to come from some great distance. His words tumbled out.

"According to the evidence, they were on their way to dynamite some powerlines. The other two boys with him will be crippled for life."

High above their heads, and riding a warm rising current of air, a solitary gull hovered, motionless, silent, unheeding of humans, and of their grief. The one sound to penetrate the anguished silence came from a rapidly moving squirrel which, racing up a tree trunk, chattered angrily at some imagined violation of his territory.

Two tears trickling down her cheeks were the only indication that Nastasia had heard and understood Paul's words. Lovingly, Elizabeth reached out and pulled her daughter's head to her shoulder. Gently, she stroked the long, greying hair, crooning words in Russian, soft, consoling, in the only way she knew to comfort her stricken daughter.

Again, Paul spoke:

"That's the reason you are to be released. The other condition is that you both stay away from Krestova."

Raising her head, Elizabeth stared at him and asked, "How is this? Where are we to stay?"

"In Vancouver. You will be on what they call parole. Father has rented the house next door to us."

Pushing away from her mother, Nastasia dashed a hand across her tear-stained face, and stood up. Fighting for control, she moved quickly behind her mother and Paul. Her words tense and harsh, she enquired, "When may we leave, Paul?"

"Right away. This afternoon. I came over on the supply boat. We are to return on it as soon as it has unloaded."

"Good. Come, Mother. Let us pack and leave this dismal place. We will meet on the dock, Paul?"

"Yes. The head matron has your papers. See her first, Nastasia."

Slowly, the two women moved away from him towards the gate. Paul stood, watching them go.

"How," he wondered, "how would they cope with this drastic change that life in a big city would demand from them?"

Shaking his head in perplexity, hands in pockets, he turned and moved towards the waiting launch.

Hounds of War
Sound full cry.
Who will answer?
Who will die?
Gambling lives,
A Madman's toss,
The Devil's gain,
Society's loss.
Guns of Hell,
Now in season.
Brave the man,
Dares to reason,
Destroy all weapons,
Live in Peace.
Let wars on Earth
From this day, cease.

14

Thou Shalt Not Kill

Vancouver in the late Thirties. A vigorous, thriving city, sprawling across the feet of green-timbered, snow-capped mountains, and sheltering one of the finest deep-water harbors on the Pacific Coast. Pride in its destiny was everywhere reflected in the numerous tall glass and concrete towers sprouting up out of the decay of Old Town — all evidence of a people's determination to shake off the misery and the shackles of the Great Depression. The Gateway to the Orient. A seaport containing within its expanding reaches, all the puzzling contradictions, the sins and the filth, the beauty and the genius of contemporary western society.

A city caught up in the midst of change. Change that was to see it grow from a careless, waterfront town, to a progressive, modern metropolis. And, over all, the war clouds. Clouds that in the months to come, were to see father and son march off to fight in the lands of their forefathers, many of them never to return. A war that was to act as the catalyst that would turn depression into affluence, and which, in the years ahead, would embark man upon a path of materialism from which there would be no turning back.

To Nickolai, walking along a quiet, tree-lined, residential street, all of this was as alien as man's future adventures into space. He had problems of his own. That which he had been faced with all his married life, was Elizabeth. After almost a year of city living, she had become more and more restless and discontented. Her ever-recurring demand was for an immediate return to Krestova, that they might assist in the struggle against

the forces of government that seemed so bent upon tearing apart
the very fabric of the Doukhobor way of life. Apprehension that
he might yet be forced back to the barren plain of Krestova, there
to participate in an ever-increasing violent struggle, together with
a sense of guilt in the knowledge that he had never really felt as
did his wife, had made Nickolai's life a hell of doubt and
frustration that was relieved only by his visits next door, where he
could chat with Paul or Maury, or spend a pleasant hour in play
with the younger children. Ruefully, he had to admit to himself
that even these defences had been broached. Elizabeth, working
herself up to a fury of self-righteous indignation, had of late
taken to following him, and, confronting her son and
daughter-in-law, would loudly deride them for their Godless
ways. Her lamentations and accusations had been avoided only
by retiring into himself, or by storming out, to walk for miles, in
the hope that, when he returned, his wife would have fallen
asleep, or into a sullen silence.

In the short time he had lived in the city, he had come to an
acceptance of the fact that a satisfying, full life could be lived
away from the farm, the tilling of the soil. Laboring as a janitor
in the same warehouse grocery firm that employed Paul as an
accountant, Nickolai had found a day to day contentment in the
reality of trading his labor for the cash with which to pay the rent
and buy the groceries that kept his little family alive. Pushing
open the small wire gate that led to his home, he moved up the
walk, then paused for a moment to survey with pleasure the
brightly-hued flower borders that enclosed a close-cropped, well-
kept lawn. Noting that a large bush, heavy with roses, had
become detached from its stake, he gently raised and retied the
branch, his mind going back to that time last fall, when he had
first decided to dig these borders and put in some plants.

Thoughtfully stroking the soft velvet of the blooms, he
remembered how his neighbors, people he never even knew
existed, the Irish family next door, and the Italians across the
street, all of them enthusiastic gardeners, had sauntered over to
chat with him, bearing in their arms rose bushes, bulbs, and
miscellaneous plants, that they figured he might be able to use.
With a smile, he recalled that they figured he might as well have
them, as their own gardens were overgrown, and the stuff would
only be thrown out. By these contacts, he had been made aware
that people were the same the world over, provided only that he
was willing to meet them on their own ground. With an inward
sense of happiness, he had to confess that he was no longer a
stranger in a strange land.

On this day, his problem with Elizabeth had taken on a new

dimension. By the time he had removed his coat, washed up, and entered the kitchen, he sensed that a showdown was at hand. No supper simmered on the cold stove. The table remained bare of dishes. Elizabeth sat in her rocking chair by the window, her packed suitcase at her feet. He stared at the grim, hard-set face. In his anxiety, his voice came loud in the stillness.

"Now what ails you woman? No supper tonight?"

Refusing to meet his eyes, she stated flatley:

"I go to Krestova."

"Krestova? You silly old woman. How can you go to Krestova?"

"If you not give me money for train, I walk."

About to retort in anger, Nickolai took a deep breath, pulled over a chair, and sat down facing Elizabeth. Quietly, taking both her hands in his, he said:

"Elizabeth. This thing you do is not good. We are no longer young. We...we have suffered enough. Now it is young people who carry on fight. We rest now. Stay here in city with Paul."

As if she had not heard his pleading words, she repeated, "I go. Train leave tonight. I go."

Defeated, and baffled by her stubbornness, he rose and walked to the window, his unseeing eyes on the neat rows of vegetables stretching across the backyard.

"O.K. Elizabeth. You go. But, you go alone."

"No matter. No one need me here."

"I need you."

"You? Huh. You same as Paul. No Doukhobor. Soon, you smoke filthy tabac. Drink the whiskey. You soon Devil's man. Not like before. Man of God." Overwhelmed by her despair, frustrated by her misery, she cried out, "You not my husband. You hear? You not my husband."

Unnoticed by either, Maury had entered, and stood in the doorway, her worried eyes on her in-laws. Before Nickolai could make a reply to Elizabeth's tirade, she broke in, a note of false cheer in her voice.

"Hi, you two. Am I interrupting something?"

Glancing over at her in surprise, Elizabeth asked, "What you want?"

"Why, I just came over to see if Father Obedkoff knows if Paul will be home soon."

Gently, Nickolai informed her, "He'll be a little late, Maury. Maybe home about six o'clock."

Not too sure of her reception, Maury walked over, determinedly pulled back the chair vacated by Nickolai, and sat down, then uncertainly gazed from one to the other.

"Look. Maybe this is none of my business, but I must say

something. You know that Paul and I love you both, and so do the kids. You're all the family we have, and...and..." Confused by the hostility evident in Elizabeth's eyes, Maury lost her nerve and finished lamely, "I...I just came over to ask you a favor."

Touched by her confusion, Nickolai asked, "What favor is it you wish, Maury?"

"Why, I thought if you weren't doing anything, you might look after the children for the weekend. Paul and I had planned to go to the Interior."

This remark caught Elizabeth's attention. With sudden interest, she said, "I too. I go to Krestova. Maybe I go with you?"

Before Maury could reply, Nickolai interjected bitterly, "Sure. You go, woman. She say, Maury, no one need her. Take her with you. I look after children."

Eyes bright with unshed tears, Maury moved closer to Elizabeth, took her lined face in both hands, and forced her to look into her eyes.

"Now, Mother Obedkoff. You listen to me. How can you say nobody needs you? How can you say that?"

Doggedly, Elizabeth cried, "Who needs me? You no need me. Husband no need me. I talk, he runs to your house. Nasta not need me. I tell her, go see husband Mike in prison, she says she got no husband." In her wretchedness, Elizabeth broke down, sobs wracking the large body. Miserably, she muttered, "No one need me. No one need me."

Saddened by the old lady's misery, Maury placed an arm about the quivering shoulder, and pulled her head down onto her breast. Her other hand gently stroked the fine white hair. Tears running down her face, she whispered, "There now. There now. I didn't know. So help me, Mother Obedkoff, I didn't know. I guess we're so busy living our own lives, we just took you for granted. Please don't cry. Listen. Listen to me." Kneeling down by the old lady's knees, Maury pulled her hands away from Elizabeth's face, and clasped them tightly in her own. "When you were over on the Island, do you know how lonely Father Obedkoff was? On Sundays, he'd take a street car out to Point Grey, and stand on the cliffs for hours staring over at the Islands. He said that way he felt closer to you. And do you know how hard Paul worked to get you released? Three trips over to Victoria. Day after day, hanging around government offices, just so he could plead with someone to let you go. How can you say no one cares?"

Dazed by this information, Elizabeth stared down at Maury.

"You mean he do all that for me? My Paul?"

"Yes. Don't you understand? He loves you. We all do. You go

away now, and Father Obedkoff would soon die. And what about Anastasia, your grand-daughter. I forgot to tell you, she's coming to dinner tonight and wants to see you."

"Huh. That Anastasia. She no grand-daughter of mine. She wear fancy clothes. Paint her face like whore. Even smoke tabac. How you say she my grand-daughter?"

Gently chiding, Maury retorted:

"That's not fair. She's a fine young lass. Not a bit like you say. And tonight, I want you to be nice to her."

Mollified by the attention Maury gave her, Elizabeth's sobs gave way to indignation. Pulling her hands away from Maury's grasp, she snorted in derision, "Huh. How you mean I not fair? That girl big smarty. Think she know it all."

Responding with a smile, Maury rose to her feet, wiped a hand quickly across her tear-stained eyes, then firmly declared, "You're so wrong, Mother Obedkoff. She's lonely, and very unsure of herself. The other day, Paul met her and she asked him if she might move up here with us. She's tired of living downtown."

Standing by the window, Nickolai had wisely kept very quiet, confident that Maury, with her good sense, would be more than a match for his wife's temper tantrums. Despite her apparent hostility and unfriendly attitude to Maury, he knew that, secretly, Elizabeth admired her way of taking life in her stride, and that she was a loving, thoughtful mother could not be denied. Although she had yet to address Maury by her given name, always referring to her as that wife of Paul's, of late she had moderated her constant harping criticism, and in fact, on several occasions, had spoken of her in terms that portrayed grudging approval.

About to speak, he was silenced by a warning hand, signifying that Maury had not yet finished.

"Wait, Father. Let me finish." Turning to Elizabeth, she asked, "Mother Obedkoff. Would you like to have Anastasia stay here with you?"

"Well. If she be a good girl, sure. I like."

"Don't worry. She's a good girl. Just mixed up. Tell you what..." Suddenly brightening, she pulled Elizabeth up from her chair, "Let's all have supper together. Paul will soon be home, and I must get over and help Nasta." As Elizabeth started to protest, she placed an arm round her waist, and led her to the door. "Come on. We'll need you to help set the table. And Father, you come over when you're ready."

Smiling with relief, Nickolai stood watching them go. The confrontation he had so dreaded had come and gone. Thanks to his daughter-in-law, this time, the battle had been won.

In contrast to the emotional crisis of the past hour, supper at Maury's was a cheerful occasion. Elizabeth, busily working at setting the large table in the dining room next to the kitchen, found herself humming one of the lighter hymns so dear to her heart, at the same time conscious of the voices of Maury and Nasta, who chattered away as they busied themselves around the stove. Surveying the finished table with its flower-patterned dishware, and heavy gleaming silverware, she had a feeling of once again preparing for a celebration, a feast. Could it be, she wondered, the advent of Anastasia into the family? No, that could not account for this feeling of well-being. Mentally counting the number of places set, she found the answer. This would be the first time in many years that she would sit down to a meal with all the family. It had been so long. So much had happened. And, for the first time in her long days of living, she thought of her own actions, and the effect they had on those around her. Nastasia allowing herself to be arrested, just so she might accompany her to jail to be by her side. Paul, taking time off from work so that he might get the authorities to release her. And Maury. How she loved that girl. Going along with all her husband wished done, uncomplaining, using her solid common sense and love for others to steady them and hold them together.

An unaccustomed wave of guilt swept through Elizabeth, as full realization of her actions came to her. Dear God, she prayed, I have not much time left on this Earth. Help me change. Tonight, she vowed, it would begin, with her grand-daughter, Anastasia. Somehow, she must reach that girl before it was too late, bring her back into God's way of life, give her pride in her heritage. But, no yelling at her. No, that would be bad. Rather, be kind. Show this little lost lamb that she was truly loved. Yes. Yes. That was the change she must make.

Lost in her deep reverie, Elizabeth was unaware of Nasta, who had quietly entered the room and placed a large bowl of steaming food on the table.

"Mother?" Receiving no answer, she repeated loudly, "Mother, you all right?"

Coming to with a start, Elizabeth asked, "All right? Sure, all right. Why you think I not all right?"

"You had such a funny look on your face... Daydreaming, maybe?"

"Not dreaming. Thinking. Nasta? You...you love your old Mother? You not think she crazy in the head?"

"Of course, I love you. But, sometimes you make it hard." Walking to the window, she called out, "Paul's home. And Anastasia with him. She's carrying a suitcase." Fervently, she exclaimed, "At last, my daughter is coming home." Turning away, she ran into the kitchen, calling to her mother as she passed her, "Mother. You run over and get Father. I'll get the supper on the table."

"No need. Father's here."

Nickolai, spotting Paul's arrival, had come in the back way. That he was still uneasy was evident from the manner in which he eyed his wife, and in the way he carefully avoided her as he moved to the table, pulled out a chair and sat down.

Watching him, Elizabeth smiled and whispered, "Old fool, Nickolai. I never leave you anymore." Walking to his side, she sat down. "Not, that is, till I pass over."

Before Nickolai could think of a reply, the others came trooping in, talking excitedly, as they moved to their chairs.

Although not yet sixteen, Anastasia looked much older. Her shoulder-length brown hair gleamed from many brushings. On her face, not a trace of makeup was visible. Before she sat down, she moved to stand between her grandparents, hugging them simultaneously, and greeting them effusively. She was happy to be there. Pleasure animated her features. Taking her seat, she dished out a large helping of pirohees and vegetables, then, addressing Nastasia, remarked:

"You know, Mother. It is so good to be home. You don't mind if I live with you? Uncle Paul said I could."

"Of course not. Now, eat your supper. You can have the spare bedroom."

Glancing over at her, Nickolai enquired, "You work, Anastasia?"

"Yes, Grandfather. In a cafe on Pender Street. Not much money though. But, it's not easy finding a job."

"Now you stay with us, you no need work." Determined to hold to her vow of kindness, Elizabeth reached across Nickolai, and patted the girl on her arm. "You Doukhobor. I teach you many things. You learn Living Book. You like."

Her voice rising in protest, Anastasia began to say, "But, Grandma, I don't..."

Sensing the beginnings of a quarrel, Nasta cut her off abruptly.

"Anastasia. You are not eating. We will talk of this after supper."

Taking their cue from Nasta, the others continued to eat in silence.

Finishing first, Paul, with a satisfied grunt, pushed back his chair.

"That was good. . .Father, I made a deal to buy the house."

"The one next door?"

"Yes. From now on, why I guess I will be your landlord."

"You pay much money for it, Paul?"

"No. The owner died some time ago, and his wife wanted to get rid of it. Actually, it was a bargain."

Pleased at this news, Maury commented, "I didn't know I'd married a business genius. Pretty soon, you'll own the whole street."

"Well. Thank you, Maury. But, the way I figure it, the rent would cover the mortgage, and by borrowing on this one, I managed to get a down payment large enough to meet their terms."

"But, Paul, how do we pay off the loan on our house?"

Worriedly, Paul studied his empty plate, then answered, "If this war they're talking about starts, why then my wages should go up, and, of course, property values will rise. We'll make it, Maury."

"You think we have another war, Paul?"

"Sure looks like it, Father. They called out the military reserves today, so it must be serious. That's the reason I was late. There were so many extra orders to get out in a rush."

Of them all, only Paul realized the seriousness of the situation. A war in far-off Europe did not appear too threatening to the others. Only Elizabeth seemed in any way effected by Paul's news. To her, it recalled an ever-recurring theme.

"I suppose now, they try to get everybody to wear uniform and fight?"

"You mean our people? No, Mother. I am confident that will never happen. The government did not break their promise to us the last time we had a war. So, I see no reason they should this time."

"Huh. You believe government too much. I no trust them."

Rising, Maury announced briskly, "Okay, nothing we can do about it, so let's clear the table and get the dishes done."

Soon, the three women were busy at the sink. Elizabeth trudged over to her house to prepare the room for Anastasia. Paul and Nickolai moved out on the verandah to sit on the steps and contentedly watched the neighborhood children at their play. Amongst these, Paul's two, Peter and Mary Beth, mingled happily, their voices shrill and laughing in the evening twilight. Despite past troubles, Paul reflected, life had really been good to him.

Later that evening, Anastasia sat with Maury in her bright, neat kitchen, waiting for the kettle to boil. The large house was quiet and peaceful, with the children upstairs asleep, and Paul on the chesterfield in the front room, deep in his after-dinner nap. Soft dance music issued from a console radio. Lulled by the music, the last thought that floated through Paul's mind as he fell asleep was that tomorrow, being Sunday, he would take the whole family in the car to Stanley Park, to enjoy a picnic. Soon, he mused, the rains would come, so he had better make the most of what was left of the fine summer weather.

In the kitchen, Maury brought out a wicker sewing basket, and commenced to knit. Anastasia busied herself by pouring water into a teapot, then set it down by the cups on the table. Interestedly, she asked, "What are you knitting, Aunty?"

"I thought I'd try one of those Indian sweaters. With winter coming on, Paul will need something warm." Holding it up for inspection, she continued, "See? This is going to be a deer standing in front of some pine trees."

"It's beautiful. But it must be a lot of work."

"Well. It will take some time. But, doing it for your uncle, why it does not seem like work. Do you knit, Anastasia?"

"No. I try to do a bit of embroidery. I...I haven't had much of a chance to learn anything like that. But I like sewing."

For a while, Maury remained silent, her needles clicking rapidly one over the other, her thoughts on what her young niece had just said. Poor child. She really has not had much of a chance to learn anything. Hers has been a troubled life. And now, she's caught between the harsh traditions of the older generation and the ever-increasing change in the lifestyles of her own generation. No wonder she is so confused.

As if in some way guessing the trend of her Aunt's thoughts, Anastasia blurted, "Aunty. Why is Grandma so, well, stubborn? So set in her ways. She just will not listen."

Thoughtfully, Maury studied her niece. Feeling for the right words, she said, "She is a very old lady, my dear, and you must remember, she has suffered much. You are young, and although I know you may have had a hard life, you, at least, have suffered no physical abuse. Not as your people have. And believe me, Anastasia, they are a fine, brave, sincere people. They are willing to die for their faith. Many, in fact, have. Did your mother ever show you the scar on her back?"

"No. I have never seen Mother undressed."

"You should ask her to show you that scar. Get her to tell you how she received it. And did you know that your grandma was very nearly killed in the same action? They cannot change, Anastasia. But you can. Be proud of your people, my Dear. And above all, try to show a little tolerance and kindness to them. God knows they have earned that."

"But, Aunt Maury. We live in a different world. People are so different now."

"They aren't. Their world still lies in the past, in their Living Book. Can you not understand, my Dear, that what you today take for granted, as...as a way of life, may seem sinful to your grandparents?"

"But why is it that Grandpa does not seem to mind how I live? He is such a dear. He never gets angry at me."

"He has always been like that. Kind and thoughtful. Somehow, I do not think he really accepted all the ways of the Doukhobors. As for your Grandmother, you can only try to go along with her. Let her live in peace. I do not think it will be for long. You know, Anastasia, under her severe manners, she does love you. That is why you must try not to make things any harder for her."

"But, Aunty, I have my own life to live."

"They are also a part of your life. Have you no love for them?"

"Oh, yes. Yes. I do love them. But they make it so hard. They would have me in a long black skirt and head scarf, out in a field digging potatoes."

Smiling at her niece's exaggeration, Maury rose, and hugged the disturbed girl.

"Time for bed. And you think of all I have said tonight. You can make things easier all around. Now goodnight."

Stifling a yawn, Anastasia moved to the door, then, with a giggle, told her aunt, "I can see why Uncle married you. Good night, Aunt Maury. See you tomorrow."

*   *   *

In the North Pacific Coastal region, there are scattered days in the winter when the grey, lowering clouds sink out of sight behind the mountainous horizon, silhouetting the Lions, the Grouse, and the Seymour peaks in all their glittering, snowy majesty against the azure blue of a sunlit sky. On a Sunday, hordes of rain-weary city dwellers pour into Stanley Park, or slowly saunter along the sands of English Bay. Those fortunate enough to own cars might take a drive along the Spanish Banks, and up through the university area, then stop off for a coke or coffee, at one of the drive-ins located on the outskirts of the city.

Nickolai, however, could find no pleasure in any of this. His one joy was to slowly wend his way along and around the docks of the waterfront, feasting his eyes on the many freighters mutely tied to their berths, awaiting the inevitable weekday clamor of cargo loading and discharge that would come on the morrow. Occasionally, when finances permitted, he would board the ferry that ran to North Vancouver and sail across the narrows, to enjoy the soft wind and the warm sun on his face.

He made a little game of trying to decipher the names boldly printed on the bows of foreign ships; visualizing in his mind the lands from which they had sailed. One unforgettable Sunday, he had come across a Russian ship, half-loaded with wheat. Eagerly, he had called in his native tongue to a group of sailors lounging on deck, who immediately invited him aboard. For two fascinating hours, he answered their queries on life in Canada, and learned from them about the drastic changes that had taken place in his homeland since his departure. Their information on the conditions prevailing in Russia saddened him for days. He knew full well that, despite his secret yearnings to return to his birthplace, he was now doomed to accept the fact that this would be impossible. If, at times, conditions had been sad here in Canada, hard, and oft-times heartbreaking, these were as nothing compared to what his Brethren must have suffered at 'the hands of a despotic regime.

On this particular Sunday, while musing on his previous encounter with his fellow countrymen, his wandering footsteps took him to one of the gigantic grain elevators that dotted the waterfront. Fascinated, he watched as boxcars were propelled inside an unloading bin, and dumped over on their sides, to disgorge bushel after bushel of yellow wheat, the rush of its descent sending great clouds of greyish dust billowing up into the air. Inwardly, he knew a pride in having been one of those early settlers who, by their back-breaking toil, had made all this possible.

Around his feet, innumerable pigeons cooed and clucked as they fed upon the spilled grain that lay in such profusion along the railroad tracks. Every now and then, a shrill blast from the whistle of a shunting engine would send them flying upwards to wheel and circle, in mad flight, before once again settling down to eat. Nickolai thought of his early life, and of the changes he had been forced to make, which had entailed so much suffering and agonized fears. Clearly, he saw it all emerging as a pattern from which there had really been no escape. He thought of his son, Paul, and felt a pride in the way in which he had established himself in this alien city. And then, of his daughter Nastasia, and of her weary acceptance of life, made so by Mike's being confined for life in the mental hospital at Essondale. His fanatical urge to destroy had, in turn, obsessed him, and his own mind had fallen prey to the obsession and had itself been destroyed. Sorrow for his daughter welled up in him as Nickolai compared his way of life to that of a vegetable-like existence in a mental hospital. He recalled Elizabeth's loudly declaiming the cruel, evil government, when news of Mike's incarceration had come to them. With a wry smile, he knew that had she not reacted in this manner, why, he would have feared that she must be ill. That was one old woman that would never change.

As he retraced his footsteps to where he would catch a streetcar for home, he wondered how many like her were left. There could not be many, surely, or the younger of the Brethren would not have been dissuaded from their criminal path of destruction.

It appeared to Nickolai that, with the untimely death of their leader, Peter the Purger, and the loss of their lands and homes—anchors which had formerly held them—many had turned to a losing, desperate form of guerrilla warfare against a government they truly believed had been the cause of their miseries. He knew, however, from many he had met in the past few months, that the majority of these young folks wanted no part in these activities, preferring to take their chances in the city, or in the larger towns.

Looking into the future, he sadly reflected that there would come a time when the Doukhobor Sect, as a viable force to be reckoned with, would cease to be. With a heavy sigh, he wondered if, at least, their music, their crafts, and their religious beliefs—all that went into their culture—might not somehow survive. They truly had so much to offer to this adopted land of theirs, this Canada, if only Canadians in time might forget the indignities and the violence of the few.

Lost in his thoughts, he realized that he had come further than usual on this walk, and that he was beginning to feel tired. Looking around, he noticed a pile of railroad ties and thankfully walked over and sat down. He still had most of the afternoon to while away. His back to the mountains, he gazed idly, unseeing, at the lines of decrepit, grimy buildings that occupied every inch of space along the tracks.

One disturbing cloud marred his thoughts. Anastasia. Only this morning, she had quarrelled bitterly with both her mother and Elizabeth. Apparently, she had come home very late, and slightly inebriated, from a dance at the Russian Society hall. Even Maury, with her usual cool tact and wit, could do little to calm these women. It was the fury of this that had driven him out of the house, to seek peace and quiet, here on the waterfront.

Anastasia puzzled him—so loving, and yet so unpredictable. It seemed to him that she must have inherited the stubbornness of his wife, and his own love of peace at any cost. If this be true, then the poor girl must be suffering from not a few inner conflicts. For a moment, his eyes followed a group of young children, playfully running along the rails and ties, sometimes climbing the ladders of the boxcars, then scampering along the tops, to disappear down the side of another. Wistfully, his eyes remained on them till they were mere specks far beyond the farthest elevators.

Could it be, he mused, that these children, this generation, were fated to be the children of no-tomorrow? Could this account for the desperation, the flouting of authority, the aching need for the pleasure of life, as opposed to that of the religious?

In his mind, he grimly pictured mankind dedicated to the killing of his fellow man, the finest brains engaged in an ever-increasing search for more and more deadly, bestial weapons of destruction.

Could this war be the end? Or would it cease, only to breed other wars, each more deadly and destructive than the last? A strong, soul-rending urge overwhelmed him, an urge to raise his arms to Heaven, to scream out for the world to hear, his frustrations, his fears — scream if he must to the endless rows of blind and uncaring warehouse, factory, and office windows, each one of which stared coldly down upon this enraged, puny human. The desire to scream "Thou Shalt Not Kill" almost succeeded in escaping from his tight, aching throat. But he remained silent. There was no one to hear.